1 Night Stand:
Love Sisters Series

1 Night Stand:
Love Sisters Series

Amaleka McCall

www.urbanbooks.net

Urban Books, LLC
300 Farmingdale Road, NY-Route 109
Farmingdale, NY 11735

1 Night Stand: Love Sisters Series
Copyright © 2016 Amaleka McCall

ISBN 13: 978-1-62286-792-9
ISBN 10: 1-62286-792-0

First Mass Market Printing February 2017
First Trade Paperback Printing August 2016
Printed in the United States of America

10 9 8 7 6 5 4 3 2 1

This is a work of fiction. Any references or similarities to actual events, real people, living or dead, or to real locales are intended to give the novel a sense of reality. Any similarity in other names, characters, places, and incidents is entirely coincidental.

Distributed by Kensington Publishing Corp.
Submit orders to:
Customer Service
400 Hahn Road
Westminster, MD 21157-4627
Phone: 1-800-733-3000
Fax: 1-800-659-2436

Chapter 1

Harmony

The wind whipped over Harmony's face so hard it snatched her breath. Her thighs burned and her arms moved one up, one down, like a track star heading for the winner's ribbon. Her breath came out so hard and fast it made her lips dry. Her chest heaved up and down, and her shirt stuck to her sweat-slicked skin.

"Ah!" A scream escaped her mouth when she realized she couldn't go any farther. A flash of panic caused her to double over and dry heave.

"Oh my God." Harmony panted, eyeing the obstacle that blocked her path. She whipped her head around and backhanded the snot running from her nose.

"Shit." She swallowed hard, listening to the footsteps behind her progress from rapid taps to thunderous thuds. Harmony turned back to the tall chain link fence. More rapid footfalls closed in behind her, hot on her heels.

Harmony saw the shadowy silhouette of a monstrous figure. She had no choice. She lifted her aching legs and climbed the fence.

With raggedy, jagged puffs of air escaping her lips, Harmony jumped down from the fence and rushed to a dumpster. She squatted behind it, hoping her pursuer wouldn't find her. The strong smell of rotting garbage and rusted metal assaulted her nostrils. Chills covered her body. She clenched her lips, trying to slow the sound of her panting.

After a few seconds, Harmony heard the footsteps slow. She could hear gravel crunching underfoot a few feet away. Her first instinct was to bolt, until suddenly she noticed the black, shiny shoes. A whimper bubbled out of her mouth. Her hands flew up to her lips. Her body trembled. The feet moved slowly at first, and then faster. Desperate to escape, Harmony crawled to her left, the feet heading straight for her. She saw the glint from the metal gun in the stranger's hand.

The first booming shot sent a deafening pain to the center of Harmony's ear that radiated through her skull. Her hands flew up to her ears. The gun sounded off again, and this time she fell into a black abyss.

***

Harmony jolted awake. Breathing heavily, she reached over to grab her cell phone from her nightstand. Squinting, she scanned her bedroom, making sure she had been dreaming. The loud ringing cut through the silence of her bedroom again.

Who could be calling me?

Harmony's head pounded and her heart raced from being yanked out of her sleep. No one ever called her at that time of the morning. UNKNOWN flashed on her cell phone screen.

"Hello?" she groaned into the phone. "Hello?"

Harmony heard the male voice, but with her mind still fuzzy with sleep, she could not register the speaker's identity. Harmony forced herself up from her pillow, wearily threw her legs over the side of the bed, and sat up straight.

"Hello?"

Harmony opened her eyes wider when she finally recognized the caller.

"Murray?" Harmony rasped, swiping her hand over her face to make sure she wasn't still running through a nightmare.

Murray Fleischer was a longtime associate of Harmony's mother, Ava Love. *Why would Murray be calling me in the wee hours of the morning?*

"Yes. Murray Fleischer here. Harmony?" he replied in his nasally, New Jersey Jew accent.

He was saying something, but she couldn't hear him. Harmony closed her eyes. Suddenly, her last interaction with her mother flashed across her thoughts:

"Leave then, you coward! You always were a coward, just like your no-good-ass father," Ava spat.

Harmony swayed on her feet like she'd taken a boxer's uppercut. Her eyes hooded over with contempt and her nostrils flared. She moved a few steps closer to her mother with her right pointer finger jutting out in front of her.

"Coward? Coward? Too bad the real coward is you, Ava Love, since you chose to keep my father from me all of my life because you were too afraid to face the fact that you failed. Too afraid to admit that you got fucked and left because all you ever were was second string. Second string singer. Second string mistress. Second string daughter. Never number one in anyone's eyes," Harmony *hissed, turning on her heels, set to storm out the door.*

Ava balked, and her face flushed red. "You're nothing without me. Nothing without your sister," Ava *screamed at Harmony's back. "You're never going to be shit but a nappy-headed wanna-be who was the mistake that ruined my whole life."* Ava's *voice cracked.*

Harmony paused. Her hands curled into fists on their own. Every muscle in her body stiffened.

A cold chill shot down Harmony's back now. She shook her head and cleared her mind of the memory. She hadn't spoken to Ava in three long years.

"I—I'm sorry, Murray. Can you repeat that?" Harmony stuttered, still confused by his call.

Murray let out a phlegm-filled cough and cleared his raspy throat. "Harmony? Harmony Love, is this you?" he replied.

A flash of panic overcame her. She darted her eyes over to the cable box; it was 4:20 in the morning. The pre-dawn light from the window cast an eerie glow over her bedroom.

"Yes, Murray, it's me."

He coughed again. This time it sounded like he was struggling to catch his breath. Old age had finally caught up to him.

Listening to Murray's labored breathing, Harmony pictured his beady eyes, wrinkled olive-colored skin, dead-rat-looking toupee, and his hooked Ichabod Crane nose. Harmony bit down into her bottom lip. She couldn't help the feeling of resentment that sprang up inside of her. Murray had been a part of her life when everything had gone awry. Harmony often blamed Murray for the events that transpired, but he certainly wasn't the only culprit.

"Oh, Harm . . . I'm so glad to know this is really your number. I thought I was going to have a hard time finding you. Ava Love really had high hopes for you. She really loved you. As her eldest, she always bragged about you. You know, despite everything, I always knew you were the smartest one. . . . " Murray rambled.

Harmony's jaw stiffened and her nostrils flared. Murray's fake small talk had always irritated her. It was always a part of his game. He'd talk you into a brown paper bag if you let him, and then he'd steal everything you had while your head was covered. In Harmony's assessment, Murray was a low-life thief who'd helped Ava destroy her life.

"Murray, what do you want? Is it Lyric? Is she okay?" Harmony finally cut him off.

They didn't need to exchange pleasantries, and he didn't need to go on and on about how much her mother cared about her. They both knew he was full of it.

Murray was silent for what seemed like an eternity. He let out another long sigh and a short snort. Harmony's face crumpled into a frown.

Is he crying?

Harmony's fingertips grew cold as she gripped the phone tighter with each passing moment. Her stomach quivered in anticipation of the bad news.

"Murray? Out with it. Is my baby sister okay?"

"Well, this is about Ava," Murray drawled. Harmony's shoulders eased with relief.

"What about her?" Harmony grumbled. She closed her eyes and sighed. *What evil thing did Ava do now? And why would it matter to me?* Harmony's temples throbbed harder.

"Harmony, you were the first person I called." Murray blew out another windstorm of wet, crackling breath, choking on his words. "I really didn't know who else to call. You know your sisters are both . . . " Murray tiptoed around the subject.

Just the mention of her sisters made Harmony's stomach tighten. *Does he realize it is four o'clock in the morning?*

"Please, Murray, just tell me what's going on," Harmony interrupted, wishing he would put them both out of their misery. "Is Ava sick? Has there been an accident? What?"

Murray belched out a sob and finally mustered up the courage and got straight to the point. "She's gone, sweetheart," he croaked. "Couple of days now, but we just found her."

Harmony felt like a brick had fallen off the top of a skyscraper and hit her on the top of her head. "What?" she asked in an almost inaudible tone. "What . . . what do you mean, gone?"

The words caught in Harmony's throat like fish in a net. She shook her head slowly, the weight of comprehension heavy on her mind. Her heart pounded through her silk nightgown. Harmony was suddenly on her feet, moving unsteadily. The temperature in the room seemed to have dropped. Her bottom lip trembled and she had to fight to keep her teeth from chattering.

"How?" Harmony managed.

Murray was saying something, but she couldn't hear him. Just that fast, her thoughts had drifted. With a flash of clarity, it occurred to her that Ava didn't have her new contact information. *How did Murray get my number?* Harmony shook her head and rid the suspicious thoughts from her mind. Paranoia and suspicion had become her natural defense mechanisms, but this was not the time or place.

Murray provided Harmony with what little details he had: Ava was dead in the house, there was no cause of death yet, and it had been at least two days before anyone had found her. He didn't know if she had been drinking again or on her usual cocktail of pills; however, the police said the house was a left in a mess.

Harmony felt like she was slipping off the slope of a tall mountain. With tears rimming her eyes, she looked down at her husband sleeping soundly. His chest rose and fell peacefully. He was oblivious to the chaos of her thoughts and emotions. In that moment, Harmony envied him.

"Murray," Harmony said, her voice unsteady. "Thank you for calling me. I know things weren't . . . I know Ava and me had . . ." The tears finally rolled down her face. Harmony cleared her throat and sucked in her breath.

"I appreciate you not letting me find out from the television or media. I will be there as soon as I can. I'll take care of her arrangements," she promised.

Her brain wasn't connecting with her tongue as usual. She tried her best to keep it together, but her voice cracked on the last sentence. Tears spilled down her cheeks and over her lips. She used her right hand to swipe at them roughly. Crying over Ava was not something Harmony thought she'd ever do, but the tears still came fast and hot. Ava was, after all, her mother.

Harmony placed the phone back on her night-stand. She flopped down on the side of the bed like a sack of bricks; the strength seemed to have left her legs. Something ached at the base of her skull. In response, she lifted her hands and placed them on either side of her neck, moving her fingertips in a circular motion at the site of the pain.

Harmony's abrupt motion caused Ron to stir. She turned her body away, giving him her back. She didn't want him to see her cry. In that moment, Harmony didn't know why she was hiding from Ron, who was her best friend. He had never been anything but supportive since they'd met three years earlier. If it hadn't been for their relationship, neither of them would have survived the crises they were experiencing at the time.

Harmony had just left a chart-topping girl group comprised of herself and her sisters. Even with all of the group's success, Harmony was practically penniless when she walked away. Ron was a washed up child star who'd fallen so deeply into his addiction to crack cocaine and prescription pills that he'd resorted to living on the steps of a church, selling off his daytime Emmy award and all of the memorabilia from his hit sitcom days when he was the heartthrob who had millions of little girl fans screaming down the streets everywhere he went.

"Harm, what are you doing up?" Ron murmured.

He reached out to embrace Harmony from behind. She cringed. Giving and receiving affection was still something she struggled with. A childhood of no love and affection had done that her.

"Hey. Hey," Ron whispered, snatching his hand back at her reaction. He sat up in the bed.

"What's up, Harm?" he asked again, reaching out and touching her back.

The dam of Harmony's composure finally broke, causing her emotions to spill forth. Her shoulders quaked with waves of rough, violent grief.

"Harmony, what is it? Is the baby okay?"

Harmony didn't have to see Ron's face to know that he was alarmed. She covered her face with her hands and belched out more heaving sobs. She shook her head and mumbled her thoughts.

"If only I had seen her one last time and told her how I felt. I should've forgiven her for everything she did. She didn't know any better." Harmony's conscience was riddled with guilt that she just couldn't understand.

Within seconds, Ron was on his knees in front of her. He tugged her hands from her face. "What's wrong, baby? Talk to me. Please."

Harmony wanted him to hold her. She wanted to know that he was always going to protect her. She finally relented and moved her hands. Through her red-rimmed eyes, she looked at Ron's beautiful cinnamon face.

He swiped a piece of sweat-drenched hair from her forehead so he could look into her eyes. "Talk to me," he whispered. "I'm here."

Harmony opened her mouth, but the words stuck to the back of her throat like she'd just swallowed a jar of arts and crafts paste.

Ron touched her cheek, encouraging her to open up to him. "C'mon, Harm, I can't help you if you don't tell me what's going on," he urged. "You're not just crying and shaking all over for nothing."

The heat from his touch soothed her, but it still wasn't enough to warm her cold heart.

"Take a deep breath and talk to me."

Inhaling deeply and exhaling a shaky breath, Harmony began. "My mother, um, Ava."

Just saying the word *mother* burned on Harmony's tongue. She noticed Ron's muscular body tense at the mention of her mother. He was one of the very few people, aside from her sisters, who knew the truth about Ava.

"What the hell did she do now?" Ron interrupted, his voice taking on a dark tone. He knew all about Harmony's relationship with Ava, none of it good.

Harmony shook her head from left to right. "No. Nothing. It's . . . she . . . Ava. I mean she's . . ." Harmony stammered, her bottom lip trembling. "Dead."

Harmony threw her hands around Ron's neck and collapsed against him with more sobs. She never would have expected to have such a visceral reaction to Ava's death. Harmony must have wished her mother dead a million times while she lived.

"Oh, shit." Ron gasped. "Baby, I'm so sorry." At a loss for words, Ron pulled Harmony up from the bed and into a tighter embrace.

Harmony clutched onto him so tightly that she could feel his chest hairs pricking her face. Her body warmed up. It felt so good to have someone like Ron at her side. Harmony closed her eyes and melted into her husband, and neither of them said another word.

Ava's image came into focus in Harmony's mind—her butterscotch skin, long and silky jet-black hair, and her eyes, those famous, deep-set, glaring, chestnut brown eyes. There was so much to think about, so many emotions to sort through. As hard as Harmony tried to put her past to rest, Ava's death seemed to reawaken memories and emotions that she had believed long dead.

Brooklyn, New York
July, 2000

Harmony was thirteen years old. Her sisters, Melody and Lyric, were eleven and nine respectively. Their musically inspired names were indicative of the fact that their mother, the great Ava Love, related everything in her life to music, even her children.

It was a blazing hot summer day and Harmony and her sisters had been outside in their backyard since the crack of dawn. Even at that early hour, the sun burned brightly, which meant it would be one of those unmercifully hot, humid summer days.

After fifteen minutes outside, Harmony already had a waterfall of sweat rolling down the sides of her face. Without a doubt, this would spell disaster for her thick mane of kinky hair. Harmony's hair had already begun folding in on itself to form what her mother referred to as "nigger naps" and a "jiggaboo afro." That day, Harmony knew, her mother would have something degrading to say about her hair not being soft and silky like her own and how she couldn't figure out why Harmony had such nappy-ass hair like a runaway slave when clearly she had nothing but "good hair" in her family. Her mother thought these harsh criticisms made her sassy and sophisticated, but in Harmony's eyes, it made her appear crude and racist.

Generally, the darker a person's skin was, the worse her mother felt about them. Unfortunately, Harmony's skin was as dark as coffee beans, and under the summer sun, Harmony would become at least three shades darker.

"Harmony, child, you look like an underground railroad escapee. Stay your ass out of the sun before we have to use your teeth to find you in the dark," her mother would say cruelly. Harmony dreaded the summer for that very reason.

Just the day before, the news had announced a heat wave would be sweeping through New York City.

"Well, if the heat wave starts at nine in the morning, y'all asses will be out there from five," her mother had barked.

Sure enough, she kicked them out of their beds at five o'clock sharp the next morning. Her mother made Harmony and her sisters call her Ava instead of "mom" or "mommy." Ava thought being called mommy made her old. In Harmony's eyes, Ava was not a stage mom; she was a stage monster.

"Start over! Goddamit! Start over!" Ava screamed like a banshee, her fair skin turning bright pink.

She folded her arms across her chest and glared at Harmony, Melody, and Lyric. They all stopped mid-motion; their faces folded into frowns. They had been practicing for four hours with no breakfast or lunch. Lyric whimpered, struggling to keep her feet in the oversized stilettos she wore. Although her youngest was only nine years old, Ava made all of her daughters practice in at least five-inch heels.

"You bitches want to be stars or you want to be in the same position next year? Practice makes perfect. Y'all think any great girl groups got to the top of the charts lying around not practicing for hours and hours? Hell no. It doesn't work like that. These record labels ain't going to even sneeze at y'all asses if y'all don't step the fuck up and get it right. Now start over!" Ava barked, pacing like a prison warden in front of them, her heels snapping like a whip on the backyard pavers.

Harmony squinted her eyes into dashes. She couldn't believe this monster had given birth to her.

"Get back into position right now or we'll be out here until the sun cooks y'all asses dead. Lord knows if Harmony bakes anymore we won't be able to see her ass at night," Ava announced.

Harmony hung her head. Those words hurt like a hard slap in the face. She rolled her eyes and bit into the side of her cheek as she reached down and rubbed the calf muscle on her left leg. She could literally feel her muscle bunch into a ball, an advance warning of the Charlie horse that would surely follow. Harmony punched at her muscle, praying the knot would dissolve.

"You better stand up straight and get into position," Lyric whispered, her eyes wide with fear. "If she sees you we will be out here longer."

Lyric's chubby baby face in that moment reminded Harmony that they had all given up their childhoods to become, as Ava pounded into their heads, "the greatest girl singing group since the Supremes."

On cue, Harmony slid her foot back into the stilettos and gritted her teeth against the pain. For what seemed like the thousandth time that morning, Ava looked at her daughters evilly and ordered, "From the top! Five, six, seven, eight!"

Like show dogs, they all responded to her commands. Each of them moved rhythmically, swaying their hips in unison. Harmony was painfully aware of the strained muscles in her legs and was careful not to twist her ankle.

The Love sisters harmonized the intro three times before Melody came blazing through the middle, one leg jutted in front of the other in her model-on-the-catwalk style. Her stilettos rang like gunshots on the ground. Melody was younger than Harmony, but much thinner and taller. Harmony always guessed that her sister took after her father, the famous Academy award–winning actor Charles Monroe. Melody was beautiful and talented, and of the three sisters, she resembled Ava the most. It was both a blessing and a curse.

Melody had slanted eyes, coupled with honey-colored, radiantly clear skin. Her body was slim but curvaceous. Even after horrendous practices, when Melody's oval face gleamed with fine beads of sweat, she still looked beautiful. Her long, sandy hair whipped around as she sang. She could move her body like a grown woman. She strutted in those stilettos like she had been born in them. Harmony envied her for her effortless beauty and grace, but Harmony also loved her sister. With each practice, however, the strain on their relationship was almost more difficult to bear than the strain on their bodies.

Melody's red painted lips were pursed into a seductive kissing pucker, and she licked them and opened them wide. Harmony could see her in the large mirror Ava kept in front of them so that they could see how they looked on "stage."

Harmony rolled her eyes again. At that moment, she couldn't love Melody even if she tried. The love was drowned out by the jealousy. Melody had begun to act more like Ava than herself.

With thoughts swirling in her mind, Harmony moved her body harder, trying to imitate Melody's effortless, graceful moves. The heat of envy rose onto Harmony's face, setting her cheeks on fire. Tears burned at the backs of her eyes. She wanted to impress their mother too. She wanted her mother to love her too, but Ava's eyes remained focused on her favorite.

"I don't love you no more. Boy, you played me for the last time. The last time," Melody belted out in a range that could hold court with any superstar. "I . . . I . . . I don't love you no more. No-o-o-o. You played me for the last time," Melody crooned, the microphone gripped in her hand as she whipped her hair and body like a

diva. She bent forward and sang her next note like her life depended on it. "I'm done playing the fool! Oh-ho for the la-aa-st time!"

With the next bar of the instrumental music, Melody fell back into step with Harmony and Lyric. They all stepped sideways in unison, their hips moving together in synchronized motion. Ava smiled, pride glistening in her eyes. Harmony rolled her eyes and winced against the pain—both in her legs and in her heart.

"Played me. For the last time." Harmony and Lyric harmonized, stepping back into their rightful places behind their newly dubbed superstar sister.

Sweat dripped down Harmony's back as the sun beat down on her. Harmony lifted her arms up and then out as they'd rehearsed. Her muscles burned. Harmony looked over at Lyric. She was also grimacing from the pain. Still, they picked up their signal and harmonized yet another note.

"Last time!"

Harmony and Lyric swayed their bodies in opposite directions and fell into step with Melody, who was out in front of them again, reveling in mother nature's hellish spotlight.

"Harmony, you missed that entire step!" Ava chastised over the music.

Harmony kept on going. She jerked her back and sashayed as hard as she could. Sweat pooled all over her body, and her underarms itched.

"Did you hear me, darkie? I said you missed a step."

Harmony closed her eyes and without even having to look, she crossed Lyric and executed their rehearsed back-up-singer moves perfectly. Harmony never let Ava's voice and cruel words ruffle her. She knew Ava's dirty tactics by now. Harmony also knew she hadn't missed any steps, that this was just one of her mother's "tests" to make sure she would be able to handle any distractions from a would-be audience. If Harmony had paused in response to Ava's distraction, she would've made them all start from the beginning.

Lyric was panting like she only had one lung. Harmony looked over at her sympathetically. Harmony could tell that Lyric's mouth was cotton ball dry because hers felt the same. Finally, Melody held her last high note, slung her head back, and lifted her arms Dreamgirls style.

Ava clapped and smiled with pride. "Bravo, Melody! This apple didn't fall far from my tree for sure," Ava complimented, beaming. "Those other two . . . we got to work on them." She snickered as Melody basked in her praise. Harmony could feel her insides on fire. Ava never gave Lyric and Harmony compliments.

"Good enough for today. Everybody go inside and get some tea and honey right away. Rest those voices, especially you, little diva," Ava called out, patting Melody on her shoulder.

Harmony sucked her teeth and let out an exasperated sigh. She kicked off her shoes and limped over to an old, rickety patio chair in their small backyard. All of the patio furniture had been purposely crowded to one side to make space for their stage. As hot as it was, Harmony was in no rush to go into the house and listen to Ava critique her appearance or performance.

Lyric took a chair next to her big sister as they watched Ava and Melody disappear into the house, laughing like schoolgirls. Harmony often wondered if Lyric was too young to understand what was really going on, although the youngest sometimes seemed quite intuitive. Harmony always hoped to spare her feelings in regard to their mother and Melody, but sometimes the bias was too obvious to dispute.

"I can't stand her." Lyric pouted. Harmony raised an eyebrow at her. "Mothers are not supposed to favor one kid over the other one, but Ava sure doesn't hide it. Melody this, Melody that. Why don't she just make her a solo singer then? I hate singing, and I hate her too," Lyric complained, folding her arms across her chest.

Harmony couldn't agree more, yet she didn't voice her opinion. Why rub salt into an already opened wound?

"She just wants us to be great. One day all of these practices will pay off when we all make it to the big stage," Harmony said, smiling as she leaned back and squinted up at the sky dreamily. It was always her plan to take advantage of what Ava was teaching them so she could become wildly famous and break away.

Lyric wasn't buying it. She sucked her teeth and blew out her breath. Harmony knew she was probably thinking she sounded like a sellout.

"Look, you're too young to understand her right now, but she loves you, Lyric." Harmony tried to assure her with a phony sincerity in her eyes. "She loves all of us," Harmony said, her voice trailing off.

Lyric looked over at her out of the corner of her eye, and Harmony could see the doubt. Harmony felt the same level of doubt in her heart, but she reached out and grabbed her baby sister's hand anyway.

"More importantly, I love you," Harmony whispered. Even if their mother didn't love them the way she loved Melody, at least they could find comfort in having each other.

It seemed like Ron had been holding Harmony in his arms for an eternity. Finally, she pulled away. Her tears had dried into two ashy white lines on her face. Ron smiled, licked his thumb, and used it to wipe away the tear marks.

"I love you, Harmony. This is going to be all right," he comforted.

Harmony smiled back. "I know. I just . . . I just have to be prepared to see my sisters again after everything that's happened," she said ruefully.

Ava's death wasn't going to be the hardest part. Facing Melody after three long years of no communication was going to be even worse. Harmony had watched from afar as her sister's career ballooned to heights she'd never imagined for any of them. It still hadn't eased or eliminated Harmony's deep-seated, and in her opinion, well-deserved resentments against Melody. After all, Harmony felt like Melody had stood on her shoulders to get to the top.

Harmony also dreaded facing Lyric, who she'd cut off six months ago on the heels of a heated argument about Lyric's embarrassing appearances in gossip magazines and on blogs. Lyric had said some pretty cruel things to Harmony during their last conversation. Just the thought of it made her shudder. If Harmony could purchase a mental suit of armor, she would. Considering her last encounters with her sisters, she would need that and more.

Chapter 2

Melody

"Take it from the top. It has to be perfect or I'll be firing a bunch of people today!" Melody screamed so loud the veins in her neck corded against her delicate skin. She squinted her eyes for emphasis as the six leotard-clad dance hopefuls scrambled to get into place. Melody twirled her pointer finger in the air and within seconds, the music blasted through the dance studio speakers. Melody took her place in the front of the pack, as usual. She stood with her feet shoulder's length apart, her fists on her waist, wearing the look of a hungry lioness on her face while she waited for the right hitch in the beat as her cue to start.

Melody stared at herself in the wall of mirrors in front of her. She knew she was special. She'd known all of her life, from the time she was a baby, that she had the juice. As a child, before she had become wildly famous, strangers had often told her that she was a beautiful girl. Melody had always believed that one day, with her looks and singing ability, she would be a huge star. Even after things had gone awry with her sisters, Melody still pursued her dream relentlessly.

Now, she topped all of the charts, this time without her sisters. She had three solo albums that had won her six Grammy awards, eight American Music Awards, five Billboard Music Awards, and fifteen MTV Music Awards. Melody had graced the cover of not just every black magazine, like *Essence, Ebony, Vibe*, and *Complex*, but she'd also broken the mold and graced the covers of *Elle, Vogue, Glamour, InStyle, GQ, Vanity Fair, Cosmopolitan, Time, Allure, Forbes* and *Sports Illustrated*, to name a few. Call her a diva or not, there was no denying that Melody dedicated her life to her craft, and she excelled because she worked harder than any other diva in the industry.

"Again. Again!" Melody yelled. She stepped forward, bent her knees, tilted her head, kicked her feet, and twisted her torso to the rhythm of the music. It was a new move that the choreographer she'd flown in from Mozambique had painstakingly worked on with her until she had perfected it. Melody was a quick study. A natural.

"You in the green, move your hips or I swear you'll be out of here," Melody shouted as she glared at the girl through the mirror in front of her.

Melody hadn't missed a step. She jumped up, landed on her feet, bent at the waist, and twisted her head in a circular motion, letting her huge mane of hair twirl around wildly. When she lifted her head to execute the next move in the routine, she noticed Gary, her manager/BFF, rushing through the studio door.

Melody rolled her eyes and her nostrils flared, partly because she'd been dancing so hard, but mainly because Gary knew better. Her rehearsals were off limits. There were to be no interruptions, under no circumstances, for any reason.

"No distractions. Move your bodies. Time is money," Melody barked, glaring over at Gary, who was now flailing his left hand effeminately to get her attention.

Melody was preparing for the kickoff of her 1 Night Stand Tour, and she was in the middle of a set for her number one Billboard hit, "Liar, Liar." She rolled her eyes at Gary again. She wasn't about to stop dancing. She was feeling the vibe, and the backup dancers had finally gotten their routine correct after hours of coaching and screaming. Gary continued to wave like his hands were on fire.

"This asshole," Melody grumbled under her breath.

Still, Melody set her jaw and bucked her waist to the swell of the music. Everybody knew that when Melody Love rehearsed, the DO NOT DISTURB sign was turned on.

Melody started to move into the next set in her routine when Gary did that stupid, desperate hand motion again—only this time he bounced on his legs like a child about to throw a tantrum. The mere sight of Gary was wreaking havoc on her concentration, and Melody made a wrong step, nearly twisting her ankle. Melody let out an audible groan this time. She finally stopped rocking her hips, kicked off her heels, and sighed. She signaled Leslie, her personal assistant, to stop the music. Melody crinkled her face into a hard scowl, letting Gary know he was about to get cussed out. He waved again, a nervous look in his eyes.

Gary and Melody had been friends since she'd gone solo. He knew firsthand how mercurial her moods could be and how fast her temper could flare.

Breathing hard, Melody stomped over. "Gary, Are you fucking serious right now?"

Gary moved like he had to pee.

"You know damn well not to disturb me while I'm rehearsing and in my zone. I was in my zone, Gary. Or did you fucking forget the tour is really fucking close?" Melody snorted at him like a bull seeing red at a Spanish bullfight.

The look on his face gave her pause. Gary was as pale as a piece of loose-leaf paper, anxiety scribbled all over his face. His natural complexion was high yellow, but right now he looked plain ghostly. He was standing stiff, like someone had put a rod up his ass and not the way he liked it either. The last time Gary looked this upset was when he had told Melody she'd been turned down for the leading lady role in the movie version of *Dreamgirls*, beat out by her nemesis in the R&B world.

"Melody, we . . . we need to . . . um . . . we need to talk." Gary stumbled over his words. His eyes roved over toward her assistant and the six dancers. "In private," he said in his stage whisper.

"Gary, I am rehearsing. Do you or do you not know the tour starts in the next three weeks? This has to be perfect. I have a reputation to maintain," Melody hissed, yanking a black hair-tie from her wrist. She smoothed her hands over her head, pulled her long weave into a high ponytail, and wrapped the hair-tie around it.

"Mel, if it wasn't important, I wouldn't dare interrupt," Gary said, his voice quivering. "It is *that* important."

Melody pulled the holder out of her hair again and replaced it, wrapping it tighter this time. Playing with her hair had always been like a nervous tic. Melody's face was stoic. She hated to show emotion, but Gary had her heart racing right now. He was obviously scared shitless about telling her the news.

Melody chuckled, although it contradicted the scowl on her face. "Oh, it better be very important," she said, folding her arms over her chest.

"It's your mother. I mean, Ava Love," he stuttered, trying his best to keep his voice down.

A hot feeling came over her. Just the mention of Ava's name made her sick to her stomach these days. She was an embarrassment to say the least. Being associated with Ava was not good for Melody's image or career as of late.

"Ava Love? What now?" Melody sucked her teeth, disgust painting her face into a mean mug. "Is that what the hell you interrupted me for? To tell me some dumb shit about Ava?" Melody had told her mother six months ago that she didn't want anything to do with her, although Melody still sent Ava a monthly allowance. Melody didn't send her the money out of the kindness of her heart, but more so to keep her away.

"Melody, I know how you are about getting emotional in front of people, so why don't we step out of the studio and talk in private?" Gary implored. His voice was high-pitched and quivering. His eyes were bugged out like he was holding back his tears.

"I swear to every God I know, this better be important, Gary," Melody hissed. She turned around. "Ladies, take your steps from the top. I have to take this call and I'll be right back. I expect perfection."

Melody knew she'd be firing some of them. They either weren't coordinated enough to dance or they were too damn pretty and thus made her look less attractive in comparison. There would be no upstaging Melody Love. When the cameras rolled and the stage lights flashed, there could be only one shining star.

Melody reluctantly followed Gary out of the dance studio doors and into the small private changing room. They stepped inside the room. The air inside of the room was stale with old sweat and leftover perfume, and now it was filled with tension. Melody's insides were churning with curiosity and anxiety.

"Mel, you might want to sit down, honey," Gary said softly, his mouth sagging at the edges.

"Just tell me what's going on, Gary. How bad can it be? I mean, shit, did she get drunk again and make a spectacle of herself for the paparazzi? Did she go harass some record executive, screaming about how great she once was? Or wait, let me guess, she got caught giving head to another much younger NBA player in the back of some sports car that she was much too old to even be a passenger in. No, I have a better one. She's gone to the Ritz and asked to be put up in the presidential suite, free of charge, because she is the mother of Melody Love."

Any of these scenarios were highly likely where her mother was concerned. Although Melody was a big name in the music industry, she was still embarrassed by her mother's outrageously juvenile behavior.

"No, Mel. It's worse, hun," Gary murmured. He lowered his head, wringing his fingers together in front of him. He cleared his throat and refused to look Melody in the eyes.

"Please. What can be worse than—" Melody was saying.

"Mel, Ava is dead," Gary said in a rush of breath, cutting her off. Melody's mouth snapped shut.

"I got the call from Murray today."

Melody didn't flinch. She didn't open her mouth. She didn't move an inch.

"Mel? Are you okay?"

Gary didn't wait. He grabbed her and forced his arms around her shoulders for a hug. Melody kept her arms down at her sides and didn't return his embrace. Her body was rigid.

"She's dead, baby girl. I'm so sorry," Gary whimpered.

His words felt like sharp stabs in Melody's gut. She set her jaw and pursed her lips. *You better not cry, Melody. Crying is for weak people. Crying is not for the famous.* She took a deep breath, swallowed hard, and pushed Gary away. She felt a very painful, hard lump forming in her throat. It took a few seconds before she could speak.

"Is that what you interrupted my rehearsal for?" she said in a low, gruff tone. She moved forward and jutted a chastising finger in Gary's face. Her eyes hooded over with contempt.

"Fucking imbecile. Never interrupt me from something as important as my tour unless Jesus lands in my backyard and wants to sing a duet with me. Understand?" Melody gritted, her face filling with blood. Her chest was tight; it was difficult to breathe. Her mind swirled with a tornado's eye of emotions.

"Don't sit your ass in here worrying about me. You have a job to do, so go do it. You need to be out there promoting the 1 Night Stand tour. I have rehearsal to attend and a career to keep on track," she snapped, turning swiftly and giving him her back.

"You can front for everybody else, but I know you, Melody Love. She is your mother and she is dead. It's okay to feel sad," Gary called out, his voice cracking.

"Fuck you, Gary." Melody almost turned around and slapped him, but she resisted the temptation and kept walking.

"Your sisters will be coming to town. You will have to face them, like it or not, Melody," Gary fired back.

His words made her pause. Melody felt a sharp pain in her heart as it filled with fear and remorse. She leaned against the wall to brace herself against the onslaught of emotions. She really didn't have time today to think about her past—mother or sisters. She took a deep breath, closed her eyes, and tried to forge ahead. The last time she saw her sisters was the day Ava and Murray announced that she would be going solo.

New York, New York
March, 2011

"Well, I called all of you down here with some news," Ava said, looking at each of her daughters seriously. "After a two year layoff, Andrew Harvey's sudden death, and loads of drama about the group's last album sales, the label has finally made us another deal," Ava announced.

Harmony smiled and reached out and squeezed Lyric's hand. Melody averted her eyes to her newly manicured nails, trying her best to keep a poker face.

"Finally," Lyric said. "I really miss performing. It takes my mind off stuff."

"But," Ava continued, noticing Harmony and Lyric's excitement. Melody folded her lips in, waiting for the bomb to drop. Her hands were shaking.

"This one is for Melody. Alone. The group is going to be dismantled for now, except maybe for an occasional Christmas album and maybe one of those huge reunion tours that bring in so much money years after a group breaks up."

"We won't close the door on getting Sista Love back together either," Murray Fleischer interjected.

Harmony's features shuttered closed. Lyric's eyebrows furrowed as she looked from Harmony to Ava, and then to Melody.

Melody finally smiled. A warm sense of satisfaction filled her chest. She was so proud.

Harmony slid to the edge of her seat, her face stony. "Just like that? She can leave us behind just like that. All of our hard work and we're just out without a backup plan? We haven't had an album or tour in two years. What are we supposed to do while she goes solo?"

Ava sighed and looked over at Murray.

"C'mon, Harmony. You knew Melody was the star from the beginning. You knew this was coming. Supremes, Destiny's Child . . . the star always leaves and moves on to bigger and better things," Ava responded.

Murray nodded his head in agreement. He coughed, clearly uncomfortable. "It's all a part of the business. Girl groups have a certain lifespan, and Sista Love's time is up," Murray said, his face flushing pink. Harmony rolled her eyes at him. Lyric let out a sigh and shook her head.

"You just used us. All of those painfully long practices, all of the things we gave up—like for one, being kids. All so you could have your favorite stand on our backs to make it to the top," Lyric screamed, her legs bouncing up and down.

"Ava, I thought you couldn't stoop any lower than some of the shit you put us through in the name of fame, but blindsiding us like this is your new low. And you, Melody, I guess it wasn't enough that you were the top earner. It wasn't enough that we lived in your shadow. It wasn't enough that your baby sister—" Harmony paused abruptly and darted her eyes toward Lyric.

Lyric shot up from her seat and gave everyone in the room one last look of disgust. Then she stormed out of the studio, slamming the door so hard she nearly smashed the glass pane in the door.

"I guess nothing was enough for you. You had to have it all to yourself," Harmony accused.

Melody placed her hand on her chest and raised her eyebrows like she was an innocent bystander being accused of a crime. "I can't control what the label wants, Harmony. They wanted me. Alone," Melody replied. She really didn't understand why her sisters couldn't just be happy for her.

Ava laughed at Harmony's outburst. "Let me tell you something. Your ugly ass should be grateful Melody let you stay in the group to even become famous. In my day, a black bitch like you wouldn't be let on stage, let alone to be *a part of a Grammy-winning, chart-topping group. You would be a broke bitch looking for a welfare check. You should be kissing the ground your sister walks on," Ava spat.*

Harmony set her jaw and took the verbal slap like a woman. She gathered her things. "I'm out of here," Harmony murmured. "You finally got what you wanted, Ava. Finally got your favorite her rightful spot at the top."

"Leave then, you coward. You always were a coward, just like your no-good-ass father," Ava spat.

Harmony swayed on her feet like she'd taken a boxer's uppercut. Her eyes hooded over with contempt and her nostrils flared. She moved a few steps closer to her mother with her right pointer finger jutted out in front of her.

"Coward? Coward? Too bad the real coward is you, Ava Love, since you chose to keep my father from me all of my life because you were too afraid to face the fact that you failed. Too afraid to admit that you got fucked and left because all you ever were was a second string. Second string singer. Second string mistress. Second string daughter. Never number one in anyone's eyes," Harmony hissed. She turned toward the door.

Ava's face flushed red. "You're nothing without me. Nothing without your sister," Ava screamed at Harmony's back. "You're never going to be shit but a nappy-headed wanna-be who was the mistake that ruined my whole life." Ava's voice cracked.

Harmony paused. Her hands curled into fists on their own. Every muscle in her body stiffened.

Before anyone could react, Harmony turned and barreled into her mother like a bulldozer. She slapped Ava so hard she fell back flat on her butt. Ava let out a high-pitched scream. Suddenly, Harmony was on top of Ava like a lion on a gazelle.

"I hate you! I hate you! I never want to see you again!" Harmony was devil-possessed; she screeched at her mother, throwing wild slaps and punches. "You ruined my life! That wasn't enough! Nothing was ever enough for you!" Harmony screamed, swiping viciously at her mother's face, taking a chunk of skin off with her nails.

Ava hollered at the top of her lungs in agony. Murray tried to loosen Harmony's grip on Ava's hair. He finally gave up and scrambled to the phone.

"Security! I need security!"

It took four studio security guards to get Harmony off of Ava. The fire flashing in

Harmony's eyes reflected pure, unadulterated hatred.

Melody cowered in the corner, shock etched on her face. She had never seen her sister like this. Over the years, Melody had heard her mother say some pretty cruel things to Harmony, and her sister had always just taken it.

Once the security guards had Harmony in their grasp, Ava seemed to become emboldened. She got up from the floor with help from Murray and began straightening her hair and clothes.

"Go on. Leave. I have all of your money and you won't get a red cent. Take the clothes on your back. Those were thanks to your sister and me, too. You have nothing, and that's just what you deserve," Ava said through bloody teeth.

"You can have that blood money, but I tell you what I will walk away with: my morals and my dignity. At least I don't have to ever live with the fact that I sold my daughters to the highest bidder, literally, just so I could feel better about my washed-up, wasted, nothing-ass life. I want to thank you for one thing—that's being such a horrible mother. Now, when and if I ever become one, at least I've learned from you what not to do," Harmony retorted, lurching forward, causing the guards to clamp down harder on both of her arms.

"And you, you disgrace. You will never prosper this way," Harmony said, her evil eyes now trained on Melody as the security guards attempted to drag her from the room. "You may have great fame, but you'll always be miserable. You'll never know peace and love. You'll be just like your mother, a prostitute for fame, and when the world is done with you—because just like every bitch diva that ever lived, one day the fans will fade and there will be no one left to cheer for you—you'll have no one to love you."

Melody stuck out her chin and lifted her chest. She wanted so badly to cry and scream and beg both of her sisters not to go, but that wasn't her style. Being tough and obstinate was who she was, and she couldn't change it.

"You're just jealous of me—always have been, always will be," Melody shot back. "Get her out of here."

As Harmony was hauled away like a common criminal, her words played in Melody's ears over and over: "You'll be just like your mother. You'll always be miserable. You'll have no one to love you."

"Forget both of those little bitches. You're the real star," Ava said to Melody, dabbing at her busted mouth with Murray's cloth handkerchief. "Who needs love when you'll have money and fame?"

"Exactly. I'm going to have it all," Melody said. *She turned away so Ava and Murray wouldn't see the tears rimming her eyes.*

Melody felt a sinking feeling in the pit of her stomach and a bad taste in her mouth. It wasn't the taste of regret. It was the taste of fear, apprehension, and already, loneliness.

Melody shook off her memory and returned to the rehearsal with a renewed sense of purpose. She watched her dancers move in unison. It was an acceptable performance, but not good enough. Melody wouldn't accept anything less than perfection.

"Let's take it from the top," she ordered, clapping her hands as she made her way to the middle of the floor. They all halted mid-step, as if she'd hit the pause button.

"Is everything okay, Mel?" Leslie asked.

"Start the fucking music," Melody snapped. *How dare she question me?* She snatched the hair-tie out of her hair and shook her head until her hair fell like a lion's mane around her shoulders.

"Hut. Let's go. No distractions and no more stopping. Period," Melody called out as she slipped into her stilettos.

All six dancers fell into line and proceeded to do the first set. Melody swung her head up and down, gyrated her hips, and moved to the music. She got to the fourth count, and before she knew what happened, her face collided with the hardwood floor. A sharp pain shot from her nose straight up to her brain. It felt like all of the bones that made up her skull had shattered. She could taste blood in the back of her throat and see small squirms of light invading her peripheral vision.

"Oh my God," Leslie screeched. "Melody, are you all right?"

Melody opened her eyes. Pain daggered through her skull. The dancers had all gathered around her, their faces contorted into different stages of shock and horror. Leslie bent down and helped Melody to her feet. The pain intensified as she stood. The room spun.

"Ms. Love, I . . . I'm so sorry. My leg caught a cramp and I almost fell. I didn't mean to use *you* to break my fall. Oh my God, I am so, so sorry," one of the dancers apologized, her hands out in front of her pleadingly.

"Are you okay?" Leslie asked again.

Melody blinked as things started coming back into focus. Blood pooled under the skin near her eyes, and her temples pulsed with pain. Melody lifted her hand to her face and touched the bridge of her nose. An explosion of pain caused her to see fireworks.

A fucking broken nose three weeks before the tour kicks off.

The reality caused a fury of white, hot heat to rise from her toes to her chest. She squinted her eyes into little dashes and looked at all of their faces. The adrenaline coursing through her veins seemed to numb the pain. Everyone in the room was seemingly rooted to the floor, scared to death.

Melody stepped out of her stilettos and bent over to pick up a lone shoe, as if to examine the heel. "I am fine," she said in a low growl, her heartbeat thumping in her throat. They all looked relieved.

"Yes, I am perfectly fine," Melody said in an unsettlingly calm tone.

Before anyone could move, Melody spun around and drove the five-inch heel right into the guilty dancer's head. The girl emitted a blood-curdling scream and crumpled to her knees.

"You're fired," Melody said, panting maniacally, blood dripping from her nose and spit spraying from her lips. "You're fucking fired." Melody stood brooding over her victim.

Everyone in the room froze. There were agape mouths, wide eyes, hands clasped over lips, and arched eyebrows.

"You're fired!" Melody raised her fists and hit the girl again. Screams rose and fell, reverberating off of the studio walls.

"Please!" the victim cried.

Melody could no longer control what had overtaken her. Her mother was dead. Her tour would have to be cancelled or at a minimum postponed. She had to face her sisters.

"You're fired. You're fired," Melody screamed repeatedly. Sweat pooled over her face and neck as she hit the girl over and over like she was hammering a nail into a piece of wood. Blood was everywhere. Tears ran down her face like a gushing stream. Spit escaped her mouth. She could taste the girl's blood as it splattered against her lips.

"You're fired!"

"You're going to kill her," someone in the room screamed.

The only sound Melody heard was the pounding of her own broken heart.

Chapter 3

Lyric

Lyric was jolted out of her sleep by a sharp pain in her side. She moaned and tried to open her eyes, but they were glued shut, and the effort to open them hurt like hell.

"Ow," Lyric groaned louder after another thunderbolt of pain lit up her left side. Her body curled into a fetal position.

"Get up," Rebel, Lyric's on-again-off-again boyfriend, shouted.

"Stop kicking me," Lyric growled when she realized that the tip of Rebel's steel-toed riding boot was the source of her pain.

"Then get the hell up. Your sister is blowing up your jack. That shit is breaking my concentration, that ringing every minute," Rebel barked.

Lyric grumbled an unintelligible complaint. Sometimes even she had to question why she stayed with Rebel, who was a washed up, one-hit-wonder rapper who was always more a stoner than a rapper in the first place.

"You ain't ignoring her call this time. She been calling for an hour straight, back to back. Blowing my fucking high for real." Rebel complained some more. "Now pick that shit up and call her back," he demanded as he dropped Lyric's cell phone next to her.

Lyric squinted her eyes against the pain and watched as Rebel kicked through the empty liquor and beer bottles, old food wrappers, and used drug paraphernalia that littered the floor. It was evident the party had gone on all night.

Lyric opened her eyes wider when she noticed Rebel digging around in her purse. "Hey," she croaked as she watched him recover a tiny foil bundle. Just the sight of the bundle made Lyric's mouth water like Pavlov's dog.

"That's mine," she rasped.

She knew Rebel couldn't hear her over the music. She would have to go fight for what was hers. Lyric tried to sit up, but the cruel pounding in her head caused her to slide right back down. She closed her eyes. She needed to get over to where Rebel stood, or else he'd hit the whole bundle and she'd be left sick and on the hunt to cop.

This time, Lyric placed her left hand on the floor in an attempt to hoist her aching body. When she lifted her head, she felt something wet and mushy on her cheek. Then the smell shot up her nostrils.

"Ugh. What the—" she grumbled, touching her cheek. She looked at her hand and realized she had put it in vomit. "Dammit."

That didn't keep her from pursuing what she needed to get right for the day. Lyric used her jeans to clean off her hand. It wouldn't be the first time she'd woken up in her own bodily fluids.

"Rebel," Lyric croaked out, barely above a whisper. Trying to yell hurt so badly. She couldn't muster enough strength to raise her voice.

"Re-bel." Lyric tried again. This time her throat ignited like she'd swallowed a fire-lit sword.

She coughed until her eyes watered. There was no way Rebel would hear her hoarse pleas. Lyric knew that she would definitely have to get over to him before he hit all of their drugs. With a prayer on her lips and the will of ten men, she rolled onto her side.

"Oh, shit," she wolfed as more pain daggered through her skull.

It hurt so bad it made her dry heave. She should've never let her friends Nikki and Gia talk her into having that party. Lyric had gotten so wasted she didn't even remember half of what she'd ingested.

Lyric put both of her palms flat on the floor and struggled to her knees. The entire room was spinning. Her stomach swirled and sweat pooled all over her body.

After several failed attempts, Lyric finally got to her feet. Her legs were unsteady, like she was standing on stilts for the first time. She braced herself against the couch.

"Rebel." Lyric found her voice.

Rebel glared back at her, giving her his back.

"Rebel, don't fucking hit all of that. That is mine," Lyric screamed, wobbling unsteadily in his direction. "Give me that," she demanded, boldly getting in Rebel's face. She'd ended up with a black eye the last time she did that.

"Fuck outta here. I wasn't going to hit it all, you fiend," Rebel spat.

Lyric couldn't care less about his name-calling. She licked her lips hungrily as he passed her the small tin foil. Lyric held it like a piece of delicate crystal as she dropped down into a wooden kitchen chair. She pushed all of the trash aside and made a spot for herself on the table. She picked up a dirty, used needle and examined it. Lyric placed what was left in the foil into the mouth of a badly burned teaspoon and lit the bottom of it on fire for a few seconds. Satisfied with the consistency of her drug, she made a fist and slapped at the center of her left arm. She didn't have time to find a belt or shoestring to tie a tourniquet. She would have to search blindly to find a good vein.

Lyric was a pro now. She pressed her already needle-pricked skin until she felt a ripe vein. She drew the murky liquid into the dirty needle. She sniffled the snot rimming her nostrils and ran her fingertips over her vein one last time to make sure she would hit the right spot. She grunted hungrily and then plunged the sharp, silver tip of the needle into the crook of her arm. She pressed the white plunger on the back of the needle, slowly releasing the special liquid directly into her vein.

The drugs hit Lyric's system right away, and all of her pain faded. Her body slumped in the chair, and her head lulled forward. The hit wasn't enough to bring her that exciting, euphoric, dancing-on-the-ceiling feeling she had experienced the first time she got high, but at least what was left of the bundle had cured her pain. Lyric closed her eyes. Her body rocked and swayed. She felt good—for a few minutes, at least.

"Yo. Answer this phone." Rebel's booming voice brought Lyric crashing back to reality. Her eyes popped open.

"I'm not going to say it again," he asserted as he put the phone in her face.

Lyric sucked her teeth and snatched her cell phone from his hand. She squinted at the screen. She rolled her eyes, although her heartbeat sped up. The entire screen was filled with missed calls from her sister, Harmony. Lyric's eyebrows folded into the center of her face.

"Fuck that traitor want?" Just the idea of speaking to Harmony made Lyric want to get high again.

"Lyric, you have to respect yourself."

"Lyric, what were you thinking letting them get pictures of you like that?"

"Lyric, you can't keep living like this. You're destroying yourself."

"Lyric, you need to be more responsible."

These were some of the last things Harmony had said to her. Lyric's insides churned just thinking about it. Harmony had become so judgmental since she'd moved out to the suburbs of New Jersey with her little husband and baby. All of a sudden her big sister was so perfect. Well,

Lyric wasn't going to let anyone judge her. It was obvious that Harmony had forgotten where she came from, and in Lyric's assessment, they had all seemed to forget the sacrifice Lyric made for their fame.

"Call her back and find out what she wants. I swear if that phone rings again, I'm going to break it," Rebel promised.

Lyric knew he meant what he said. She stared down at the phone for a few contemplative minutes, trying to imagine what her sister wanted after six months of no contact.

Lyric inhaled deeply and exhaled loudly. Her high had officially been blown. She tapped the screen, closed her eyes, and lifted the phone to her ear.

"Lyric? Oh my God, I've been trying to reach you since yesterday," Harmony huffed into the phone.

Lyric twisted her lips and squeezed her eyes shut tighter and didn't respond. She thought her sister had some nerve. Just like that, Harmony calls after disappearing and expects some wonderful family reunion.

"Hello?" Harmony inquired, like she was making sure Lyric was still there.

"Yeah?" Lyric snapped. "What do you want, Harmony? I'm busy."

"Lyric, are you alone? I mean, um, is there someone there with you?" Harmony asked, her voice strained.

"Why? Why does it matter to you *now* if I am alone or not?" Lyric spat. She could hear Harmony sigh.

"I . . . I have to tell you something, and it can't wait for me to travel all the way there."

Lyric looked over at Rebel, who was now sprawled out on the couch, snoring. He was a waste. She might as well have been there alone.

"Just tell me. Doesn't matter if I'm here alone or with a bunch of people. I mean, it must be important since I haven't heard from you in months."

"You're right, baby sis—"

"Don't fucking call me that. I'm grown. I'm not a fucking baby and haven't been for a long time," Lyric exploded. There were a few long seconds of silence.

"Okay," Harmony relented.

Lyric could tell her big sister was crying. *Good. Traitor. You should be crying.*

"Now that we are clear, Harmony, what is it that I need to know?" Lyric asked, her lips twisted. She was trying hard to keep up the angry-girl act when truthfully she was elated to hear Harmony's voice. Lyric was so lonely since everything that happened. She felt totally abandoned by her entire family.

"It . . . it's Ava," Harmony managed.

Lyric held her breath. She didn't even want to think about the big explosion she'd had with Ava the last time she saw her.

"She's, um, she's dead." Harmony gulped.

The silence was deafening. Lyric's ears began ringing. She could no longer hear the music. She could no longer hear Rebel snoring. She could no longer hear Harmony screaming her name on the other end of the phone. Instead, all she could do was keep her eyes closed and think back.

New York, NY
January, 2004

"Oh my God," Lyric squealed as she exited the long, shiny black limousine that had transported her, her sisters, and Ava from Brooklyn to Broadway in Manhattan.

"Right. I can't believe we are standing outside of Elektra Records," Melody gasped, craning her neck to gawk at the shiny, glass-front skyscraper.

"This is going to be our big break. I know it," Lyric said giddily.

"We are going to be all over the world singing," Harmony chimed in.

"And make enough money to shop, shop, shop," Melody added. All three of the girls were squealing and giggling with delight.

"Be quiet," Ava chastised.

The girls closed their mouths and wiped the smiles off of their faces. "Now don't start being over confident and go and put blight on this opportunity. Andrew Harvey was a friend of mine back in the day, but I still had to beg him for this chance," Ava continued. "Nothing in this business is free. Remember that. Now straighten up those clothes, make sure there is no lipstick on your teeth, remember your damn routine, and let's go. This is that one shot I was never so lucky to get."

Harmony, Melody, and Lyric were suddenly back in business mode. Still, the girls walked into the building trying hard to stifle their muffled snickers of excitement.

When the elevator dinged on the twenty-sixth floor, Lyric felt like her heart would stop. They all exited the elevator in a clown-car jumble, with Lyric bringing up the rear. She stopped and stood in awe of the silver letters on the wall that read ELEKTRA RECORDS, INC. Lyric's heart throttled up, pumping wildly—a dizzying mixture of fear and excitement.

"C'mon," Harmony whispered, grabbing Lyric by the arm so she wouldn't get lost in the maze of glass, black lacquer, and modular furniture that made up the posh suite of offices.

"Sit down," Ava instructed, directing the girls to a beautiful, oversized white leather sofa that was positioned directly across from a tall, frosted glass counter that had ELEKTRA RECORDS etched into it.

Ava walked up to the glass counter and peered over it at the beautiful receptionist. The receptionist held up her right index finger and continued speaking into the little contraption that extended in a line from her left ear to her mouth. When she was finally done, she smiled warmly at Ava.

"Hi. Um, we have a meeting with Mr. Harvey," Ava whispered politely, her voice jerky and unsure. It was not like her at all.

The receptionist smiled again. "And your name, ma'am?" she asked perfunctorily.

"Oh, um, Ava. Ava Love."

The receptionist hit a few keys on her computer keyboard and squinted at her screen. Her smile faded. She punched a few more keys for good measure.

"Hmm. That's strange. I don't seem to have you on Mr. Harvey's calendar," she said apologetically, dragging out the last word as she broke the news.

Ava shifted her weight on her heels. She ran her tongue over her teeth and parted a phony smile. "That's impossible. I spoke to Andrew myself," Ava replied. She was still trying to smile.

The receptionist paused, her lips flattened into a straight line. "I'm telling you, you're not on his calendar," she said flatly. "I've looked in three places and there is no listing for an Ava Love."

Ava fanned her well-manicured hand in front of her face. Lyric and her sisters looked on, recognizing their mother's mood swing.

"Well, check again. Look up Love Sisters or Sista Love. It's a singing group. My daughters," Ava said brusquely. "He sent a car for us, for God's sake." She looked over her shoulder at her daughters, shame creasing her brow.

"I'm telling you—" the receptionist started to argue.

Just then the door to Andrew Harvey's office swung open and the sound of men laughing broke up the tense moment between Ava and the receptionist. Andrew Harvey was ushering three men in suits out of his office.

"I'll definitely be in touch. Can never have the iron in too many digital fires." Andrew Harvey laughed, shaking hands with the three men as each exited his office and stopped for one last handshake.

Ava whirled around and rushed toward Andrew Harvey without regard for his guests.

"Andrew. Andrew," Ava shouted.

Andrew Harvey's facial features flattened and he shot the receptionist an evil look. The receptionist bounced up out of her seat, standing so fast that she sent her office chair rolling into the wall behind her with a bang.

"Miss! You can't just—" She raced around the counter to stop Ava.

"Andrew, it's me, Ava Love," Ava hollered, charging forward. *"Ava Love. Donna Summer, All Systems Go tour. Eighty-seven. Ava Love. Plato's Retreat, Studio Fifty-four."* Ava laid her past and his out there shamelessly.

Andrew Harvey smiled weakly, clearly embarrassed. He put on a good face for his departing guests. The businessmen all eyed Ava suspiciously but reserved their comments.

Within seconds the receptionist was in front of Ava, blocking her forward progress. *"I told you that you were not on his schedule. I am going to have to ask you to leave now or I'll* call security," the receptionist threatened, all professionalism out the window.

Lyric threw her hands up to her mouth. Harmony darted her eyes from her mother to Andrew Harvey, then to the receptionist. Melody stood up with her hands fisted at her sides.

Ava looked past the rail-thin receptionist like she was a tiny buzzing fly that was annoying her but posed no threat. Ava kept her eyes trained on Andrew Harvey.

"You told me to come today, Andrew. Remember? You sent a car for us, so why do I feel like I'm begging for a minute of your time?" Ava said, confusion playing out on her face.

Andrew Harvey darted his eyes over to where Harmony, Melody, and Lyric sat frozen with fear, clutching onto one another like their world was about to end. His frown suddenly eased. He licked his thick lips and flashed his oversized porcelain veneers. Suddenly, it seemed as if Ava's outburst was acceptable.

"Yes. Yes. Ava Love. I'm so sorry. It was an oversight on my part," Andrew Harvey sang, placing a comforting hand on Ava's shoulder. "It's okay, Sonja. This is all my fault. It's okay." He called off his receptionist. She glared at Ava before stomping back to her desk. Ava twisted her lips at the girl, victorious.

"Ava Love," Andrew Harvey huffed, taking in the sight of her. He chuckled knowingly, a joke only he and Ava understood. Lyric and her sisters all breathed a sigh of relief. "Yes. The wild child, Ava Love," Andrew Harvey continued dreamily like he was recalling some far away time. Ava blushed, giggling coquettishly.

"Come on in," Andrew Harvey said invitingly as he stood aside and ushered Ava toward his office with his left hand. "And bring those little beauties with you," he said, licking his lips hungrily again.

Once inside of Andrew Harvey's office, Lyric, Harmony, and Melody looked around in awe. The wall of windows behind his huge, elevated Presidential-style cherry wood desk offered a breathtaking view of the New York City skyline. It felt like they could see as far a Brooklyn from there. Andrew Harvey had beautiful mahogany shelves filled with music awards. Grammys, American Music Awards, Billboard Music Awards: you name it, Andrew Harvey had one on his shelves. There were also more than ten platinum plaques hanging museum-style throughout the expansive office.

This is the real deal, *Lyric thought as she spun around, wide eyed. At thirteen, she had never seen anything like this. She could tell by*

Harmony's agape mouth and Melody's slow, awestruck pirouette that her sisters were also in awe.

"So, whatcha got for me, Ava?" Andrew Harvey asked, his eyes stuck on Lyric.

She noticed. It made her feel tingly inside. She didn't know if the feeling was good or bad. Either way, she noticed.

"Well, you remember how in my day I could hold those notes, baby. Mariah Carey who? I had her beat. I was the queen of that whistle register back then. I was something. Remember that time at Studio Fif—"Ava was saying.

"Um. Yeah, so these are your little girls, huh?" Andrew Harvey interrupted, walking over and examining the girls one by one. Ava quickly shut up and switched gears.

"Yes. These are my pride and joy," Ava sang.

Lyric pinched Harmony's hand and they looked at each other quizzically. Pride and joy? Really?

"Yes, sir. This is Harmony, seventeen, Melody, fifteen, and Lyric, thirteen. They sing, dance, act. All three are triple threats, just like their proud mother," Ava beamed, walking over, fussing over the girls' clothes. She stepped behind Harmony and pushed against her back, making sure she stood up straight.

Andrew Harvey smiled as he moved slowly down the line, examining the girls like slaves for sale at auction. He stopped in front of Lyric. His smile was so wide Lyric could see that beyond the shocking white veneers covering his front teeth, his back teeth were all yellow and nasty looking.

Andrew Harvey placed his pointer finger under Lyric's chin and urged her face upward. Lyric wanted to cough, the strong scent of his Ralph Lauren Safari men's cologne threatening to make her gag. She remembered that cologne scent because the one time she got to meet her father, she'd seen it in his overnight bag.

Lyric's knees knocked together as she stared up into Andrew Harvey's face for a few quick seconds. He was ugly. His eyes were dark, cupped by fleshy pouches. Lyric could tell Andrew Harvey was old by the wrinkles branching out from the corners of his eyes and the strip of baldness that ran straight down the center of his head. But it was the craters in his cheeks and his large, flat nose that made him look like a monster to her.

"She your youngest, huh?" Andrew Harvey asked, a sly grin on his lips. "She's the prettiest. Yeah, nice and innocent," he drawled.

Lyric kept her head tilted upward but averted her eyes away from his greasy, pockmarked face. Her cheeks quivered and suddenly she wanted to pee. Lyric could feel the heat of her mother and sisters' gazes on her.

"Yes. Yes. She's the baby," Ava answered cheerfully, putting emphasis on the last word. She stepped over to where Andrew Harvey stood staring down into Lyric's terrified face. "But look, um, look here. Melody here is the lead. She's got the most talent, and to me, she's my best looking child," Ava said, pushing Melody toward Andrew Harvey.

As if he'd been snapped out of some sick trance, he finally moved his hand from Lyric's chin and turned his attention to the other girls. He gave Melody and Harmony the once over.

"Eh. Typical black girls. Nothing very exotic about them. So far, doesn't appear to be marketable," he said, disinterested. "Girl groups are a dime a dozen these days, Ava. You know that. I just don't see the it factor here."

"Oh, no. You're wrong. They've got what it takes," Ava said anxiously. "Get into position." Ava clapped.

Lyric and Harmony clumsily took their places behind Melody. All three girls lowered their heads and placed their hands on their hips just like they'd rehearsed.

"And five, six, seven, eight," Ava counted down.

On cue, Harmony was the first to lift her head. Lyric counted down silently, and when she got to two-one- thousand, she lifted her head next. Lastly, Melody lifted hers, and when she started rocking her body, her sisters fell into perfect step with her.

"Ewww, ewww. Yeah, yeah," Lyric and Harmony harmonized.

"Many say that I'm too young to let you know just where I'm coming from," Melody crooned.

"Giving him something he can feel," Harmony and Lyric harmonized perfectly behind her.

The girls gave a flawless performance. Ava clapped joyfully at the end. She immediately turned to Andrew Harvey. She could see that he was enthralled.

"See? What did I tell you? You can't lose with us," Ava beamed.

He shook his head up and down, never taking his eyes off of Lyric. It was becoming so noticeable that Lyric shifted uncomfortably under the heat of his gaze.

"I tell you what. Why don't you have them step out so we can talk?" Andrew Harvey said to Ava.

"Oh my God," Melody whispered excitedly. The girls giggled as they filed out of the office.

Ava and Andrew Harvey seemed to be in their private meeting for an eternity before his office door swung open. Ava's face was serious and slightly paler than before. She walked over to her daughters and cleared her throat.

"We got the deal," Ava said flatly, as if she hadn't just announced the best news of their lives. Something flickered over her facial features. Fear? Regret? It definitely wasn't the excitement or elation her daughters expected to see after such a big announcement.

"What? Huh?" Are you serious? A record deal? Us? Like, a real deal?" The girls shot questions at their mother rapid fire. Finally, the reality sank in.

"Ah!" Harmony was the first to scream.

Melody followed with a squeal of her own, while her legs moved as if she were running in place. Lyric jumped up and down in the middle of her sisters.

"We got a deal. We finally got a deal," they screamed.

Ava didn't move or join in their excitement. Instead, she peered precariously over her shoulder at a smiling Andrew Harvey, his return glance as conspiratorial as a wink. Ava took a deep breath and exhaled it.

"Lyric, baby." Ava interrupted their little party. All of the girls stopped celebrating and turned their attention to their mother. *"Mr. Harvey wanted to show you something in his office. He said he sees something special in you,"* Ava said, struggling to get the words out. Ava looked at her youngest daughter with a strangled expression on her face.

Lyric's eyebrows shot up into arches. *"Me?"* She looked at her sisters in disbelief.

Almost at the same time, they all turned and looked at Andrew Harvey and then back at Ava. Harmony's face was crumpled into a shocked frown. Melody's eyebrows were furrowed.

"He wants to see Lyric?" Melody asked incredulously, disappointment replacing the shock. *"Alone?"*

"Yeah, me? Melody is the lead, the star," Lyric said, still completely incredulous of the request.

"Listen. We just got a deal from him, so if he wants to see Lyric alone, don't question him. And don't question me," Ava whispered harshly.

Lyric turned around to find Andrew Harvey still waiting for her in his office doorway. He licked his lips and played with the diamond pinky ring on his right pinky. This time he did wink.

"Go on," Ava encouraged, her hands shaking.

"Can I go with her?" Harmony asked maternally. She was seventeen and the oldest. She had always taken care of Lyric and looked out for her.

"He asked to see Lyric. Alone," Ava repeated firmly. "Now go," Ava hissed at Lyric.

Lyric walked forward gingerly, feeling a sense of dread creeping over her like a dark cloud. When she made it to the doorway, Andrew Harvey put his hand on her shoulder and welcomed her.

"This won't take that long," he said. "You're a very special girl. I could see that the minute I laid eyes on you. You're a star."

Right before he closed the door, Lyric looked back at Harmony with terror dancing in her eyes. Harmony turned her face away and looked over at Ava. There was a clarity in her eyes that had not been there before. Melody folded her arms across her chest and rolled her eyes. As young as they all were, something about Andrew Harvey's request had made them so uneasy that they'd quickly forgotten that they had just landed their first major record deal.

***

"Lyric. Lyric, are you there? Lyric!" Harmony screamed on the other end of the phone. Lyric jarred back to reality. She took a shaky breath.

"I'm here."

"Are you okay?"

Lyric's jaw went stiff. "Why wouldn't I be?" she retorted. "Did you expect me to cry and scream that my mother was dead? Nah. I'll leave the phony tears and histrionics for you and the megastar," Lyric spat cruelly.

Lyric heard Harmony breathe heavily into the phone and knew she was making her sister uncomfortable. Mission accomplished.

"Okay. I'll be in Brooklyn tomorrow. I'll be at Ava's to gather some things," Harmony supplied.

"Good for you." With that she moved her cell phone from her ear, pressed the red button and disconnected the call. She needed to get high immediately.

Chapter 4

Harmony

"I left all of the new class descriptions in alphabet order. All you have to do is hand them out during your last drama class tomorrow. Oh, and please, please make sure you put up the dance and voice class cancellations for the next three days and the replacement class schedule. You know these parents get crazy when they feel like they've paid and they're not getting the full value of their little bit of money. I really don't want to come back to an email inbox full of parent complaints," Harmony rambled, moving around her house like an electrified ball of nervous energy.

"Aubrey's clothes are laid out for seven days, but use your common sense. If the weather changes, of course you'll need to switch things up. Please spend at least the first few hours with Aubrey at the day care. It's her first time being away from me for that long during the day, and I just don't—" Harmony shot off more instructions like a drill sergeant.

"Hey. Hey." Ron grabbed her from behind, halting her jittery movement. "I know what needs to be done. I will take care of things at Dance and More. Remember, we opened the school together. If I didn't know the business model, what kind of owner would I be? I'll handle the parents, the classes, the substitutes, and even the costume lady for the recital," Ron said reassuringly.

Harmony slapped her forehead with the palm of her hand and closed her eyes. She groaned. "I forgot about the fittings for recital costumes," she said through her teeth.

"But I didn't. That's my point. I can handle it. And I will take very good care of Aubrey. She's mine too, you know. I will not leave her dirty, hungry, and naked. You just have to trust me," Ron said smoothly.

Harmony closed her eyes and inhaled. "I know. I'm sorry. I'm just anxious. It's not about you," she apologized.

Ron turned her around and looked into her eyes. Harmony returned his gaze.

"Harm, this is all going to be okay. You're not going to the guillotine; you're going to bury your mother. Once you've done your duty as a daughter, you can move on." Ron soothed her. "A lot of people wouldn't even be doing all of this with everything you've been through at her hands."

Harmony cringed. Suddenly she was shivering. Ron was right. Harmony couldn't figure out why she felt so compelled to make sure Ava had a decent funeral after everything she'd done. Harmony had spent her entire life convincing herself that she hated her mother, but maybe deep down inside she loved her more than she could understand.

"I know, Ron, but things are just so—" Harmony's voice hitched.

"They're the way they are supposed to be. Period. You didn't do anything wrong," he replied. "Once the arrangements are made, Aubrey and I are going to come be right by your side through it all. I am not going to let you go through this alone. But this trip, this meeting with your sisters for the first time in so long, well, that is something you have to do on your own," Ron said, grabbing her hands and using them to pull her closer to him.

"You're right," Harmony murmured, falling against his chest.

"I love you, Harmony Bridges," Ron whispered into her ear. "I'll never stop loving you. I'll be here for every good time and bad time."

Harmony's insides warmed up. His words were like the sun on a patch of ice.

"I love you more, Ronald Bridges, and I thank God every day for you," she replied, moving her face in front of his.

He placed his mouth over hers, and their tongues moved together sensuously. In that moment, there was peace wrapped around them like a warm down blanket in the winter. This was all Harmony needed. His love.

"Ma-ma," Aubrey cooed from her playpen. Harmony quickly moved her lips from Ron's like a teenager who'd just gotten caught stealing her first kiss.

"There goes our little CBer. She's got perfect timing," Ron joked, groaning playfully.

"Stop. Don't call my baby a cock blocker, Ron." Harmony laughed, playfully hitting him on the arm as she unhooked herself from his embrace. She rushed over to her baby girl, smiling brightly.

"Hey, sweet girl," Harmony sang, lifting her chubby-faced baby out of what they called baby prison.

"Yup. A natural born CBer," Ron continued, pointing below his belt to the rise in his pants that was now shrinking.

"Oh my goodness, Ron. Stop. Look how she's looking at you like she understands," Harmony replied, shaking her head.

They both shared a good hearty laugh. It was just what Harmony needed to take her mind off of Ava, Melody, and Lyric, even if only for a few minutes.

Harmony bent down and gave Aubrey one last kiss. She stood over her daughter's crib and stared at her baby's little chest rising and falling so peacefully, so innocently. Harmony shuddered at the explosion of love that lit up inside of her like a fireworks show every time she looked at her baby girl.

Harmony wrapped her arms around her torso and hugged herself, wondering if her mother had ever felt that crazy, dizzying, throw-you-off-kilter type of love for her when she was a baby. *Probably not.*

Harmony suddenly recalled being two years old, standing up in an old-fashioned wooden crib that was pushed into the corner of a small, cramped room filled with show costumes. Harmony was screaming and extending her little arms out desperately, while her mother moaned and groaned from the tiny bed like the man on top of her was killing her. Even as young as she was then, maybe only two years old, Harmony still remembered the twisted look of disgust and frustration on her mother's face as she shoved a cold bottle of milk into her mouth and slammed her down onto the crib's bare mattress.

"You ready?" Ron whispered, interrupting her thoughts.

Harmony was startled. Ron walked over and put his chin on Harmony's shoulder so that they both were staring down into the crib at their little sleeping beauty. Harmony sighed loudly.

"As ready as I'm going to get," she replied.

They tiptoed out of Aubrey's nursery. Ron handed Harmony her pocketbook. "I've already taken your suitcase downstairs," he told her. "You sure you're all right to drive?"

"It's only New Jersey to Brooklyn, honey. I'll be fine. Besides, some driving time will help me clear my head," she assured.

Harmony pointed one last time to the to-do list she'd written on the white dry-erase board that hung on the wall outside of their kitchen.

"You just don't quit, huh?" Ron shook his head. "Let's go, woman," he said, grabbing her car keys from one of the hooks under the board.

Harmony chuckled and followed her husband outside. Ron put Harmony's suitcase into the trunk of her hybrid SUV and opened the driver's side door for her.

"Remember, I am just a phone call away," he said, using his thumb to lift her chin so that he could kiss her one last time.

Harmony held the sides of his face and kissed him deeply. She turned and prepared to get in her car. Just then, the sun glinted off of the gold Narcotics Anonymous emblem that Ron wore on a Cuban link necklace. It had been a gift from Harmony after he'd made it through his first full year of sobriety. Harmony looked at it, then into his eyes.

"Don't forget your meetings, Ron. I won't be here to go with you, but you know I am sending my support in spirit. Those are important. They've gotten us this far," she reminded softly.

"Would I miss my meetings? Those meetings and you saved my life. I would never throw all of that away," he assured, winking at her and kissing her on the nose. "You worry too much," he followed up.

"Maybe I do," Harmony agreed with a smile.

With that, she slid into the driver's seat of her car. Ron closed the door and stepped back. Harmony started the car and took one last look at the love of her life. She waved and smiled.

"What would I do without that man?" she whispered just as she stepped on the gas.

Harmony always said it was fate that had brought her and Ron together. The rain had been coming down in torrents the day she'd rushed up to the steps of the Trinity Church, soaked and shivering. Her tears had mixed with the rain and ran in streams down her face. Until then, Harmony had never been one to pray or even know anything about religion or God, but that day, having just been tossed onto the Manhattan streets like a piece of trash at the behest of her mother and sister, Harmony had wandered the streets of Manhattan until she'd ended up there. With nothing but the clothes on her back, about two hundred dollars in her purse, and nowhere else to go, Harmony stood trembling and squinting up at the gothic revival style building, with its tall pointed arch, rose windows, flying buttress, and ornate eighteenth century façade, compelled to go inside. The church, nestled at the corner of Broadway and Wall Street, seemed so out of place in the middle of Manhattan's modern skyscrapers. *Perfect*, Harmony had thought, since she felt out of place herself.

Harmony climbed up the gray slate steps of the church and took shelter from the rain under its front overhang. As Harmony twisted the bottom of her shirt and let the water drip into a pool at her feet, she noticed the homeless guy crouched in the corner of the church's doorway. He leaned down on a black garbage bag, with his head covered by a dirty gray hood. A cold chill had shot down her back. Just like the man, she had no place to go. No home. No real money. No family. Nothing.

Once Harmony was satisfied that she wouldn't drip all over the inside of the church, she reached out to grab the carved brass handle of the church's doors. Suddenly, the homeless guy jumped up onto his feet as if he'd been hit with a jolt of electricity.

"Hey!"

Harmony was startled. She clutched her purse against her body.

"Can you spare some change?" he yelled at her, swiping his hood off of his head so that she could see the hunger in his bugged-out eyes.

Harmony froze, unnerved by his sudden move toward her.

"Anything you got, I'll take," he said, back-handing the clear mucus rimming his nostrils.

Harmony's eyes widened, stunned at how young he looked. *Aren't most homeless people old veterans or older mentally ill people?*

"I . . . I don't have anything." Her bottom lip trembled. She didn't know if it was from being cold and wet or the gravity of her situation becoming reality in that moment.

"I'm not asking for a free handout, miss. I got some stuff to sell," the homeless guy said. He scrambled back over to his corner spot and started digging in his big, black garbage bag.

"Really. I don't—" Harmony shook her head and clamped down harder on the door handle.

"Wait. Wait," he called over his shoulder at her. "Just hear me out. I'm not begging. I got stuff to sell. Real valuable stuff. I'm not asking for something for nothing," he pleaded.

Harmony's shoulders slumped. *What can he possibly have that is valuable if he's living on the street?* She inhaled and exhaled. She waited like he'd asked, silently kicking herself for being such a bleeding heart all of the time. That same compassion had let her mother and Murray take advantage of her all of these years.

"I'm telling you I don't have any—"

"You remember the show *Our Family, Your Family*? It was on from 1996 until 2004. You had to have seen it." He cut her off as he continued to dig deep into his bag.

Harmony's brows knitted. Of course she'd heard of the show.

"I was on that show," he announced.

Harmony sucked her teeth and tilted her head to the side.

"I'm serious. I was the son. Kyle. That was me. My stuff is still worth money. It was the longest running black sitcom on television," he rambled, finally finding whatever he was digging for.

Harmony's lips were twisted sideways.

"I have proof." He extended something toward her. "Since you don't believe me."

Harmony looked at his "proof." She stood stiff, her mouth slightly open. Her hand slipped from the church's door handle. *Our Family, Your Family* had been her favorite show growing up. It was the one thing she would sneak to watch whenever Ava didn't have her practicing dance moves or singing ranges. Harmony remembered wishing and dreaming that she could be one of the kids in the family, and that Ava could be as loving and supportive as the mother on the show.

"Here. See. This is an original studio audience show program and one of my original scripts," the homeless guy said, holding his goods up to her face. "I can let this go for ten bucks."

It had taken a few blinks for Harmony to realize that he might be telling the truth. She looked at the booklet then back up at his face.

It is him!

Even through his scarred and ashen skin, overgrown beard, and wild unkempt hair, Harmony had recognized Ronald Bridges, one of the stars from her favorite childhood show. No matter how terrible he looked, Harmony could never mistake that gorgeous face. She had had such a crush on him when she was a pre-teen.

"Y—you're . . . " Harmony stammered, her mouth fully open by then. He sniffled and used his dirty sweater sleeve to wipe his nose.

"Yeah, it's really me," he said, shame causing him to lower his eyes to his feet. "Ron Bridges. In the flesh."

Harmony's lips turned downward with pity. Ron Bridges. *The* Ron Bridges was standing in front of her, a complete shell of his former gorgeous, heartthrob self. His filthy, stained jeans, run over sneakers, and dirt-filled fingernails made Harmony itch just looking at him.

"I . . . I just, um, hit a rough patch. But I got a couple auditions lined up. That's why I need the money. Carfare." He sniffled some more and moved restlessly on his legs. "A few bucks and I'll be on my way. Just need to get to those auditions. Movies. Yeah, um, movies. I moved on from sitcoms years ago, you know. After being on TV for eight seasons, it was time for the big screen," he rambled.

Harmony knew he was lying. She could recognize the signs of drug use when she saw them—that runny nose, those wild eyes, the skin lesions, the constant arm rubbing. Harmony knew he had the monkey riding his back, but she still envisioned him as his old self.

"You don't remember me, do you?" Harmony asked him. "Kids' Choice Awards, 2002."

Ron halted his jerky movements. "You know me?" He squinted and moved a few steps closer to her.

"Well, maybe not personally. I was in the group Sista Love. My sisters and I were still trying to get a big deal then, but we got lucky enough to get the gig. We performed for the pre-show, and we did some red carpet interviews. We interviewed you. Well, my sisters interviewed you. I was too star struck to speak to you, but I was right next to you. I'll never forget it," Harmony recalled dreamily.

"Oh, shoot. Um, yeah. Sista Love. That girl group, right? You were like the backup singer for that girl. The real pretty one. What was her name? Uh, Mel . . . Melody Love, right?" Ron said, snapping his finger at the memory.

Harmony's heart sank. She shifted her weight from one foot to the other.

Backup singer? That's what the world sees me as, huh? Always in Melody's shadow. Her hands curled into fists so tight her nails dug moon-shaped craters into her palms.

"Yeah. I guess you can say that," she said. "Backup singer sounds about right."

"So, you still in that group?"

Harmony shrugged, holding his gaze. Her heart thumped wildly, and she had no idea why.

He smiled at her. "Look at us. Two superstars standing on the steps of a church, cold, wet, and—" He looked down at himself. "As for me, dirty. But you, I'd say beautiful."

Harmony's cheeks got hot. She looked out at the street. She didn't know what to make of his compliment. Anytime someone called her beautiful, she had a hard time believing it. She'd spent her whole life being called black and ugly.

"Nasty night for a superstar girl group member to be out here." Ron jerked his chin toward the buckets of rain coming down just outside of the church's covered steps.

"I could say the same thing about a superstar TV actor," Harmony replied without looking at him.

"Touché."

She turned her eyes back to Ron, her face serious. "I was a big fan, and I know at least ten thousand girls that were too. I always wondered what happened to you," she said, nodding toward Ron's corner shelter and his black bag of worldly possessions.

Ron hung his head again. "The business," he murmured, tugging at a frayed piece of string hanging from his hoodie. "It chews you up and it doesn't just spit you out; it violently spews you out like the worst projectile vomit you could imagine."

"That's for sure." Harmony nodded her understanding. "I guess all we can do is pray for ourselves."

With that, she opened the church's doors and stepped inside. Although she later found out he had never ventured inside of the church, that day, Ron had followed her inside. They had been inseparable ever since.

Harmony drove past the Barclays Center in Downtown Brooklyn and was in amazement at how much her hometown had changed. The Brooklyn landscape reminded her more of the Village in Manhattan now, with the bustling crowds and new, brightly lit shopping center. Even the Atlantic Avenue train station had gotten a facelift. Harmony stared out of her window at all of Brooklyn's new residents too.

There was a time when living in Brooklyn and seeing a white person in that part of town was as rare as a Big Foot sighting.

"Gentrification is real," Harmony whispered, still slightly awestruck at how quickly everything had changed.

Harmony remembered when she was growing up that same area of Brooklyn was off limits to yuppies with their little teacup Yorkies and Schwinn bicycles with baskets on the front. And outdoor cafés? In Brooklyn? Unheard of back then.

Harmony reached down and pressed a few buttons to find her favorite radio station. Right away, she recognized the voices of the Hot 97 radio personalities. Harmony turned it up.

"So, we heard that Melody Love will be postponing her 1 Night Stand Tour," the popular female radio host said, as if she was revealing the best kept secret in town. A collective groan filtered through the radio station.

"Yeah, her moms passed away a couple of days ago," the male host added. "Suspicious, I heard. Ol' girl was some old school eighties backup singer, right? Damn, I was looking forward to Melody's tour. Her last album was lit, and those collabos with Sly always had the clubs jumping. Damn, I hope it ain't canceled for real.

The Barclays was going to be their first stop," the male host said.

"Well, I'm about to spill the tea on all of that, okay? I heard that Melody wasn't even close to her moms these days. Sources said they had a big blowup not too long ago. She fired her moms and everything. I also heard she canceled the tour because she attacked one of her dancers in the studio over Sly. Supposedly, Sly was banging one of those dancer chicks, and we all know how jealous the diva Melody is. I heard Melody beat that ass and came out of that whole thing with just a black eye, but the dancer, well, I hear she's in *bad* shape," the female radio personality gossiped.

"I wonder if Sly will go with her to her mother's funeral. I mean, they are the couple everyone loves to hate. I don't know why he doesn't just put a ring on it already. Every dude out here wants her," the male host chimed in.

Harmony exhaled loudly. She definitely knew she was back in New York, because every radio station either played Melody and Sly's music incessantly or they were the topic of the gossip. Harmony shivered. The dread of going from living a low-key life in a small suburb of New Jersey to being back in the spotlight because her sister was a megastar was going to be a nightmare.

When Harmony pulled up in front of her childhood home, her stomach immediately twisted into knots. She reached over to her passenger seat and fished around in her purse for her pocket-sized container of Tums. Harmony put two of the antacid tablets on her tongue and looked out the window at the house. Her mouth hung open slightly at the sight.

"What the hell, Ava?" Harmony whispered as she took in the rusted and broken wrought-iron front gate, several cracked windowpanes, and the dilapidated front steps. "Not you, living like this."

Ava's house was always one of the best kept brownstones on the block, but from what Harmony could see, Ava had let things go for too long.

After driving up and down the narrow, tree-lined Brooklyn block, Harmony finally found a parking spot. After six tries at parallel parking, she'd finally managed to wedge her car between a van and a tiny smart car.

"Thank you, Jesus, for my driveway," Harmony whispered, worn out from the effort it took to park.

Before she got out of the car, Harmony punched out a text message to Ron.

> I made it to Brooklyn. I'm okay. Miss you already. Kiss my baby for me.

Harmony smiled when she got a kissy face reply from Ron. As she exited her car, Harmony said a quick prayer for strength.

"Here goes nothing," she mumbled, grabbing her purse and locking up.

When she made it to the front of the house, Harmony lifted the broken gate so that she could push it open without it scraping the ground. She could tell by the scratches on the concrete that not every visitor had taken the time.

Once inside the yard, Harmony stood at the steps and looked up at the dirt-covered windows, the chipped paint and shattered glass panels on the front door, and the cracked cement on the stoop. She hadn't expected her mother, the great Ava Love, to be living like this at all. It didn't surprise Harmony that Ava had died alone, but it did surprise her that Ava hadn't kept up appearances, since that was what she'd preached to her daughters all of their lives.

"Don't any of you ever leave this house looking raggedy, poor, or broke. I don't care if you

don't have a dollar in your pocket; you better look like you do. Your hair always needs to be combed, pressed, laid down neatly. Your clothes always need to be pristine. And your faces— beauty is all women have most of the time. You should always have a flawless face," Ava preached.

Harmony reached out and held onto the rickety stair railing as she climbed the uneven steps. She walked up to the front door, closed her eyes, held her breath, and used her fist to knock. After few minutes, Harmony could hear shuffling on the other side of the door. Each time a lock clicked, more hairs stood up on her neck.

"Ah, Harmony. I knew you'd be the first to come," Murray greeted her, smiling sunnily.

Harmony didn't return the smile. She had already promised herself she was not going to pretend with him. "Murray." She nodded, standing at the door's threshold like a stranger.

"Come on in. This is still your home," Murray sang, stepping aside slowly.

Harmony's heart sped up as she crossed the doorway. She could smell remnants of Ava's signature scent, *Anaïs Anaïs* perfume. Harmony held onto the wall for support as she moved through the darkened foyer. Her teeth chattered, although it was probably 90 degrees inside the house. Harmony's head swirled and her stomach cramped. She felt out of place, like she'd been bound, gagged, and dragged there against her will. As she moved on unsteady legs, Harmony clumsily bumped into the tall, silver cylindrical vase that Ava kept umbrellas in, sending it toppling over with a crash.

"Harmony, are you okay?" Murray turned around as fast as his old, hunched body allowed.

Harmony was already on her knees, cleaning up the mess of umbrellas, when suddenly that corner of the house, Ava's scent, and the contents of the umbrella holder brought a memory crashing down on her.

Brooklyn, New York
September 2001

"Harmony. Harmony, wake up," Melody whispered, shaking Harmony's shoulders.

Harmony groaned, exhausted from another entire day of dancing and singing practices. She was too tired to be bothered.

"Harmony," Melody hissed in her ear.

Finally, Harmony opened her eyes a crack. "What?" she whined, shrugging her shoulders in frustration.

"Wake up. Look what I got," Melody said, pushing something toward Harmony's face.

Harmony scrunched her face and opened her eyes a bit wider. "What is that?" she asked, her voice still gruff with sleep.

"You have to get up to see," Melody whispered, climbing onto Harmony's bed.

Harmony sucked her teeth and sat up. Her pink chenille quilt fell down around her waist as she sat up and leaned her back against her tufted headboard.

"I got this while Ava wasn't looking. Today, at the store," Melody whispered excitedly, shoving her secret contraband toward Harmony's face.

Harmony blinked a few times to make sure she was seeing correctly. She smiled weakly.

"How did you do that?" Harmony reached out tentatively to take the forbidden item from her sister's hand.

"Easy. I just put it in my pocket when she wasn't looking. Ava never watches me. She is always too busy watching you," Melody told her, snatching the goods back before Harmony could take it.

Harmony tilted her head and twisted her lips. "Why did you wake me up if you weren't going to give me any?" she grumbled. She should've known better.

Melody chuckled evilly. "Who said I wasn't going to give you any?" She stuck her tongue out.

Harmony rolled her eyes. "Because I know how you are. Everything is for you. I'm going back to sleep. We are not supposed to have that anyway," Harmony said, gathering up her blanket.

"Okay. Okay." Melody tugged at the blanket to keep Harmony from pulling it over herself.

"Well, are you going to open it or not?" Harmony asked impatiently.

Melody smiled slyly. "Not this one. I got this one for you," Melody announced, pulling another forbidden item from behind her back.

Harmony's eyes went wide like a kid at Christmas. "Oh my God. My favorite," Harmony whined. "I'm really not supposed to have this kind, but I love it so much," Harmony whispered, conflicted.

"Hurry up and eat it while Ava is 'sleep." Melody looked over her shoulder to make sure no one was there. Harmony snickered. Melody tossed the little treasure to her. Harmony picked it up and eyed it like it was a shiny, freshly cut rare diamond. She sniffed the tiny package.

"Oh my God. Cherry, my favorite of all." Harmony sighed.

"Eat it. Hurry up," Melody urged.

Harmony darted her eyes toward their bed-room door. *"Okay, but you have to look out for Ava,"* *Harmony said apprehensively.*

"I will," *Melody assured, climbing off of Harmony's bed.* *"I'll go outside and listen out."*

"No," *Harmony whispered harshly.* *"If you go out there she might hear you and wake up. Just stand inside, right by the door, so you can hear her footsteps."*

"No. I will pretend I have to pee and make sure she's not coming," *Melody said.*

Harmony's shoulders slumped.

"I'm telling you I won't let you get caught. I pinky swear promise." *Melody held up her right pinky finger.*

Harmony played with her bottom lip with one hand and clutched her secret treasure in the other. She looked down at the shiny package. It was calling out to her. She looked back over at Melody. She wanted to trust her sister.

"Okay. I'm going to eat some of it," *Harmony relented.*

"Okay. I'm going to go look out. Eat up," *Melody whispered.*

Harmony watched as her sister carefully opened their bedroom door and tiptoed out. She took a deep breath and took one last leery look at the door before she tore open the wrapper on the long, red Jolly Rancher stick. She held it up to her face and smiled. When Harmony put the candy on her tongue, the flavor explosion gave her chills. She hadn't had a piece of candy in years. She wanted to savor the moment and the candy for as long as she could. It was like being in a dream. Harmony bit off a piece of the hard, sticky candy and folded the rest into the wrapper. She was sucking on the sweet piece of heaven like it was the last piece on earth.

Harmony slid out of her bed and slid the leftover piece of candy under her mattress. She already had it planned out that she'd eat a tiny piece each night after Ava went to bed until it was gone.

Harmony was dancing around with her candy in her mouth when the door to her bedroom swung open. Harmony whirled around, smiling.

"It is so—" Her smile quickly faded into a terrified grimace.

"What is it that you have?" Ava snarled, rushing over to Harmony like a hurricane-force wind.

Harmony was frozen with fear. Her entire body trembled. She darted her eyes toward

Melody, who was standing in the doorway, moving her hands and shrugging her shoulders as if she had no idea how Ava knew about the candy.

"You sneaky little spook. You're always being a sneaky, disgusting, nappy-headed little bitch," Ava spat cruelly. She grabbed Harmony by the arm. "Get downstairs! Now!"

Harmony knew what that meant. "No, Ava. I'm sorry. Please."

"Oh, you're going to be more than sorry when I get through with you," Ava hissed.

Harmony took one last look at Melody, and she could've sworn her sister was smiling.

"Get in the corner. You know the drill," Ava demanded.

"Please don't," Harmony whimpered.

"Not only did you eat candy when I don't allow it, but you stole it too. You put us all at risk. You put your sisters' careers at risk." Ava reached down into the silver umbrella holder she kept in the corner of the foyer and retrieved her leather belt.

"This hurts me more than it hurts you," Ava said as the belt came down with a fury on Harmony's back. Ava said that same thing every time she gave Harmony a whipping for just being alive.

***

"Harmony? Are you okay?"

Murray was at her side, trying his best to help her up from the floor. Harmony had Ava's leather belt gripped so tightly in her left hand that her knuckles paled. Her chest heaved, and she could feel sweat rolling down her back. Ava was always careful to hit Harmony in a place that wouldn't show if she had to perform.

Being back in the house reminded Harmony just how much she had given up. She had often wondered what being a normal kid with a childhood filled with laughter, tears, play dates, candy, and best friends was like. Ava didn't allow Harmony, Melody, and Lyric to do normal kid things. They couldn't eat candy because a rough piece might pierce their throat muscles or ruin their pristine smiles. They couldn't go swimming because it would ruin their chest muscles and voice boxes. They couldn't even eat foods that kids liked. Ava only allowed them to eat salads and very lean meat because they all needed to be perfectly proportioned. Fat girls, after all, would never make it in the music industry. Harmony, Melody, and Lyric never went to the movies or amusement parks—that would be a waste of their time and a strain on their voices. Forget the zoo, class trips, and eventually even school. They were all homeschooled by a lady Ava hired and brought home with her after she'd been on the road trying to breathe life back into her own fading career.

Harmony had only attended public school for three years, from age five to seven, before her mother had pulled her out. Melody and Lyric never got a chance to attend school and meet other kids their age. The girls had no friends, but they did have each other and their music. According to Ava, that was all they needed.

Harmony was the songwriter, Melody the lead performer, and Lyric, well, she was kind of forced to be a part of the group so she just fit in where she could.

"Let me get all of this out of your way," Murray said, noticing the tears rimming Harmony's eyes. He gently eased the belt out of her hand and shoved it back down into the umbrella holder.

Harmony blinked a few times. *That's the past. That's the past. That's the past. You are not your past. You are not your past.* She stood up and ran the flats of her hands over her clothes. She held her head high and used her thumb to make sure her tears didn't fall.

"I've got some things laid out in the living room." Murray jerked his chin toward the doors.

Harmony waited until he was done cleaning up her mess. She was, after all, a guest in Ava's house now.

When Murray was done, he slowly inched the rest of the way down the hallway to the French doors leading to the living room. Harmony followed him inside. She stood stiffly like a stranger. Everything seemed so old now. Harmony looked to her right and noticed Ava still had the tall, glass-encased stereo system with the record player on top and shelves of LPs on the bottom. Ava would turn it on every morning before the sun came up to make Harmony and her sisters practice. It was covered with a thick, gray layer of dust now. Harmony could tell it hadn't been used in years.

"Sit. Sit," Murray said invitingly. "I just pulled out some old pictures here. You know, in case you girls wanted to do a program for the services."

Harmony sat at the very edge of the leather couch. She instantly remembered how happy she was when she, Melody, and Lyric had gotten their first advance check from the record company. It seemed like so much money back then. Ava had rushed out and bought all brand new furniture for the house, but the couch, the leather couch, had been Ava's prize. According to Ava, leather furniture meant that she had made it in life.

"Look at this one. She was a real beauty in her day," Murray mused.

Harmony reached out and took the picture from his hand. She stared at it. She twisted one side of her mouth and shook her head slowly, blown away.

Ava's personality certainly contradicted her looks. Outwardly, Ava was a stunning woman, in a regal, Lena-Horne-mixed-with-Diahann-Carroll sort of way. She had blemish-free butterscotch-colored skin. Her eyes were striking, both slanted and deep set. She had perfect heart-shaped lips, and even after three kids, her body had remained a shapely hourglass, boasting a flat stomach, round hips, and cellulite-free legs.

Harmony narrowed her eyes at the picture, recalling how Ava never left the house without a full face of flawlessly applied makeup. Her hair was naturally long, and most of the time she wore it in a regal chignon, only letting it hang when she went on a date. Ava preached that real women always wore heels and makeup. Ava never wore flats or sneakers; instead, she donned the most fabulous stilettos and pumps. Her shoe collection could give Imelda Marcos a challenge.

Murray laughed out loud and extended another picture in Harmony's direction. "Now these were the days. She always said she was the most happy when she was performing."

Sure wasn't most happy being a mother. Harmony swallowed before her thoughts turned into words. She was trying to remain polite, so she took the picture. In it, Ava smiled beatifically as she stood with Donna Summer and the husband-and-wife duo Ashford and Simpson. Ava wore a short black mini dress with a feathered bottom and a beautiful pair of sparkly, silver T-strap dance shoes.

Harmony knew about her mother's career, but she couldn't recall ever really seeing Ava in action. According to stories Harmony heard growing up, Ava Love had been a chart-topping disco diva in the late '70s early '80s. Ava had graced every major stage in every major city in the United States, but she never got any further than an opening act for Donna Summer. Getting pregnant with Harmony had dashed her dreams, and in Ava's assessment, changed her life for the worse. Ava had never failed to remind Harmony of the burden of her existence.

Harmony passed the picture back to Murray. "And this one," he said.

Harmony put her hand up. "I've seen enough, Murray. I'm just going to wait for my sisters so we can get all of this over with," she said flatly.

Just then, Harmony and Murray both heard tires squealing, car doors slamming, and the buzz of voices outside. Murray and Harmony exchanged a furrowed-brow look. Harmony stood up first. She rushed to the two floor-to-ceiling windows in Ava's living room. She pulled back the dusty, moth-eaten curtains and peeked out of the window. Harmony sucked in her breath.

"Melody has arrived."

Chapter 5

Melody

"Melody! Melody! Is it true there might've been foul play with your mother's death? When is the last time you saw her? Did she forgive you for firing her? Did she ever accept your relationship with Sly?"

"Melody! Melody! Did you cancel your tour because of problems in your relationship with Sly?"

"Melody! Melody! Where's Sly? Did you break up over his affair with a dancer?"

"Melody, is Sly going to support you through this difficult time?"

"Is this the home you grew up in?"

"Where's Sly?"

"Are the wedding rumors true? Did Sly finally propose?"

The paparazzi were relentless. They had followed Melody from her Tribeca loft all the way to Brooklyn. From the time Melody's caravan of vehicles turned onto Ava's block, the shameless reporters and cameramen quickly jumped from their cars, leaving them haphazardly abandoned, surrounding Melody's Range Rover like a police tactical exercise to prevent the escape of a fleeing suspect. The fiendish reporters banged on the windows, the doors, and the hood. They hurled questions at Melody like handfuls of mud. Even through the heavily tinted windows, one explosion of flash after another lit up the inside of the car.

Melody peered out the window at the crowd of hungry photographers. She let out an exasperated breath. There were times she loved the attention and lived for the camera flash, but this wasn't one of them.

"V, will you go secure my exit and entry into the house please? I need to make a clear beeline straight inside," Melody said to Virgil, her six foot seven inch tall head of security. "I don't want to give them anything printable."

"Sure thing."

He swung his door open, using his muscular arms and barrel chest to force the throngs of cameramen back before they could push their cameras through the door to steal a picture of Melody.

"Melody!"

"Melody!"

"Melody!"

Melody leaned her head back against the headrest and closed her eyes behind her dark shades. *Sly, Sly, Sly.* Every other question the blog, tabloid, and newspaper reporters shouted at her had to do with her boyfriend, Sly. The world was obsessed with their relationship. Every two days, even when Melody took a break from touring and didn't have any new music out, there was some story about her and Sly. Simple nights out at restaurants always resulted in tons of pictures and speculative stories about them. If they were out together and Sly walked a few steps ahead, the stories about their impending breakup would surely follow. If Melody was spotted out alone, even for a rare shopping excursion in a European city, she'd read about how she used retail therapy to get over Sly's latest infidelity. It was non-stop.

Sly was a popular street rapper turned music mogul who owned his own record label and was ten years Melody's senior. Melody was a beautiful, wildly talented diva who had the entertainment world on lock with her dancing, singing, and acting. Theirs was the type of forbidden love affair that steamy romance novels were made of. Melody had girls everywhere envying her for being with Sly. To the public, Melody and Sly had the perfect love. They even had their own social media hash tags: #Mel-ly #RelationshipGoals.

Melody and Sly had met by chance at an industry party in the city. It was one of the first industry parties Ava had let the girls attend. It was 2009, and Sista Love was in between record deals. Ava thought the exposure from the girls finally participating in the industry nightlife would do some good to breathe life back into the group's waning popularity. Ava had made Rocky Beats, their new producer, promise he would chaperone and look out for the girls.

Melody sat on one of the burgundy, high-backed, velvet wraparound couches in club's VIP section, taking in the sights with Lyric and Rocky when Sly and his entourage made their very noisy entrance. Even over the music, their deep baritone shouts of, "Yo!" and "What's up?" and "Damn, these bitches hot in here tonight," could be heard loud and clear.

Of course, Sly was in the center of a phalanx of dudes, some as big as Shaquille O'Neal, which meant they were security, and at least fifteen more who were either his friends, staff, or just those hangers-on that are so popular with music entertainers.

Even from a distance and in the midst of his crowd, Melody had noticed Sly. She felt something tingle inside of her. The sensation was so strong it had made her cross, then re-cross her legs. Melody picked up her glass of club soda and sipped it, trying to seem disinterested. In reality, she was stretching her eyes to get a good glimpse of him. Finally, Sly stepped from behind the human wall of his entourage to take a few pictures and was in Melody's full view. She drank in every detail with her eyes.

Sly wore a black motorcycle jacket with silver panels on the shoulder, a T-shirt from his clothing brand that read FUCK THE WORLD DON'T ASK ME FOR SHIT, *black fitted jeans, and a vintage pair of all-black, high-top Jordan dunks. His long platinum chain hung almost to his belt line, and even in the dark club, his sparkly diamond piece, in the shape of his record company's logo, sparkled. Melody watched as the scantily clad gold diggers fixed their hair, applied fresh coats of shiny lip gloss, and made sure they were exposing enough cleavage before they rushed over to Sly and his people, begging for attention.*

"Is that Sly? Like, Diamond Records Sly?" Lyric leaned in and yelled over the music into Melody's ear.

"I'm not sure who he is, but if you watch the groupies flock, you'd think he was Jesus." Melody shook her head.

Melody, of course, knew who he was. The whole world knew Sly. He had the kind of rags-to-riches story that made him an icon. He also had the kind of swagger that made his presence known without so much as a word.

It wasn't Melody's first time being in the same place and the same time as Sly. They'd locked eyes and flirted from a distance at industry events more than once over the years. She'd even gotten word from an A&R that worked at her label that Sly had asked about her age and where she was from. As soon as Ava had gotten wind that Sly had asked about Melody, she had warned Melody that Sly wasn't good for her image. After all, with some people, Sly had made a name for himself as a misogynist because of some of his music lyrics blatantly referring to women as hoes and bitches.

Melody put her glass down on the table in front of her and shook her thoughts of Sly. "Harmony missed a good one," she shouted in Lyric's ear, trying her best to keep her eyes *from roving over to Sly. She didn't want anyone to catch on that she was even interested in Sly. He was too old for her anyway. She was only nineteen at the time and still a part of a girl group that wore matching beaded costumes and sang about dance moves, having big booties, and boys with cars. Sly was at least ten years older and had gone from drug dealer to rapper to music mogul all probably before Melody could even read a chapter book.*

Melody was lost in thought, listening to her little sister blab about people in the club, when it happened. Sly boldly walked straight over to their table.

"Rocky. What up, man? I been trying to contact you, man," Sly yelled over the music, extending his hand toward Rocky for a pound. Rocky stood up, slapped hands, and chest bumped with Sly. "You got me feeling like you been ducking my calls."

"Nah, it's not even like that. Man, you know how it is. Been locked in the lab with these ladies creating some new fire with them and a few other projects got me hiding out," Rocky replied, pointing to Melody and Lyric, his scapegoats.

Sly turned his attention to Melody. The heat of his gaze caused her to shift in her seat. After a few seconds, that tingly feeling was back. She quickly averted her eyes away from his, but not before it registered in her mind that Sly was gorgeous. His smooth dark skin, perfect pearly white teeth, and neatly cut, scalp-hugging curls made her bite down on her bottom lip.

"Ah. These the little chicks that be singing that man-bashing music, right? What was that song they had? Ladies World? Talking about ladies should fight for the right to be on top or something like that?" Sly chuckled.

Melody didn't find him funny. She raised one eyebrow and tilted her head sassily. "Yup. That's us. I would call it man-bashing music only if you're going to admit to being the dude that makes woman-bashing rap songs. What's the one song? I Don't Wife No Bitch?" she snapped back.

Sly put his hand up to his mouth and busted out laughing. "Yo, sweetheart got balls," he sang, laughing right after. "And she hella beautiful too. I like her. I like her a lot," Sly said to Rocky, his voice taking on a serious tone. He kept his eyes trained on Melody the whole time.

"Who said I like him, though?" Melody turned and said to Lyric.

She had already gone down the lane of sassy, so there was no turning back. Ava had always preached that playing hard to get made men more interested than being an easy catch. So far, it had worked.

"Oh, I'm not worried about you liking me, ma. They never do at first," Sly replied as he boldly took a seat at their table, right next to Melody.

"Okay. We got a straight path to the front door," Virgil huffed as he rushed back into Melody's vehicle and slammed the door.

Melody lifted her head and shook off her daydream.

"For the second time, I'm telling you I don't want them with any pictures of my face. At all," Melody said flatly. "I don't care if you have to smash a few cameras. I'm holding you and your people responsible."

"We will do our best."

Flanked by Virgil and protected by a wall made up of her security team, Melody exited her car with her head low and her forearm up to shield her face. The cameras still flashed and the reporters still screamed her name and their invasive questions.

Melody finally made it to Ava's front door. Murray already had the door held open, waiting for her.

"Melody, I'm happy you decided to come," Murray said, smiling weakly.

Melody noticed how frail Murray looked now. Long gone was the shark of a man who stepped over and on people to get what he wanted.

"No small talk, Murray. I'm here to take care of business and protect my own interest. We are not friends."

Murray coughed and held his hands up in surrender. There was no sense in hiding the fact that they hated each other. When Melody had fired Ava as her manager, she had fired Murray too. He had later sued her for millions based on contracts Ava had made Melody sign. Melody had to ultimately end up meeting Murray in the middle. After that, she wanted nothing to do with him, and it made it difficult for her to deal with Ava too.

"Everything is laid out in here," Murray told her, pointing to the doors leading to Ava's living room. Virgil and three members of her security team rushed into the living room first. Virgil nodded and then Melody entered.

"So what's been done—" Melody was saying until she noticed her sister. Melody froze, swallowing the rest of her words.

"Harmony." Melody was wide-eyed. Her stomach muscles immediately clenched.

"Melody." Harmony nodded politely. The sisters both stood in the middle of their childhood home like two cowboys in a standoff preparing for a duel. The silence was so heavy they seemed to struggle under the weight of it.

"Murray didn't say you were here, and frankly, after everything, I didn't think you'd be coming." Melody was the first to break the silence.

"That's the past," Harmony said tightly.

"Mmm. *That's the past*. We've come a long way now, haven't we?" Melody replied smartly.

Melody was making reference to the fact that Harmony had also sued Murray, Ava, and essentially the group for back royalties, song-writing credit, and to have her name added to publishing for the group's catalog of music. That little stunt had caused the record company to owe Harmony a couple million dollars, and it had cut Melody's checks from the record company significantly. Melody assumed the money was how Harmony ran off, never to be seen again.

"Actually, I have come a long way," Harmony shot back. "Can you say the same?"

Melody opened her mouth to say something, but Murray interrupted.

"Girls, girls. Let's not go down this road right now. This is about burying Ava," Murray said feebly, standing in the space between them with his shaking arms out in both directions like a boxing referee.

"You damn right it is, or else I wouldn't be here," Harmony mumbled.

Melody scoffed at her sister's comment.

"Remember the first tour you girls sold out?" Murray asked. "You all had packed the Garden when no one expected you to. You all were the headliners, no more an opening act. One of the proudest moments," he recalled with a smile. Melody and Harmony both softened at the thought, each trying hard to stifle their smiles just thinking about it. "Those were the good times," Murray said.

He walked over and took a picture from Ava's coffee table and held it up so that they could see. "I took this one of you girls backstage while you all listened to the crowd chanting your names. 'Sista Love! Sista Love!' they screamed. Melts my heart just thinking about it."

Melody looked over at Harmony. Melody didn't even realize she was smiling, and so was Harmony.

Madison Square Garden
New York, NY
August, 2007

"Sista Love! Sista Love! Sista Love!"

"Oh my God. I cannot believe the entire Madison Square Garden is sold out for us," Melody said excitedly as she twirled in front of the floor-length mirror, staring at the beautiful silver-sequined hot shorts and one-sleeved crop top she was wearing.

"Yes. I have chills just listening to that," Harmony replied. She wore a one-piece silver sequined mini-dress with a high neck.

"We are going to blow it out of the water tonight," Lyric added, shimmying her hips in her silver sequined leggings and bra top.

"Did I not say this day was coming?" Ava interjected from behind them. All three girls whirled around nervously. "Be easy, now. I didn't come to yell or play warden right now. I came to say I am proud of you girls," Ava beamed.

Harmony was the first to let out a sigh of relief. Lyric followed, and then the tension in Melody's shoulders eased.

"You did say this day was coming, and you made good on your promise, Ava." Melody rushed over and threw her arms around her mother's neck.

Ava stumbled back a few steps, caught off guard by the show of affection. Ava's arm stayed stiff at her sides. She wasn't good at being, as she called it, touchy-feely, but she did at least crack an awkward, weak smile.

"All this mushy stuff ain't for me. Besides, you can't smear that beautiful makeup job Troy did," Ava said in response.

Harmony and Lyric didn't dare try that stunt, but they were both smiling as they watched.

"Okay, ladies. Showtime in six minutes," Abe, one of the stage managers, stuck his head in and announced.

Lyric fanned her hands in front of her. "Oh my goodness. I am so nervous."

"We've performed a million times. We got this," Melody told her.

They all came together and locked arms in a team huddle.

Melody led the chant. "All we need is each other."

"All we need is each other," Harmony and Lyric repeated.

They all said it together in unison three times before they got the cue that it was showtime. Right before they exited their dressing room to head to the stage, Melody looked back over her shoulder and saw Ava with her face in her hands, sobbing.

The crowd roared as Melody, Harmony, and Lyric popped up from the stage floor on the special platforms. They stood in a triangle formation, with Melody at the point, like always. The beat to "Liar, Liar," their first hit single, dropped and the girls immediately moved their bodies in response. Arms up and out. Kick step and left. Pose. Turn. Kick step right. Pose. Hip sway. Hip sway. Twerk. Twerk. Turn.

The crowd roared. The energy in the Garden was electrifying. All of the nervousness was out of the window. The girls' movements were fluid. Each step went off without a hitch. Melody, Harmony, and Lyric were flawless; their execution perfect.

"For the last time!" Melody huffed into the microphone as she got to the last line of their first song.

The crowd went so wild the sound vibrated the stage.

"How y'all doing tonight, New York City?" Melody screamed into her microphone. That sent the crowd into an even louder frenzy.

"I said how y'all doing tonight, New York City?"

More screams of, "We love you!" erupted from the crowd. When the beat to their next song started, the lights dropped mysteriously.

A hush fell over the crowd as everyone tried to figure out what was going on.

"Heeey," Melody crooned. Suddenly big flumes of fire flew up at either end of the stage, and Melody and her sisters were in the spotlight. "Ladies, we gotta fight." Melody held her note.

"Fight for our rights," Harmony and Lyric harmonized in the back.

This time the crowd simply lost it. Girls screamed so much they fainted. Even the guys in the crowd flailed their arms, and some jumped up and down.

Melody, Harmony, and Lyric gave a perfect performance. They flowed through their costume changes without one hiccup. It was one of their proudest and happiest moments. After their last set, they were lowered down into the stage floor to raucous cheers and chants from their fans. Once they were out of the spotlight, they stepped off of their stage spots and ran to one another. They all hugged each other excitedly.

"We did it!" Melody squealed.

"Oh my God. I live for this," Lyric said, smiling so hard her cheeks hurt.

"Yes. We killed it," Harmony added, locking arms with her sisters.

"Bravo. Bravo. Perfect," Ava complimented as they bustled into their dressing room amid laughter.

"Thank you," Melody said. *"We could've never done it if it wasn't for you."*

Ava's face flushed red and she waved Melody off. "No. No. It was all of your hard work," Ava finally acknowledged.

All of their hard work had finally paid off. It was one of the rare occasions, after their first record deal, that they all seemed genuinely happy.

"Well, good times fade just like beauty, fame, and everything else." Melody fanned her hand dismissively as if she could fan away the memories too.

Harmony looked at her watch. "Murray, did you ever get in contact with Lyric?"

"I sent my guy down to Harlem where she was staying. No luck. He left the message that we would all be meeting here today," Murray replied, shrugging his shoulders. "I can't promise that she'll even get that message. He said she's around some pretty shady characters."

"I spoke to her. I don't think she took the news so well. I told her I'd be here today too," Harmony said.

Melody chortled. "If either one of you think that Lyric, the wild child, is coming here after what she did to Ava the last time she was here, think again," Melody said, looking over the rim of her dark shades that she still hadn't taken off in the house.

Harmony tilted her head quizzically.

"Oh, what? You didn't know about the assault and the attempted murder?" Melody asked with her eyebrows arched.

Murray began coughing uncontrollably. Harmony looked at Murray and back to Melody.

"Oh, yes. Your baby sister is completely off her little rocker. I won't even get into the half-shaved head, purple dyed hair on the side of the head that still has hair, piercings in the face, neck, and everywhere else. Oh, and the totally insane behavior. I had to send the police over here more than once when she was living here with Ava. Now, you and I may have told Ava we wished her dead—you even had a little scuffle with Ava, but your baby sister, Miss Wild 'n Crazy, actually tried to kill her. It wasn't a fight; it was attempted murder," Melody reported.

Harmony's eyes were stretched and her left hand moved up and down her right arm, squeezing every so often as she listened.

"Yes. I didn't want to get into all of that when we spoke the other day," Murray added.

"But—" Harmony was saying when a loud crashing noise cut through the air and interrupted her.

"What the hell?" Melody clutched her chest.

Harmony snapped her mouth shut and jumped to her feet. "It came from the back, by the kitchen," she announced.

Melody's security team immediately sprang into action. Another rumble of noises made Melody and Harmony move closer together. After a few minutes, they heard the familiar voice.

"Speak of the devil and the devil shall appear," Melody murmured.

Chapter 6

Lyric

"Fuck off me, asshole," Lyric snapped, wrestling her arm away from the huge security guard that had grabbed her breaking into Ava's back door. Harmony and Melody rushed into the kitchen with Murray slowly bringing up the rear.

"Fuck y'all hire security around this bitch for?" Lyric shot, still struggling with the seemingly unfazed giant holding her. "And he didn't do anything, so let him go." Lyric glared in the direction of the security guard that was holding onto Rebel.

"It's okay. You can let her go," Melody instructed, shaking her head like a disappointed parent.

Harmony's mouth hung open like she had just seen a ghost. Lyric rolled her eyes and turned her attention back to Melody.

"Oh, I should've known it was *you* that had security with you. We wouldn't want something to happen to the world's biggest superstar, now would we?" Lyric taunted. "Should've had some security for your mother," she mumbled.

"Hey." Harmony finally smiled and nervously stepped over to Lyric with outstretched arms.

Lyric threw her hand up and glared at her eldest sister. "You see what I mean about them? They love to pretend life was just so perfect," Lyric said to Rebel, who'd flopped down in one of Ava's kitchen chairs under the looming presence of Melody's security team.

"Let's save all of that. I'm not here for your little phony family reunion. I really came to grab some of my things from my room before y'all toss it out. I know how people do when somebody dies. They pillage shit and throw away the rest. Other than that, I wouldn't even be here."

Harmony dropped her arms and her facial expression flattened. She looked at Melody for help. They both looked at Rebel through disapproving eyes.

"Oh, and for the record, we would've come through the front door like everyone else, but the icon here has her own personal paparazzi

SWAT team posted up outside. I could barely walk down the street."

Melody shook her head and folded her arms across her chest. "Okay, so if the only reason you're here is to grab your stuff, no one is stopping you," she countered, stepping aside. "I just don't see why you needed to bring *him* here."

"I brought him for the same reason Sly would've been here if he wasn't out there probably with some other singer chick. Unlike you, Melody, some of us are in *real* love and not the pretend-for-the-paparazzi kind," Lyric defended.

What did her sisters know? When they both decided to abandon her and go forward with their happy lives, Lyric had met Rebel at a party and they'd quickly become friends. At first, Lyric just liked hanging out with him because he had a hit song on the radio, always traveled with his own party, and knew how to have a good time. She had escaped the pain of her life just being around Rebel. He hadn't been the first one to give her a drug, but he certainly had introduced her to heroin.

"What are you doing?" Lyric had asked him that fateful day.

She was still rubbing sleep from her eyes after waking up at his Harlem apartment to find him sitting on the side of his bed with a needle in his hand.

"This is that china-white I be rapping about," Rebel had told her. "This shit make you forget it all."

Lyric's curiosity was immediately piqued. Anything that would make her forget it all, she was game.

"That's scary though. Sticking yourself with a needle," she said, her eyes wide.

"Only the first time," he promised.

With that, Rebel plunged the needle into this arm. Lyric winced, but only for a second. When she saw the lazy grin that spread across Rebel's face as he fell back on his bed, it seemed like an internal happiness she was longing for. She wanted to feel relaxed just like that. The weed she smoked every day, and even the pills she popped, didn't seem to last long enough anymore.

"Can I try it?" she had asked Rebel.

"Nah. You too young and gorgeous to be fucking with this shit. I promise you, I will never let you get fucked up on this shit. Stick to the little girl shit," Rebel had replied.

Lyric had stormed out of his house that day with a promise of her own—that she'd never come back, never speak to Rebel again. She hadn't kept that promise, and neither had he.

Melody looked like she'd been gut-punched by Lyric's statement about Sly. Harmony stepped up to break up the tension.

"Lyric, we are not stopping you from gathering your things, but—"

"Good." Lyric cut her off and stormed past both of her sisters.

"Listen, sweetheart, we—"

"Save it, Murray. I really don't care," Lyric said tightly, brushing past him so hard he stumbled back a few steps.

Lyric defiantly stomped up the stairs that led to the bedrooms. She was so overwhelmed with a mixture of anger, sadness, loneliness, and hurt that her blood roared in her ears. Lyric swiped angrily at the tears threatening to fall from her eyes. She wasn't going to let them see her get emotional. That would only make them pity her, the one thing she promised she would never allow again.

Once Lyric made it to the top of the landing, she paused, halted by the sight in front of her. A

cold chill shot down her spine when she noticed
Ava's bedroom door sitting wide open. Lyric
sucked in her breath as she took in everything
that was out of place—the folding chair that was
propped right outside of the door, the fallen
remnants of police tape still hanging on the
side of the doorway, a lone abandoned rubber
surgical glove from either EMTs or the medical
examiner right at the doorsill. It looked like a
crime scene. Lyric knew all about crime scenes.
This scene was identical to the one set up when
her best friend Ashley Krueger, daughter of a
famous rock star and actress, had OD'd and died
in her parents' penthouse suite.

Lyric moved slowly toward Ava's room, some
unknown force propelling her forward. She
didn't know why she even cared to see or to
know how Ava had spent her last few minutes
of life.

Lyric sucked in her breath at the wild tan-
gle of sheets and pillows on Ava's unmade
bed, the shattered vanity mirror, the clothes
hanging sloppily out of the dresser drawers,
and all of Ava's makeup and prized perfumes
thrown on the floor, some shattered. Ava
would've never had people in her house with
her room in that condition.

The reality that Ava was gone hit Lyric like a gust of gale-force wind. She cupped her hand over her mouth to quiet her whimpers. She didn't want Harmony and Melody to know she was this distraught. Lyric backed out of Ava's room, turned, and ran down the small hallway to her old bedroom. She busted inside, slammed the door, pressed her back against it, and slid down to the floor. She drew her knees up to her chest and rocked slowly. The memories and the sobs came so hard and fast that Lyric choked.

Saddle River, New Jersey
2005

Lyric, Harmony, and Melody climbed out of their hired Lincoln Town Car in wide-eyed amazement.

"Now this is a house." Melody gasped, her eyes lit up.

"Do you see this driveway? It's as big as a highway. I have never seen a circular drive-way," Harmony said, awestruck.

Lyric was quiet. She looked up at the beau-tiful, pale yellow sandstone mansion with its six regal white Roman columns, smooth white-and-gray speckled marble steps, and what looked like over one thousand windows. Lyric couldn't get excited because fear gripped her insides like a clenched fist.

"Andrew Harvey is living like a damn king. I have never seen a fountain like that unless it was in a museum or on TV," Melody said, still whirling around, taking in the scenery. "And look at the beautiful greenery. It must cost a fortune to have your bushes carved into your initials and little animals like that. This is how I want to live when I grow up." She shook her head, enchanted.

"For real. Definitely something to live up to," Harmony added. "Right?" She nudged Lyric with her elbow. "Why you so quiet? You see this house? Do you understand what it means to get invited to an Andrew Harvey private party?"

Lyric shrugged away from Harmony. "So? Everything excites y'all. It's just a stupid house," Lyric grumbled, folding her arms over her chest.

She hated everything about Andrew Harvey. From their first meeting until now, every time Lyric had to be in his presence she went into a dark place mentally.

"What's wrong with you?" Melody whispered harshly, frowning. "You better change that mood. This party is in our honor. We finally went platinum, and a big player like Andrew Harvey is throwing us a party," Melody chastised.

"Ladies, right this way." A man dressed in a tuxedo interrupted their little spat. "Mr. Harvey is awaiting your arrival."

"And he got his own Geoffrey like the one in The Fresh Prince of Bel Air," Melody whispered as they followed the man.

When Lyric, Melody, and Harmony crossed through the beautiful glass front doors, Lyric felt a nauseating sense of déjà vu.

"Oh my God. The inside of this house is even more amazing." Melody gasped. "Look at these floors." She tapped her foot on the gilded floors. "You think this is real gold?"

"Plated. Gold plated." Andrew Harvey chuckled from behind them. The girls all seemed to spin around in unison, like a dance routine.

"Mr. Harvey," Melody said, beaming. "Oh my God. We love your house. We have never seen anything like it."

Andrew Harvey laughed. "I can tell."

Lyric reached over with a shaky hand and furtively grabbed Harmony's hand. Harmony looked at her and questioned Lyric with her eyes.

"There's my special girl." *Andrew Harvey stepped in front of Lyric and placed his hand on her shoulder. Lyric clutched Harmony's hand in a death grip.*

"Wait until you see the cake and the spread I had made up for you girls," *he said, keeping his eyes on Lyric the entire time.*

A small amount of acidic vomit leapt into Lyric's throat. She forced herself to swallow it back down.

"Ava said to send you her apologies. She wasn't feeling well," *Harmony told him.* "She told me to look out for everyone," *Harmony emphasized.*

"Oh, she didn't come?" *Andrew Harvey asked, looking over the girls' heads as if he was making sure.* "Don't worry. I'll take good care of all of you. You don't have to act as the mother. You're just a kid yourself. You need to enjoy yourself." *He smiled and placed his hands over Lyric's shoulders.*

Harmony tugged on Lyric's hand, pulling her away from him.

"So, is the party out there?" Harmony jerked her chin toward a wall of glass doors that led to Andrew Harvey's expansive backyard, patio, and saxophone- shaped pool.

"Yes, yes. All of you girls make yourselves at home. This is all about you and that beautiful platinum plaque you've earned," he said cheerfully, extending his left arm toward the action.

"Let's go!" Melody cheered, rushing for the doors. Lyric and Harmony followed her.

The party was packed with people. Lyric, Melody, and Harmony stood flabbergasted by the attendees. There were famous actors, singers, dancers, radio personalities, and even politicians in attendance. Beautiful girls dressed in traditional French maid outfits and high heels walked around serving drinks and hors d'oeuvres held on silver platters. The gorgeously laid out spread of food began at the right of the door and extended the full length of the property.

Melody and Harmony were giggling about the ice sculpture with Sista Love carved into it. Lyric had never seen so much lobster, giant shrimp, king crab legs, and oysters in her life. Seafood was her favorite. There were four carving stations—pork, lamb, prime rib, and *venison—manned by men in tall white chef's hats and white chef coats.*

"Let's give it up for Sista Love." The D.J. announced their arrival.

Everyone in attendance turned their attention to Lyric, Harmony, and Melody and began clapping, whistling, and cheering. Melody drank up the attention, waving like a beauty queen at a pageant. Lyric's face turned dark red. She lowered her head shyly.

"This is so crazy," Harmony whispered as she plastered an obligatory smile on her face. "Like, are we really in the same party as Tiasha?" she said through her fake smile.

"Yes, and she's a megastar. Can you imagine? I feel like I'm dreaming," Melody answered.

After two hours of eating, drinking, dancing, swimming, and hobnobbing with the rich and famous, Lyric had finally let her guard down. Andrew Harvey kept his distance, and she barely saw him. Lyric began to think she had been afraid and tense for no reason.

It was just what needed to be done a couple of times, for the deal, but it's okay now. He's not thinking about me, *she had finally convinced herself. Lyric had loosened up and even shared laughs with her sisters and a few other celebrities in attendance.*

"Dang. I have to pee so badly," Lyric told Harmony as they stood in the shallow end of Andrew Harvey's pool, holding their virgin Pina Coladas and singing along with songs from their album.

"You better not pee in this pool. What if it's filled with the stuff that turns red if someone pees in the water?" Harmony warned. They busted out laughing.

"Okay. I'm going to go inside," Lyric relented. "Watch my drink."

She climbed out of the pool and was immediately met by one of the pretty servants who was holding fluffy white oversized towels out in front of her. Lyric smiled at the girl, took a towel, and wrapped it around her body. She rushed toward the house, her full bladder threatening to bust.

"Bathroom?" Lyric fidgeted, doing the pee pee dance in front of another tuxedo-clad staff member.

"Right this way." He pressed a little button on a silver earpiece and spoke some code into it.

High tech, she thought. Lyric followed the man down a long hallway that had high ceil-

ings, a beautiful Oriental rug runner down
the center, and was decorated with walls of
gorgeous paintings that she could tell were
probably one of a kind and expensive. The
man turned another corner and walked down
another seemingly endless hallway. This one
was adorned with glass-encased sports memorabilia that, again, was probably worth more
money than Lyric could fathom.

"Is it this far to the nearest bathroom? I
really gotta pee." Lyric winced.

The man didn't respond. Finally, after six
more turns, the man stopped in front of two
beautiful wooden doors with beautiful long,
shiny gold door handles. Lyric's eyebrows
folded into the center of her face when he
opened the doors to a bedroom decorated in
all off-white and gold. The huge four-poster
bed in the center seemed swallowed up in the
expansive room. Lyric blinked a few times. The
room seemed bigger than her entire house.

"I just needed the bathroom," she said,
looking into the room apprehensively. "A half
bathroom or guest bathroom would've been
fine." She didn't want to intrude into someone's
bedroom.

"Straight back."

"Um, really. I, um, I could've just used the guest bathroom closest to the pool," Lyric stammered, turning and pointing back down the hallway she'd just walked through.

"Mr. Harvey insists on special guests having privacy," the man said with no emotion behind his words.

Lyric looked into the room again. Now her bladder was one second from truly busting. She took a deep breath and reluctantly rushed through the doorway.

"Please wait for me. I don't know how to get back."

The man didn't respond. He simply shut the door behind her. The click of the door made her stomach twist. Lyric's heart pounded wildly in her chest. If she didn't have to go so badly, she would've turned and ran straight back to the party.

Lyric raced through the huge bedroom and made it to the white and gold-trimmed bathroom door.

"Is everything in this house trimmed in gold? Crazy," Lyric whispered, pushing the door to the bathroom.

"Dang." She gawked at the huge white marble soaking tub.

"A gold toilet? Guess when you have money . . ." Lyric spoke to herself as she let her towel fall on the floor and pulled down her bikini bottoms.

"And who has bathing suits waiting for people at a party?" Lyric kept talking to herself. She closed her eyes and relaxed on the beautiful toilet as she released her overflowing bladder.

Lyric finished and walked over to the long, marbletopped double sinks. "Fancy," she whispered, examining the sophisticated hand-engraved gold faucet. Lyric put her hands under an automatic soap dispenser. She smiled because the liquid soap fell into her hand in the shape of a heart. Lyric looked up into the beautiful beveled mirror and smiled at her reflection.

"They were right. This is how I want to live."

Lyric finished washing her hands. She turned around, picked up her towel, and exited the bathroom, singing cheerfully.

"You like my house?"

Lyric gasped, staggering backward off balance. She braced herself just before she hit the floor.

"Hey, hey. It's just me." Andrew Harvey stepped closer to her with his hands out to break her impending fall.

Lyric pushed his hands away from her. "Why did you sneak up on me? What are you doing in here?" *Lyric huffed breathlessly. Her chest moved up and down like she'd run a race.*

"I was looking for you. You're my special girl," he said, moving closer.

Lyric took a few steps backward. Her hands started trembling.

"I thought I would bring you something to make you relax a little bit this time." He held a little pill between his pointer finger and thumb and extended it toward her.

"Please. I don't want to," Lyric pleaded, moving backward as he advanced toward her. "I just want to go back to the party. I was relaxed out there. I don't need the pill. I just want to go have fun like everybody else."

"You don't want to what? Keep a record deal? Make your mother happy? Keep performing? Be famous? Keep your sisters happy?" Andrew Harvey asked, his tone steely.

Lyric shook her head. "But we can just sing and keep—"

"That's not how the business works," Andrew Harvey snapped.

Lyric jumped when her back hit a wall. She couldn't go any farther.

He reached out and gently swiped her wild, wet hair from her face. "You're beautiful," he said. "Here, be a good girl and take the pill."

"*Please don't,*" *she gulped, trying to move away from his touch. She could barely breathe. His cologne and sweat, mixed with the chlorine soaked into her bathing suit, made her stomach swirl.*

"*Take the pill,*" *he whispered, using his huge hand to clutch the back of her head so he could hold it in place.*

"*No.*" *Lyric struggled.*

That just made him clamp down harder on a handful of her hair, until he was holding it painfully tight. Tears sprang to her eyes.

"*You're my special girl,*" *he murmured, putting the pill between his teeth and lowering his mouth over hers.*

Lyric writhed under his grasp and moaned into his mouth. She almost choked as the pill tumbled awkwardly onto her tongue. Andrew Harvey used his long, lizard-like tongue to push it into the back of her throat. Lyric tried to fight some more, but she was no match for his girth and his strength.

"*Shh. Let me take care of you,*" *he whispered, moving his mouth from hers and trailing his tongue down her neck.*

She was shivering all over now. This wasn't the first time, but it felt just as disgusting, and she felt just as caught off guard as the first time.

"This is what your mother agreed to for you girls to get the deal," Andrew Harvey told her while he used his right hand to loosen the string at the back of her bikini top. "If you want me to stop, you'll have to explain to Ava why you girls lost your deal, all of your tour dates, and all of the money," he threatened.

"Please," Lyric cried pitifully. Her teeth chattered uncontrollably. "I'm only a kid," she whined. "I'm just fourteen." She sobbed as he licked down her neck to her newly budding breasts.

Lyric felt like bugs were crawling all over her body. Something began to tingle in her head. She started seeing a rainbow of colors flash before her eyes. She tried again to fight him off.

"Get off of me," she groaned, weakly punching at the bald spot in the top of his head. "I'm a kid," she whimpered. Her speech began to slur. "I'm just a kiiid."

"I'm going to make you a woman," Andrew Harvey breathed into her ear. He pressed his protruding gut against her roughly and worked his fingers into her bikini bottoms.

Lyric's body went partially limp. She could feel him exploring her with his fingers, but she could no longer fight. She was escaping. She was flying. For the first time, she was high.

Andrew Harvey carried her over to the bed and threw her down. Lyric smiled lazily, and her head rocked from side to side.

He licked his lips hungrily. "Yes. After tonight, you'll be a woman."

"Lyric, let me in."

Harmony pushed against Lyric's bedroom door. Lyric was balled into a fetal position on the floor, rocking and sobbing. Harmony pushed harder and was able to wedge her way through a small opening.

"Go away," Lyric cried, covering her face with her arms. She rocked harder now. "You don't give a shit about me. You didn't come back to Brooklyn to check on me."

"No, baby sis. I am not going to go away and leave you like this," Harmony said softly.

Lyric coughed out more sobs. She was angry at herself for being weak . . . again. She hated to let anyone see her like this.

Harmony lowered herself onto the floor. "C'mere," she urged, tugging on Lyric's arm.

"No. Leave me alone." Lyric resisted, stiffening her body and tugging away from Harmony. "That's what all of you are good at anyway. Leaving me all alone. Don't act like you care now." Lyric wept.

"Oh, sweetheart. I'm sorry. When I ran away I was running for my life, Lyric. I wanted to just kill myself. I had nothing. No one. I wanted you to come with me, but you were gone. I had to go, and I had to go fast or else I wouldn't be here right now. I was running from the pain too, baby sis." Harmony's voice cracked. She bent down and wedged her left arm under Lyric's body and scooped Lyric into her arms.

"Just leave me alone. I don't need your love now. I needed it then. It's too late for me now," Lyric wailed. "Just leave me alone now."

"I'm never going to leave you alone again," Harmony cried, pulling Lyric close to her chest. She squeezed Lyric tightly and rocked her.

"I have never said it before, but I know that you sacrificed yourself for us, Lyric. I was there. I didn't do anything to stop it, and it tears me up inside every day," Harmony said through her tears. "It tears me up that I was too weak, too abused, too broken down to just grab you and run." Harmony's body shook with sobs. She could feel Lyric's tears dancing down her neck and chest.

"She gave my life to him. She just gave him my entire life, and I was a baby," Lyric bawled. "I sacrificed everything, my entire soul, so that we all could be famous, and look at me. I have nothing. I have nothing left. All of you left me." Lyric struggled to get out of Harmony's grasp.

"He took my innocence. Over and over again she sent me to him, and when I was all used up, that was it. No more deals. No more fame. No more money. Everyone just left me." Lyric's words were like daggers. She kicked her legs and tried again to break away from her sister's tight embrace. The pain cut through her like a surgical tool, spilling her insides.

Harmony's body quaked with sobs. "I am so sorry, Lyric. I swear, if I could go back in time, I would. I should've protected you. None of it meant anything to me. If I knew you were being hurt . . . but she had so much power over me back then. I couldn't stand up to her because I was too busy trying to make her love me. I wanted the same thing you wanted. I just wanted my mother, our mother, to love me. I wanted anybody to love me," Harmony blubbered through her sobs.

"She was supposed to be our mother. She was supposed to protect us. She never said sorry. She never said sorry to me for ruining my life, and now she's gone. I hated her. I wanted to kill her, and now she's gone," Lyric said, her body shaking like a leaf in a wild storm.

"I know. She's gone. And it's too late now. I know." Harmony stroked her baby sister's head and clutched her tighter. "She's gone. She's gone," Harmony repeated and rocked harder. "We have to stick together now and heal, baby girl. There is nothing we can do to change the past, but we can at least heal." Harmony sniffled. "We just have to try to heal. I know she didn't ever say it, Lyric, but she did love you. I love you."

Lyric went silent, her body stilled. She melted against Harmony and took comfort in her sister's affection. She wanted to be angry and resistant, but she was too weak. The sheer emotion of being in the house, being around her sisters, had left her drained.

"Don't leave me," Lyric finally whimpered. "I need you."

"Never again. I will never leave you again," Harmony promised. "Never again."

Chapter 7

Harmony

Harmony's heard jerked up at the sound of knocking on Lyric's bedroom door. She cringed, not wanting to disturb the peace that had finally settled over Lyric. Another round of knocks made Harmony open her red-rimmed eyes and glare at the door. She watched as the doorknob turned and the door creaked open.

Melody appeared in the doorway, staring at Harmony and Lyric, baffled. Melody gestured with her hands for an explanation. Harmony raised her eyebrows then closed her eyes and shook her head as a signal for Melody not to ask or say anything. Harmony mouthed the words *give us a minute*. Melody folded her arms across her chest and poked out her left hip like a mother waiting for an explanation from a child. She stared at Harmony, sitting on the floor, holding Lyric in her arms like a toddler who needed comforting after falling and scraping her knee.

Harmony jerked her chin at the door. She couldn't afford to set Lyric off again. Melody finally relented. She put her hands up, palms out, and slowly backed out of the door and closed it.

Harmony turned her attention back to her baby sister. She lowered her chin onto Lyric's head and continued her silent comforting. Harmony felt like she had been wrung dry of every emotion she had inside of her. Since arriving at Ava's house, Harmony had felt anger, sorrow, hurt, regret, and now a deep, cutting guilt that threatened to reverse all of the mental wellness work she'd done over the past three years. As Harmony clutched Lyric in her arms, like she had back then, she couldn't help but think about what happened to Lyric at Ava's hands. At all of their hands, for that matter. All in the name of fame.

Harmony closed her eyes and recalled how she had watched, day-by-day, as the sparkle of innocence slowly burned out in Lyric's usually big, bright doe eyes.

After their first audition for Andrew Harvey at his office, Ava had announced that they'd landed a deal. Their excitement had been short lived, when Andrew Harvey had requested a private meeting with Lyric. Harmony remembered how her insides had felt like they were being run through a meat grinder as she paced outside of his office door, worried about Lyric being alone with him.

Ava and Melody had both tried to pretend not to notice the stifling tension that had seemingly choked them all, but Harmony had certainly felt it. When Andrew Harvey's office door had finally opened that day, Harmony had stopped cold. Lyric's eyes seemed dead, lifeless. She moved like a robot, like her legs weren't her own. Gone was the usual little-girl gleam in her eyes and bounce in her step.

"Lyric?" Harmony had rushed over to her. "What was that about?" she whispered.

Lyric hadn't answered; instead, she looked, wide-eyed, over her shoulder at Andrew Harvey. When Lyric looked at him, the expression of terror on her face reminded Harmony of a look she'd seen on the face of a horror movie actress being chased by a deranged killer.

Harmony remembered how Andrew Harvey had winked at Lyric. His wink had made Harmony feel like she'd been kicked in the chest. He had clearly been hurling a threat with his eyes. Lyric had whipped her head back around, her eyes stretched to their capacity, her nostrils wide and pulsing.

"Lyric, are you okay?" Harmony had pressed.

"She's fine. I'm her mother, not you." Ava had wedged herself between Lyric and Harmony. "Let's go celebrate now. We must not forget you girls just landed your first deal. Today, you can all have a sweet treat." Of course Ava would allow them to have sweets to overshadow the reality.

That night, at home, Harmony had crept down to Lyric's tiny bedroom and found her balled up, knees to chest, sobbing on the floor.

"Lyric?" Harmony had whispered gruffly, trying to make sure Ava didn't hear them.

"Lyric, what's the matter?" Harmony got down on the floor and tried to pull Lyric's arms from her face. "Why are you crying? What did he do to you?" Harmony asked, her own tears burning the backs of her eye sockets. Lyric never answered that night as Harmony scooped her into her arms. She didn't have to. Both girls had sobbed into the night, and there would be many more of those to follow.

"Lyric, honey," Harmony said softly. "Let's go downstairs and face this together. I'm going to be right here."

Lyric stirred like Harmony had roused her from a deep sleep. She pulled herself out of Harmony's grasp and sat up. Harmony finally got to take a good, close-up look at her baby sister. Harmony felt an explosion of pain in the center of her chest. She knew it was her heart breaking at the sight. Gone was Lyric's blemish-free, smooth caramel skin. She had tiny scabbed-over sores on her cheeks now, and silver piercings with little sliver balls at the ends protruding from each eyebrow, her bottom lip, and a round one ringing her septum. Her half-shaved head and purple hair made her look older, harder. Lyric's eyes were swollen and ringed by dark circles. Her nails were bitten down to the quick, and the tops of her hands had veins protruding like the hands of a ninety-year-old woman.

"I'm going to hold your hand through this entire thing. I promise, Lyric. I'll never abandon you again," Harmony comforted, scanning her sister carefully.

When Harmony's eyes landed on Lyric's arms, her eyebrows shot up into arches. Lyric noticed the flash of shock that filtered across Harmony's face. Lyric folded her arms across her body so that her track marks were partially hidden.

"Are you okay? I mean, living okay?" Harmony asked, concern lacing her words.

Lyric scrambled up from the floor in a huff, brushing herself off. "I'm surviving," Lyric answered evasively as she moved around her room, gathering her things she wanted to take.

Harmony stood up too. "I know that you've been caught up in the life, Lyric, but I want you to know that you don't have to be. I can get you some help," Harmony offered, again lowering her eyes to Lyric's arms. If Harmony had been able to do it for Ron, she could do it for her little sister too.

Lyric let out a contradictory chuckle. "First of all, I don't need help. Second of all, let's take things slowly, Harmony. You don't rush in and start judging me and I keep speaking to you, although I really don't want to," Lyric retorted.

Harmony put her hands up in surrender. She didn't want to undo the tender moment they had shared. "Fair enough. I just want you to know your options. I just want you to be okay."

"I've been doing okay this far."

Harmony walked over to Lyric's old dresser and grabbed a picture that was stuck in the top left hand corner. She brought it close her face.

"I remember this like it happened yesterday." Harmony shook her head, one side of her mouth twisted upward. "Wow. Every corner of this place has a memory. Couldn't escape it even if I tried." Harmony exhaled.

Lyric stopped moving and crossed the room. She stood next to Harmony and they both stared down at the picture. "I remember this too. Those outfits were a mess," Lyric remarked, trying to skirt around the real memory that was swirling around the picture.

"Yeah, a mess," Harmony said in a low tone as they were both thrown back in time. Together.

Harlem, New York
October, 2003

"The Apollo Theater!" Melody announced. "So many big stars started off performing here. We have to kill this performance tonight."

Harmony rolled her eyes. "My legs are so sore from practicing. I am dreading those heels. And this weave has my head pounding. I feel like a poodle with all of this hair on my head."

"Yeah. I have blisters on my feet," Lyric chimed in, lifting her foot for emphasis.

"Shut up complaining!" Ava boomed from the doorway behind them.

Harmony jumped and Lyric fell backward onto the tiny, threadbare couch inside the old backstage area.

"Do you ungrateful bitches know how many strings I had to pull to get you all this gig?" Ava gritted, pointing an accusing finger in Harmony's face. "All you can do is find it in your little selfish devil hearts to complain all the damn time. As for you and your weave, I paid a lot of money to have you look like something other than an ugly, gorilla-face spook," Ava spat cruelly.

Harmony lowered her head in shame. Melody and Lyric both looked away.

"I have feelings too, goddammit! I go through all kinds of hoops and ups and downs to try to make sure all of you get somewhere in life, and all you can do is find it in your black, ugly heart to complain?" Ava went on, her vituperative words aimed directly at Harmony.

Harmony's jaw rocked as she fought to keep her tears from falling.

"You better learn how to be grateful because the way I see it, all your dark face is fit to do is clean somebody's house. Now get ready for the show. There are six other groups in this talent show, and if you all don't stand out, you'll be tossed aside like next week's garbage." With that, Ava stormed out of the room.

Lyric walked over to Harmony and wrapped her bony arm around Harmony's shoulder.

"You and me will never part. Ma-key dada," Lyric sang. At first Harmony didn't budge. "Here come that Mister; Celie, you better clean this house," Lyric mocked.

Harmony lifted her head a little. "I'm poor, black, I might even be ugly, but I'm here. Dear God, I'm here." Harmony followed up with her own line from the movie The Color Purple. Lyric was the first to laugh. Harmony followed. That trick had been working ever since the girls had snuck and watched the movie. They would pretend Ava was Mister, Harmony was Celie, and Lyric was Nettie. They never included Melody in their game.

"Don't worry with old Mister. She need a man," Lyric joked. Harmony laughed harder this time.

"Y'all better be quiet." Melody broke up their fun. "We have a show to do, and I'm not trying to come in last with this talent showcase tonight. I don't know about you two, but I'm going to be rich and famous one day," Melody said, pouting her lips and kissing at herself in the dull, scratched-up backstage mirror.

Lyric and Harmony looked at each other and sniggered. If they had ever included Melody in their game, she'd be the drunken version of Shug Avery.

The Apollo crowd was a tough one to please. It was like they would rather boo and hiss than cheer and clap. As soon as Harmony, Melody, and Lyric filed onto the stage in their homemade matching pink army-fatigue patterned outfits, boos rose and fell over the audience. Harmony looked out into the audience of scowling faces and felt like running off the stage. She knew that would only draw more cruelty from her mother later. Harmony looked over at Lyric, who looked like she was about to pee on herself.

Melody stepped out in front of the group and opened her mouth to belt out her first note. Melody's voice cracked. The crowd was relentless. The booed and groaned and hissed and yelled, "Get them off!"

Sweat dripped down the sides of Harmony's face like a faucet had been turned on in her scalp. Harmony and Lyric danced their hearts out behind Melody, and they tried to harmonize their notes perfectly, hoping that would calm the ruthless audience. It didn't work. Melody was completely off her game. She tried another top range and fell flat. Melody just couldn't hold the crowd at bay.

Harmony finally took things into her own hands. She stepped in front of Melody and picked up Melody's lead lines. Harmony held her head back and belted out the high notes like her life depended on it. Harmony closed her eyes and let her raw talent rip from her body and someplace deep in her soul. She didn't dance. She didn't move. She didn't worry about Melody's hurt feelings. Harmony just sang. She sang and sang until her insides vibrated with the music. It was the first time the music had soothed a painful ache somewhere deep in her heart.

A hush quickly fell over the crowd. They were enamored with the girl in front of them, each word of the song she sang mesmerizing them further.

Harmony moved to the next stanza of the song, her voice holding court with the likes of Mariah Carey and even a young Whitney Houston. The crowd's sound went from boos and jeers to cheers. Harmony was feeling the energy so much. She had connected with the audience in ways she had never been allowed. She carefully stepped down the stage stairs and into the audience aisle.

"Oh, I love you!" Harmony bent at the waist and sang, pouring her heart into the performance.

The crowd went wild. Slowly people began to get to their feet.

"I said I love you!" Harmony carried the "you" as she climbed back on stage and stood in front of her sisters. Melody's face was a dark shade of red, and her eyes were hooded. Melody could barely keep up with the dance moves. She was fuming.

When their performance ended, they received a standing ovation and the loudest cheers of the night from the audience. Harmony beamed. The energy in the small theatre gave her chills. It was something she had never experienced before—acceptance.

"Why did you do that?" Melody rounded on Harmony as soon as they were off stage. Harmony could see fire flashing in Melody's eyes.

"Do what?" Harmony snapped back. "Save our performance?"

"No! Steal the lead from me and make me look like some stupid backup singer!" Melody shouted, getting in Harmony's face.

"I didn't steal anything. I took over because you were failing and we were about to get booed out of here," Harmony said through her teeth, standing almost nose to nose with Melody. "And if that had happened it wouldn't be blamed on you. I would be the one called all kinds of names and punished for the failure. So,

I stepped up and did what I needed to do to save myself," Harmony said with feeling.

"What is going on here?" Ava rushed and got between them.

Harmony backed down. She knew that when it came to Ava, she had no wins against Melody.

"She . . . she made me look like a fool out there," Melody whined, stomping her feet like a brat. Harmony knew better than to say anything. Ava looked at Melody sympathetically.

"Tell me exactly what happened. What did they do?" Ava demanded, glaring at Harmony and Lyric.

"I was singing my lead, and all of a sudden she"— Melody pointed an accusing finger at Harmony's face— "just pushed me out of the way and started singing my part. She even left position and went down into the audience like . . . like she was really trying to make me look bad or something," Melody relayed.

"She's lying!" Lyric tried to interject. Ava held up her hand. "But—" Lyric was saying.

"Enough!" Ava walked over to Harmony, her eyes narrowed into dashes.

"What did you do?" Ava asked stiffly.

Harmony's teeth chattered like someone had pumped ice water into her veins.

"She ain't do nothing," Lyric answered. "She was just helping."

"I'm not going to tell you to be quiet again. I asked Harmony what she did," Ava gritted, never taking her piercing gaze off of Harmony. *"Look at me when I'm speaking to you!"* Ava roared.

Harmony's head snapped up. Her cheeks twitched as she met Ava's gaze.

"I asked you a question."

Harmony glared back at Ava stubbornly. *"I saved the show,"* she answered crisply.

Harmony suddenly felt her face light up with heat and her head snapped sideways. Her teeth clicked and her eyes squeezed shut on their own. She crumpled to the floor like a deflated balloon as more blows rained down on her.

"Don't hit her! She didn't do anything! She saved the show!" Lyric screeched, grabbing Ava's strong hand.

Ava whirled around, and with the strength from her coursing adrenaline, she shoved Lyric so hard that Lyric fell backward at top speed. Caught off guard and unable to brace herself, Lyric's body crashed to the floor at full force. The back of her head crashed into the uncovered concrete floors. A sickening crack resounded through the room.

"Lyric!" Harmony squealed, forgetting her own safety and rushing to her sister's side.

"Lyric! Lyric! Wake up!" Harmony cried out, shaking Lyric's shoulders. There was blood coming from Lyric's nose. Her body was completely limp. Harmony looked up, terror etched on her face.

"Call an ambulance! Now!"

Within a few minutes the ambulance arrived. Lyric had regained consciousness but was dazed and confused. Ava had insisted she was okay, but the EMTs still loaded her onto the stretcher for transport to the hospital.

Just as the EMTs got set to wheel Lyric out of the building, the talent show director came rushing toward Harmony, Melody, Lyric, and Ava.

"Hey! Wait!" the director called after them. They all turned in her direction. "I just wanted to let you girls know that you won tonight," the director huffed, out of breath from running. She turned and looked directly at Harmony.

"Your performance was light years above the rest tonight, honey. I watched you pull off a save most people wouldn't have been brave enough to even try. You didn't let your sister's failing deter you. I was in awe of how selflessly you stepped in and saved her from that crazy audience. It was something special to watch," the lady said to Harmony. Harmony blushed.

"You've got a special bunch of girls here. And that one," the director said, turning to Ava while pointing to Harmony, "she is fearless and fierce. That voice is something special, not to mention she's a beauty," the director complimented with a wide, toothy grin.

Ava's face turned a deep shade of pink. She couldn't even look Harmony in the eyes. The lady handed Ava the tall trophy with a gold-plated winged lady at the top and the $500 first prize check.

Harmony rolled her eyes at Ava and turned her attention back to Lyric.

"We won?" Lyric croaked weakly reaching her hand out for Harmony.

"Yes, baby sis. We won. And I'm here. I'm never going to leave your side. I'm here forever."

Chapter 8

Melody

"You ladies finally decided to break up your little *Color Purple* reunion?" Melody asked crisply, watching Lyric and Harmony enter the room together, arm in arm.

Melody swallowed hard to stave off the tornado of hurt feelings swirling in her stomach. She hated that Harmony and Lyric had always shared a close, special bond. When they were kids, the two of them were inseparable. Melody remembered feeling left out of their little giggling secrets and their secret code language. She knew they excluded her, mostly because Ava treated her so differently, but that didn't change the fact that Melody had grown up feeling a deep disconnect from her sisters and most of the time a cavernous loneliness that often made her secretly cry herself to sleep at nights. Everyone always mistook her for the strong one when deep inside, she felt she was the weakest of them all.

"Yeah. I think we can finally get down to the business of planning now," Harmony said.

Melody eyed her sisters suspiciously. Lyric had a large duffle bag slung over her shoulder, and Harmony clutched a stack of pictures. Melody felt a hot flash of jealous rage ignite in her chest.

"So everyone just grabbing keepsakes without me?"

"These are not keepsakes, and we're not keeping you from taking anything that you want from the house, Melody," Harmony replied flatly.

"I don't need anything from here anyway." Melody waved her hand. "Anything that Ava had I can buy ten of," she said defensively.

She'd also perfected her defenses as a kid too. Whenever her sisters left her out of things, Melody would pretend it didn't bother her, that she had bigger and much better things to do than worry about them. She would use Ava as a weapon against them too, since she knew how much Ava's favoritism bothered them.

"Ava, who is your prettiest child?" Melody would ask in a whiney baby voice.

"You already know it's you. Harmony is like a black mamba, and Lyric just looks like a regular ol' black girl," Ava would say.

"Who is your favorite?" Melody would ask, all the while eyeing her sisters for their hurt reactions.

"You, child. You're the most like me," Ava would say, beaming.

"Okay. Can we get down to the planning?" Harmony asked, blowing out a windstorm of breath and flopping down.

"I think we should bury her in gold. It was her favorite color," Melody blurted.

Harmony and Lyric looked at one another, seemingly contemplating what Melody had said.

"Oh, come on. We all remember every single awards show red carpet outfit. Ava loved her gold gowns. We can't just put her in some old frumpy suit or some terrible cotton-blend flowered dress like some elderly church lady. She lived for the sparkle, the shine, and the gold dresses," Melody told them, moving the tips of her fingers for emphasis.

"You're right," Harmony relented. "Ava Love was a gold lamé–loving somebody."

"Remember the first time we went to the Grammys?" Melody asked. They all looked around at one another. "That gold gown Ava wore that night was so fabulous it was the talk of the town afterwards. Ava was stunning. No one believed she had three children, and they were certainly shocked to see her make such a comeback through us. Ava was so proud to finally be on a red carpet too . . . "

Los Angeles, California
February 2006

Ava's shiny gold lamé gown fit her like it had been painted on. One thing about Ava Love, she still had a body most women her age would die for. All it took was one panty girdle and she looked as svelte as some of the young people. The high neck, ruched mid-section, and fabulously long train gave Ava's gown a regal feel. To round out her outfit, Ava slipped into a pair of thin-strapped gold stilettos and held onto a simple rectangular gold clutch with a diamond bumblebee clasp at the top. Her hair was drawn back in her signature chignon with a simple rhinestone pin stuck in the center.

"You look gorgeous, Ava," Melody complimented proudly. "I bet there aren't many people who can say their mother looks this good." Ava's cheeks flushed and she batted her eyelashes.

"Thank you. You look stunning yourself. All grown up and just as gorgeous as you want to be. You certainly look older than seventeen, and

I mean that in a good way." Ava returned the praises.

Melody drank in her mother's admiration. She whirled around in her strapless, floor-length royal blue satin gown, feeling like a princess. The sparkling Swarovski crystal hand beading at the breast line of the dress showed off Melody's white frosted eye makeup and the 20-carat Lorraine Schwartz earrings that Andrew Harvey had gotten for her on loaner from the famous jewelry designer. Melody was simply gorgeous and she knew it. There had already been rumblings and speculation through the media about what she would wear. Everyone expected Melody and her sisters to wear their usual matching outfits homemade by Ava Love. Not this time. Andrew Harvey had made sure Melody and the girls had gowns from exclusive designer collections.

Harmony and Lyric watched as Melody and Ava basked in their own shine. It wasn't new to them. Harmony and Lyric didn't get the same compliments, nor did they expect it. They were both stunning in their gowns as well. Harmony's champagne-colored fully beaded gown played up her beautiful, gleaming brown skin and the simple, regal low-slung bun she wore at the nape of her

neck tied in the classy look. Lyric was adorable in an emerald green satin skater dress
that showed off her long, slender legs and
her youthfulness. Ava had arranged for a
well-known hair stylist to fix Lyric's hair into
a stylish pixie cut after Lyric had rebelliously
taken scissors to her own hair the week before
and hacked it so badly a pixie cut was all
that could be done to it. Luckily, the pixie cut
really brought out her face and the glow of
her light, chestnut brown eyes.

Sista Love and Ava stepped onto the 48th
Annual Grammy Awards red carpet in high
fashion style and with grace. They all posed a
million different ways for the cameras. They'd
even stood close together and threaded their
arms at the waist behind each other's' backs
like the Rockettes. They smiled so brightly that
they didn't seem to have a care in the world.
Ava waved to the cameras like she was the
star. Melody giggled with her sisters, and they
changed places for different poses. Melody even
pretended to fix Lyric's hair and Harmony's
dress a time or two. To the world, Ava and
her daughters seemed like a close-knit family
surrounded by love and admiration for one
another. It was their best acting job to date.

That night, inside the Staples Center, when
the presenter read off the nominees for Best

R&B Vocal Performance by a Duo or Group, Ava, Melody, Harmony, and Lyric all held their breath. Melody's heart drummed against her chest bone so hard it made her dizzy. She reached over and grabbed Ava's hand as each nominee was announced. She had seen Harmony and Lyric do the same with one another.

When the presenter said, "And the winner is . . . Sista Love!" all three of the girls exhaled. They looked around in disbelief. Melody's mouth dropped open. Harmony bolted up in her seat, and Lyric cupped her mouth with her hands. To say they were shocked was an understatement. In two short years, Sista Love had gone from a no-name bunch of sisters practicing in their backyard and performing at small local talent shows to make ends meet, to being a Grammy award–winning singing group with a real record deal. It was like someone needed to shake Melody awake from what seemed like a never-ending dream.

"We won?" Melody gasped, slowly rising from her seat, her hands trembling fiercely.

Ava jumped up, clapping profusely. Melody threw her arms around her mother's neck. This time Ava lifted one arm and hugged her back. All three of the girls slid out of the row of seats into the aisle and rushed to the stage excitedly.

Melody shot to the front and stepped to the microphone first.

"Thank you." She was panting, on the verge of tears as she accepted the little gold gramophone from the escort model. Harmony and Lyric stepped up behind Melody.

"Oh, wow. I really didn't expect this tonight. I am so new to this industry. I want to thank my wonderful, beautiful, dedicated mother, the great Ava Love," Melody said, extending her arm toward the audience and pausing while the audience clapped. "I also want to thank the label and Mr. Andrew Harvey for getting me here. You promised you would and you did. Thank you to the fans. I never would've made it without all of you," Melody finished up. "Thank you, everybody!" she shouted into the microphone in finality.

She never thought to give Lyric and Harmony a chance at the microphone. The excitement of it all and her nerves had caused the oversight. They were all escorted off the stage by the same model who'd handed Melody the Grammy award.

Once they were backstage, Lyric kicked off her heels and bolted for the bathrooms.

"What the hell?" Melody asked, her face contorted in confusion.

Harmony rolled her eyes at Melody. "You thanked everyone but us. Did you ever think that we would want to say something, Melody? You made it all about you, as usual," Harmony gritted.

"I said everything that needed to be said for all of us," Melody defended.

"That's the thing, Melody. You don't speak for all of us. You never did," Harmony hissed, storming off in the direction Lyric had gone.

Melody's shoulders slumped with disappointment. It was one of the greatest moments of her life, and the usual jealousy, competition, and division had trampled all over it.

"Don't worry about them." Ava sashayed over.

Melody spun around and met her mother's gaze. Tears rimmed Melody's eyes. She was so proud, but at the same time, she was conflicted that her sisters never seemed to be happy for her.

"Tonight was just the beginning of what's in store for you, Melody. Everybody doesn't have what it takes to be a star, but you, I always knew that you did," Ava said, taking the Grammy from Melody's hand and hugging it against her chest. "Finally," Ava whispered, closing her eyes. "I finally got one."

***

"So, we all agree Ava will be buried in gold, just like she would've wanted." Melody clapped, snapping herself back to reality.

Harmony and Lyric murmured their acquiescence. Murray shrugged his approval.

"Now for the program. We should have a few musical selections," Harmony said.

Melody held up her hand. "Please. Not that god-awful 'Amazing Grace' or 'Wind Beneath My Wings.' For Ava, it'll have to be something upbeat, lively," she said.

"Well, I guess you could've planned all of this by yourself," Lyric snapped, standing up to leave. "Always controlling everything and everybody. We don't work for you."

"Well, Lyric, when you're the one paying for everything, that's what happens," Melody shot back.

"Yeah, you're paying for everything *now*, but what happened all these years while your *mother* remained in this old, broken down brownstone and you bought homes all over the world?" Lyric spat accusingly.

Melody opened her mouth to speak.

"Save it. I really don't care what you have to say. I'm out of here," Lyric huffed, slinging her bag over her shoulder. "Rebel! Let's go!"

Harmony jumped to her feet. She shot Melody an evil look. "Wait, Lyric!" Harmony grabbed Lyric's arm and turned her around.

"For once can't we just all come together without all of this catty bullshit? Without trying to see who is more in control than the other?" Harmony sounded off. "I get it. I totally get it." Harmony shook her head. "We didn't have the best person to foster loving and supportive relationships, but it's up to us now to change that. We are *sisters*," Harmony preached.

Melody raised her hand to her mouth and faked a yawn. Melody didn't want to hear it. In her assessment, Harmony was a hypocrite, because Harmony was the first sister to disappear and cut off contact with everyone else. Melody hated that Harmony hadn't given a damn how she felt when everyone went their separate ways. Harmony and Lyric may not have been Ava's favorite like Melody was, but it still hurt Melody that she had always been left out of her sisters' special bond.

"I'll have the flowers, limousines, and everything else taken care of. All I need from you all is your contribution to the program and for you to show up," Melody said flatly. With that, she stood to leave.

"Good day. *Sisters*."

Chapter 9

Lyric

"Ding-dong, the witch is dead. The wicked old witch is dead," Lyric slurred loudly as she staggered into the funeral chapel with one shoe missing and runs in her black sheer stockings. "I said ding-dong, the wicked witch is dead," Lyric sang shrilly, trying to clap but unable to bring her hands together at the same time. "Why is everyone so sad? Hey, we should be celebrating."

Hushed murmurs and gasps rose and fell amongst the guests. Harmony was on her feet within seconds and practically sprinted down the aisle from where she'd been sitting in the front row.

"What? Everyone thought Ava Love was a pure, sweet old lady that just died quietly?" Lyric continued, her words coming out as if they were too heavy for her tongue. She followed it up with a loud cacophony of shrill high notes—"The wicked witch, evil mother, is dead!"— and then more maniacal laughter.

"Lyric," Harmony said through clenched teeth, grabbing onto Lyric's arm roughly. "What do you think you're doing? You're making a fool of yourself."

"And here comes Captain Saaave-a-Hoooo," Lyric sang, dragging out the vowels.

Harmony clamped down harder, backing Lyric down.

"You can't fix everything, Harmony," Lyric garbled, stumbling and bumping into a wall as Harmony gripped her arm tightly and pushed her backward toward the door. Harmony and Lyric stumbled out of the chapel door and spilled out into the lobby. Lyric was still making noises and singing off key as Harmony dragged her by the arm.

"Lyric, what the fuck are you doing?" Harmony whispered harshly, finally shoving Lyric into a corner in the funeral home lobby. "This is not the time or the place for this bullshit," Harmony chastised, trying to use her body to block any sneaky paparazzi from getting a picture.

Lyric let out a loud, raucous laugh, garnering a few suspicious stares from people coming and going. "Did you know that there were many people that wanted Ava dead? You should tell everyone here." Lyric spoke like she had a mouthful of hard marbles in her cheeks. "Tell them all of the enemies she had, including you and me and me and you and you and me," Lyric rambled, giggling stupidly.

Harmony sniffed, her face folding into a frown. "What have you been drinking?" she asked in a stern parental tone.

"What have I been drinking? What have I been drinking you ask?" Lyric repeated, garbling her words and raising her voice to almost a shriek. "I'll tell you *just* what the hell I . . . I . . . been driiiinking!"

"Shh!" Harmony grabbed Lyric's arm again and yanked her like a tantrum-throwing toddler into the ladies' room. "Excuse us!" Harmony yelled at the occupants, her eyes bugged out and wild. With agape mouths and furrowed foreheads, all of the ladies quickly scampered for the door.

Harmony shoved Lyric into a stall. "Sit down!" she demanded.

"Naw, you want to know what I have been drinking, right? Well, sister, I'm going to tell you," Lyric mumbled almost incoherently. She tried to get out of the stall, but Harmony shoved her back.

"I said sit down! You need to dry out before the service starts! You're a damn mess right now! And where the hell is your other shoe?"

Lyric fell back, off balance, her legs splayed like a newborn baby deer trying to stand for the first time.

"Ouch!" Lyric howled then laughed. "Why you pushing me, sis-ter? What? You don't want to hear the answer to what I've been drinking? Huh, big sis-ter?" Lyric said, sticking out her tongue mockingly.

"You're being ridiculous right now, Lyric," Harmony said, disgusted. "I don't even think water or coffee will work for you right now. This is more than just a drink. You're on something."

"I'm still going to tell you what . . . what I've been drinking," Lyric sing-songed, putting her thumbs up to her ears and wiggling her fingers like a little kid teasing another.

Harmony rolled her eyes and crossed her arms over her chest. "I can't believe you came here in this condition, Lyric." Harmony sighed.

"I've been drinking good ol' blackberry brandy. Straaaight. Straight. Straight down the hatch. Straight as a string. Straight," Lyric said, the words tumbling out of her mouth almost on top of one another.

Harmony's back went stiff and she breathed out heavily.

"What? Did I say the magic words?" Lyric put both of her hands on her cheeks and opened her mouth into an O in mock surprise. "Black-berry bran-deee," Lyric emphasized.

Harmony shook her lowered head.

"Don't tell me you don't remember why my own mother made me drink the stuff when I was only seventeen years old," Lyric said, emitting a contradictory chuckle. "I am positive you remember. Right, sis-ter?"

"Lyric." Harmony lowered her voice to a soft, comforting tone. "I know this is all hard for you. We are all battling these memories, her death, our relationships, but we have a lot of people—"

"I don't give a fuck about the people!" Lyric boomed.

Harmony jumped, wobbling slightly on her heels.

Suddenly Lyric's eyes hooded over and her right pointer finger wavered unsteadily in front of her face. "Fuck the people and what they think! The world needs to know the truth about Ava Love! You want to protect her after every-thing?" Lyric shouted, pointing at Harmony accusingly.

"Lyric, that's not what I'm—"

"Shut up! *Your* mother . . . *your* fucking mother made me drink blackberry brandy to try and give me a homemade abortion. I didn't even know I was pregnant! She said it would work and that I wouldn't feel the pain. Do you remember that, Harmony? Huh? When I was deathly ill from being pregnant by the man she sold me to so that we could be famous. Huh? Does anybody remember that I was seventeen and pregnant by a disgusting troll that was fucking old enough to be my grandfather? Huh? Does anybody remember how I bled and screamed in pain and she didn't even want to take me to the fucking hospital and then lied and made it look like some off-the-hook teenage whore? Do you and Melody remember all of the nights *your* mother, *her* mother, grabbed me out of my bed and sent me to him so you bitches could have record deals and fame and so *your* mother could live out her sick fantasy of being famous? Huh? Do you remember?" Lyric screamed through her tears while her chest heaved.

Lyric punched the metal wall of the bathroom stall. Harmony jumped, her shoulders shuddering with sobs.

"I don't even have shit to show for all of it. Used up. Broke. Damn near homeless. Nothing left. And now she's gone, so I can't even tell her how fucked up she was and how I've never been the same since I was thirteen years old."

"Lyric," Harmony croaked, her hands up in surrender. "Not now," she whimpered, barely able to get the words out. "We can't go down this road right now." Harmony's words came out in a shaky whisper.

"Then when?" Lyric rasped, lowering her head into her hands to stop the spinning. "When?"

Brooklyn, New York
May 2008

Lyric bent over the toilet for the fifth time and vomited. When the entire contents of her stomach had all come up, she fell to her knees, panting. Her hair was pasted to her forehead with sweat and her heart pounded.

"Oh God. Help me. I'm dying," Lyric prayed out loud.

She felt terrible. She closed her eyes and sprawled out on the cold tile floor, hoping it would relieve the burning hot feeling engulfing her entire body.

"You ain't dying nothing," Ava said, suddenly looming over her.

Lyric's eyes popped open. Her legs kicked out and her palms slapped the bathroom floor.

"*Ava, you scared me.*" *Lyric gasped. She had been so busy throwing up and trying to recover that she hadn't heard her mother come into the bathroom.*

"*Now stand up here, girl, and let me see your breasts,*" *Ava demanded.*

Lyric slowly sat up on the floor. "*Huh?*"

"*Let me see your breasts I said,*" *Ava repeated, a cigarette dangling between the shaky fingers of her left hand.*

Lyric knew Ava only smoked when she was stressed out about something. Lyric braced the wall, and with a few starts and stops, she finally got to her feet. Ava's gaze bore down on Lyric until her entire face was flaming hot.

Lyric lifted her shirt so that her bra was exposed. Ava raised both eyebrows when she saw how much of Lyric's breasts were spilling out of her now severely too small bra. Ava reached out and poked Lyric's right breast.

"*Ow!*" *Lyric winced, stepping back a few steps.* "*Why did you do that?*" *Lyric asked. The real question that ran through her mind was why a simple poke like that hurt so badly.*

"*Take off that tiny-ass bra,*" *Ava grumbled.*

Lyric turned her back to Ava and did as she was told. When she unleashed her breasts from the confines of the much too small bra, the pain hit her. Lyric hadn't realized before then how sensitive, swollen, and painful her breasts had become.

"Turn around here," Ava instructed.

Lyric sighed loudly, embarrassed by her mother's seemingly perverse examination. "Why? What does my breast have to do with this stomach virus?" she whined defiantly.

"I said turn around here," Ava shot back.

Lyric twisted her lips and flared her nostrils as she did a slow turn, her breasts hanging freely and now painfully in front of her.

Ava squinted and shook her head. "Goddamn it," she grumbled before she took a long pull on her cigarette. Her hands shook more fiercely now.

"What? What is it?" Lyric asked, her eyebrows knitted together. "Why are you looking at me like that?" Lyric crossed her arms over her breasts to hide them from her mother's disapproving glare.

"When was your last period?" Ava asked, drawing in another lungful of smoke and blowing it out right away.

"I don't know." Lyric shrugged, waving her hand in front of her face, annoyed by the inquisition and the disgusting cigarette smoke.

"Think," Ava growled.

Lyric's eyes went up and to the left. "Oh, I remember I had it for the Staples Center show in L.A.," Lyric suddenly recalled.

Lyric watched as comprehension washed over Ava's face. Ava's hands shook so badly her cigarette slid from her fingers. She jumped back and hopped a few steps when the hot tip hit the top of her left foot.

"Shit! You mean to tell me you haven't seen a period in two months?" Ava's bottom lip trembled and she was barely able to use her foot to stub out the cigarette because she was so off balance.

"I—I didn't think about it," Lyric stammered, taking a few steps back. Her heart was racing now. She was in trouble according to the evil, squinty-eyed, twisted look on Ava's face.

"Fuck!" Ava paced, her hands on her hips. Lyric was too scared to say anything. Ava finally stopped moving.

"Don't tell nobody about this, you understand me?" Ava jutted her long, red-painted nail at Lyric.

Lyric shrugged. "About what? Having a stomach virus?" she asked innocently.

"This ain't no virus, stupid. Don't you know what it means when you don't bleed for a month?" Ava snapped, disgusted.

Lyric's eyes darted around like she was trying to think real hard. No one had ever had any talk with her about her body, why she bled each month, what it meant. She hadn't ever been to school to have sex education, so Ava's question seemed like one of those hard Jeopardy questions to Lyric.

"Just don't tell nobody, not even Melody and Harmony. I'll take care of this," Ava said. She left Lyric standing there, confused.

Two nights later, Ava shook Lyric out of her sleep. "Come with me," Ava whispered. "And be quiet."

Rubbing sleep from her eyes and shuffling her feet, Lyric padded behind Ava and followed her downstairs to the kitchen.

"Sit down," Ava instructed.

Lyric flopped down into one of the kitchen chairs.

"Drink this and drink it all," Ava said, placing a steaming coffee mug on the table in front of Lyric.

"What is it?" Lyric groaned. "It stinks."

"Just drink it," Ava whispered harshly. "And drink it all."

Lyric picked up the mug and apprehensively regarded the steaming hot liquid inside. She sniffed it. "Eww." She balked.

"Drink it," Ava hissed. "I'm not going to tell you again."

Lyric rolled her eyes and lifted the mug to her lips. She blew over the liquid to cool it off some.

"No. It has to be very hot for it to work," Ava corrected. "Drink it as hot as you can stand it."

Lyric carefully and slowly slurped in the first bit of the liquid. She squeezed her eyes shut and stuck out her tongue. "Oh my God! This is disgusting!" Lyric gagged and waved her free hand in front of her face.

"Shh! Be quiet and finish it," Ava urged through clenched teeth.

"It's burning my chest and my stomach and my whole body," Lyric complained, writhing in the chair. "This is like drinking poison." She gagged some more.

"Unless you want to be around here dead, you better drink it. I'm not going to say it again. If you drink this, everything will be better and you won't feel no pain," Ava gritted, tapping her foot impatiently.

Lyric slowly lifted the mug over and over again until all of the drink was gone. Her head felt like someone had dunked it under water. Her vision came into and went out of focus. Her ears rang. She felt like she didn't have control over any of her body parts. She tried to stand up from the table, but her legs didn't work, and she slipped back down into the chair. Lyric couldn't feel her tongue, let alone speak.

"C'mon." Ava grabbed one of Lyric's arms and put it around the back of her neck.

"I . . . I . . . can't," Lyric slurred.

"I got you," Ava replied. She hoisted Lyric from the chair.

"Whoa," Lyric said loudly as her legs slipped from under her, almost causing both of them to spill onto the kitchen floor.

Ava groaned as she struggled to move Lyric along. Finally, Ava had gotten her from the kitchen to the living room. Lyric flopped down on the couch, and Ava lifted her legs and pushed her the rest of the way onto the couch until her body was stretched out straight.

Lyric moaned and groaned until she finally fell asleep. Two hours passed, and Lyric awoke screaming.

"Help me! Help me!"

Ava came racing from the kitchen. Lyric was covered in blood from the waist down. Her entire body was drenched in sweat.

Harmony and Melody raced from their bedrooms and down the stairs.

"Help me!" Lyric cried, her knees drawn up into her chest and her head hanging from the side of the couch.

"Lyric!" Harmony yelped, racing over to her. "What's going on?"

"Move! Go back upstairs," Ava scolded, snatching Harmony by the shoulder to move her away.

"Get off of me!" Harmony wrestled away from Ava. "She's bleeding and she's pale as hell! She needs a hospital!" Harmony barked.

Melody stood staring, her eyes stretched to their capacity and her mouth open stupidly.

"I know what she needs!" Ava spat. "It's going to be fine."

"It hurts! Help me! Help me!" Lyric screamed some more.

Harmony stomped out of the living room and into the kitchen.

"Where are you going?" Ava yelled at her back. "Harmony! Don't you—"

"Hello, 911? I need an ambulance fast. My sister is bleeding," Harmony huffed into the phone.

Ava rushed into the kitchen to disconnect the call but it was too late. Harmony had already given the operator the address.

"You nosey bitch!" Ava hissed. "You'll pay for this."

***

"I'm so glad you're okay." Harmony smiled, leaning at the side of Lyric's hospital bed and stroking Lyric's forehead.

Lyric smiled weakly. Thank you, she mouthed silently to Harmony. Harmony smiled back at her.

Just then, a man in a white lab coat and a woman in a frumpy black pantsuit entered the room. Ava jumped up from her seat in the corner of the room and rushed over to the strangers.

"Ms. Love?" the man asked.

Ava plastered on a fake smile and stuck her hand out. "Um, yes. I'm Ms. Love."

"I'm Doctor Seitz, and this is Ms. Carlisle from our social work department," the doctor said. Ava's features quickly shuttered. She dropped her hand at her side and her smile was gone.

"We wanted to speak to you about what happened."

Ava shifted her weight from one foot to the other. "What do you mean?" she asked, her words coming out shaky.

"Well, your daughter was pregnant and severely intoxicated. We also found the drug RU-486 in her blood. Do you know what that is?"

Ava's entire body trembled now. She could barely keep still. "I, um, think I've heard of it before, but I would have no idea where she'd get something like that." *Ava fabricated on the spot so fluidly that even she seemed to believe it.*

"It's a pill that terminates pregnancies, Ms. Love," *the doctor said sternly.*

Ava put her hand up on her chest like she was shocked and devastated at the same time.

"Were you at home when she ingested the alcohol and the pill?" *the doctor probed. The social worker scribbled wildly on a yellow legal notepad.* "This could've been a deadly cocktail, Ms. Love. It seems more like a suicide attempt. I mean, with all of these pregnancy options around, this was extreme."

Ava swallowed hard and ran her hands over her clothes. "You know how it is. . . . These teenagers," *Ava replied, wringing her hands together in front of her.* "I have three girls. I can't be with them all of the time. I tried to talk to them about these things—pregnancy, staying away from boys—as much as I can, but like I said, they are teenagers." *Ava shook her head and chuckled nervously.*

Harmony stood up and glared at Ava evilly then shook her head in disgust and stormed out of the room. Melody followed her out.

Lyric turned her head to the right and closed her eyes. Tears ran over the bridge of her nose, down the side of her face, and pooled in her right ear.

Your daughter was pregnant. . . . Your daughter was pregnant. . . . A pill that terminates pregnancies. . . . A pill that terminates pregnancies.

The doctor's words played over and over in Lyric's head. She had been pregnant! She had only had sex with one person in her life. Getting pregnant came from sex, that much she knew. Lyric's heart monitor began to squeal loudly in response to her broken heart.

Harmony bent down in front of Lyric and grabbed her around the shoulders. "It's just one day. When this is all over, you're going to get some help. *We* are going to get some help. But we have to bury her, Lyric. Rehashing all of this pain is not doing us any good," Harmony said, giving Lyric a soft pep talk.

Lyric's breaths came out in jagged puffs. "It wasn't you," she rasped. "It didn't happen to you."

"I know," Harmony agreed, her voice going low with shame. "I used to pray that it was me, that one of those nights it would be me instead of you. Believe me, Lyric. I would've taken your place in a heartbeat if I could've," Harmony assured, stroking her sister's head.

"What the hell?" Melody boomed from behind them.

Harmony closed her eyes and let out a long, exasperated breath.

"The service is about to start. How many of these stupid little hug fests are you all going to have?" Melody spat, peering at them over her dark shades.

"As many as it takes for her to be all right," Harmony said tersely, standing up to meet Melody eye to eye. "Now go get her a cup of black coffee, find her a pair of decent stockings and some shoes, and hold off the service for another thirty minutes. And if you can't do shit for yourself, then tell one of your flunkies to do it. But do it," Harmony said with force.

Melody stomped out of the bathroom, mumbling under her breath.

"Thank you," Lyric said barely above a whisper, her words still clumsy. "I mean it, Harm. Thank you."

Chapter 10

Harmony

"Are you sure you're ready to go out there?" Harmony asked as Lyric took the last sips of the black coffee.

Lyric kept her eyes closed, but she shook her head in the affirmative. Harmony could tell her sister wasn't one hundred percent sober, but even fifty percent would have to do.

"Can you stand up by yourself?" Harmony asked.

Lyric chortled. "I'm good, Harmony."

"Well, I had to ask. You weren't so good an hour ago," Harmony said, letting out a light chuckle of her own. Harmony's shoulders eased a bit, seeing her sister in better shape.

"Okay, well, let's go face this together," Harmony said, extending her hand toward Lyric.

Lyric slapped her hand away playfully. "How old am I again?" she joked, standing up on her own.

"Well, excuuuse me," Harmony sing-songed, placing her hand on her chest in a clutch-the-pearls manner. They shared a light laugh and headed for the door.

Just as Harmony pulled the door open, Melody came rushing at them.

"I can't hold this service off anymore. I mean, it's been over an hour. What's taking so long?" Melody panted like she'd been running.

"Nothing. We are ready," Harmony replied. "You sure are doing a lot of running around here for yourself today. Don't you have people for all of this back and forth?" Harmony asked, annoyed by Melody's persistence.

"Okay, everything is set for the service. She looks much better. Now let's walk in together," Melody said, ignoring Harmony's subtle dig.

Harmony raised a suspicious eyebrow. It wasn't like Melody to be acting like a regular everyday layperson and not a high-falutin' celebrity. Melody also wasn't the one to readily request or participate in any sisterly bonding moments or to be seen with her sisters.

What is she up to?

Harmony shrugged off her paranoia and didn't say anything. All three sisters exited the bathroom doorway together. Lyric and Harmony did their usual arm-in-arm routine, and Melody walked alongside them at first. When they were about to round the corner that spilled into the funeral home's lobby, Melody quickly hooked her arm into Harmony's free arm, making them look like the Three Musketeers.

Harmony's eyebrows shot up into arches. She opened her mouth to say something, but there was no time before the first surge of flashes exploded in front of her.

"Smile," Melody said through her teeth while smiling beatifically. Harmony looked like a deer in headlights. Lyric's head whipped from side to side, her eyes also wide with surprise.

"It's Sista Love!"

"They're back together!"

"Look at them!

"Melody, will there be a reunion?"

"Melody, are you going to have your sisters make an appearance on the 1 Night Stand tour?"

"Melody, where have your sisters been all of this time? Will you be doing a press tour about your reunion?

"Melody, are all of the rumors about bad blood between you and your sisters lies?"

"Melody, will there be a new album from the group?"

Goddammit. She set us up! I knew she was up to something, Harmony thought. Her jaw rocked. She bent her arm and pulled it toward her chest, tightening her lock on Melody's arm until she was sure it was painful.

"Who invited them here? This is your mother's funeral, not some publicity stunt, for God's sake," Harmony whispered through her teeth while trying to keep a smile on her face for the cameras.

"I didn't call them here, but if I can use this as an opportunity to get you girls back out there, why not?" Melody did the same, speaking through her smile while one explosion of flash after another went off in front of them.

"Are we going on tour with her?" Lyric asked, a hint of childlike excitement in her voice. "Is that what they just said? Is that what she's saying?"

"I wouldn't bank on it," Harmony whispered out of the side of her mouth.

As Harmony, Melody, and Lyric finally made it through the gaggle of paparazzi to the funeral chapel doors, Harmony spotted Ron and Aubrey. Harmony's pulse quickened. She swiftly unlatched herself from her sisters and frantically pushed through the gawking crowd and made her way to her husband and baby. Ron's eyes lit up when he spotted her.

"Hey!" Harmony sang, throwing her arms around his neck and squeezing him tight. "Oh God, I'm so happy to see you," Harmony whispered as she melted against him.

She inhaled his Jazz Club cologne, and suddenly all of the tension from the day's events seemed to ease. Ron smiled and moved his face so he could kiss her. Harmony's entire body tingled. Oh, how she loved her husband.

"Mama," Aubrey cooed, reaching her tiny arms toward Harmony.

"Awww," Harmony crooned, grabbing her baby girl and squeezing her against her chest. "Hi, sweet girl. How's my sweet girl?" Harmony used her high-pitched baby voice to speak to the baby.

"Oh my God. I've missed you both so much," Harmony said, turning her attention back to Ron. She was on the verge of tears. This time, happy tears.

"Oh, we've missed you too. Trust me. It felt like you were gone twenty days instead of two days. Sheesh. I didn't realize how easy you made life," Ron replied, shaking his head like he'd had it rough in her absence.

"But we survived. What about you? Are you okay?" Ron asked, his eyes darting around the packed lobby. "And everything here?" he continued, jerking his chin toward the crowd.

Harmony sighed. Her shoulders slumped. "It has definitely been emotionally taxing. One minute up, next minute down. You just never know how much pain and resentment or even good memories you've buried until you have to relive it." She sighed. "And all of this . . . this circus doesn't make it easier." Harmony nodded toward the hungry paparazzi and all of the members of Melody's entourage that were zipping around as if the funeral was one of her concert productions.

Ron shoved his hands deep into his pants pockets and nodded his understanding. Harmony noticed the strained look on his face.

"Enough about me. I don't want to be selfish. How about you? Are you okay? Being back in New York. I mean, the last time you were here . . ." Harmony's voice trailed off.

"No. No. I'm fine." Ron waved his left hand and smiled. Harmony eyed him with suspicion. "Hey," he touched her chin and looked down into her eyes. "Trust me. I know what I need to do to always be here for you and Aubrey," Ron assured, winking at her.

Harmony tried to search his face for any signs that he might be struggling with being back in his old stomping grounds, but she knew that Ron had mastered his poker face years ago. She didn't want to be pushy and cause an argument, but she also knew all too well that addiction was a disease that needed to be treated every single day. It didn't matter that Ron had been clean for three years. Harmony knew it would only take one single trigger to make him relapse.

"We are ready to start," One of Melody's assistants came over and said to Harmony. Harmony nodded.

When the woman walked away, Harmony turned to Ron. "This is how it's been. All of *her* people telling us *little* people what to do."

Ron grunted and placed his hand on the small of Harmony's back as they made their way into the funeral chapel. "Well, hopefully it won't be for that much longer. After this is all said and done, we will return home to our simple life in our little honeycomb hideout and forget about the rich and famous and all of their pretentiousness." He followed up with a peck on Harmony's cheek.

A cold chill shot down Harmony's back, and she shivered. She still hadn't told Ron that she would need to stay in New York a while longer than they'd both expected. She had promised Lyric that she wouldn't abandon her ever again, and she meant it. Harmony knew that if she left Lyric now, she would probably lose her forever.

She also knew if she neglected Ron for too long, it might send him spiraling backward and she'd lose him forever too. Harmony closed her teeth down on her bottom lip and bat-sized butterflies fluttered in her stomach just thinking about how she could save her little sister and also keep her family intact.

Chapter 11

Melody

Melody watched as Harmony walked into the funeral chapel with her little family. She noticed Harmony's husband's supportive hold on Harmony and the love in his eyes. Rough waves of jealousy suddenly swirled inside of Melody like a high tide, making her feel like she was choking. Her eyes went dark and her mouth flattened into a straight line. All of the money in the world couldn't buy her the love she'd been looking for, the kind Harmony seemed to have now.

Melody hid behind her dark shades, furtively staring at Harmony, her husband, and her little sweet-faced baby. Melody's temples pounded and her stomach curled into knots. She was supposed to have everything. She was supposed to be the happiest. That's what Ava had promised. Melody was supposed to be the only one worthy of the perfect life. Those words had come out of her mother's mouth. They were all lies.

Melody turned away. She couldn't stand to watch Harmony with her head on her husband's shoulder and his arm around her. It was making Melody physically sick.

Melody shifted in her seat. Her insides ached with loneliness. It was the kind of loneliness that couldn't be assuaged even as she sat in a room full of people. Melody knew deep down inside she couldn't even pay for the type of love and companionship she longed for. She had Sly, but Melody knew he wasn't all hers. She knew that they did an unhealthy relationship dance and fronted for the public like they had the perfect love. Melody wanted Sly to love her and only her.

The pastor Melody had hired stepped up to the microphone and opened up the service. "Tonight we celebrate the life of Ms. Ava Love, and I want to begin with the theme of tonight's memorial, and that is, Everybody Needs Somebody and We All Need God."

"Amen," a few people in the crowd shouted.

"We all need love, do you agree?" the pastor asked.

Melody reached down next to her and forced her hand into Sly's hand. It was a bold move, but she wanted to let him know she needed him.

Melody could see Sly's perplexed reaction out of the corner of her eye, but she ignored it. She told herself that he would get it, that in that moment he would love her like she needed to be loved. Melody curled her fingers around his the way she imagined a couple in love, like Harmony and her husband, would do it.

Sly didn't return the affection; instead, he shifted and twitched in his seat like the public display of affection made his skin itch. Melody knew that they usually staged their public affection, agreeing to hold hands when leaving their building in the city, sitting cozy next to one another at a basketball game, or Sly admiring Melody from a distance while she walked a red carpet. They were all public relations–advised activities. This handholding now hadn't been discussed or planned. Melody felt her heart drop, but like usual, she put on a brave face.

"We all need love, but you won't know love if you don't know God first," the pastor preached.

"Amen," Melody murmured. With that, she released her hold on Sly's hand and turned her body away from his. She would find love for herself, no matter what she had to do to get it.

After the service, Sly did his usual—took his people and left. He planted a dry kiss on Melody's cheek and told her he would come later to the private repast she was having at her estate in the Hamptons. Melody wandered out of the funeral chapel alone. Her security team immediately surrounded her, ready to escort her to the waiting fleet of cars outside.

"Give me a minute." Melody called them off when she spotted Harmony and her little family huddled together. Melody bit into the inside of her cheek, inhaled deeply, and plastered on a fake smile as she sauntered over to her sister.

"All of these days we've been together and you didn't tell me about this little sweetie," Melody said cheerfully, stepping up to Harmony and Ron. Melody noticed Harmony's body stiffen and her facial expression flatten.

"Now who is this little doll? Is this my first niece?" Melody inquired, extending her arms toward Aubrey.

Harmony looked at Ron nervously as she clutched her baby against her chest, suddenly guarded.

"Come here, sweet girl," Melody pressed. This time she put her hands on Aubrey's arm and tugged her gently away from Harmony.

Harmony sucked in her breath and reluctantly released her protective death grip on her baby.

"I'll give her right back." Melody was familiar with the horrified look Harmony wore on her face. She had seen that look so many times when they were kids—like the time Harmony had gotten a beautiful black Barbie doll for Christmas, one that Ava didn't think Melody would want, but when Melody decided she liked Harmony's doll better than hers, Ava took it away and gave it to Melody. Melody got to keep both dolls, hers and Harmony's, that year.

"Oh my goodness," Melody cooed, holding the baby's face in front of hers. "You are the most gorgeous little thing. You look *just* like your daddy," Melody babbled in a baby voice.

Harmony shifted her weight from one foot to the other, her hands moving aimlessly at her sides.

Melody pressed Aubrey against her, closed her eyes, and inhaled the baby's scent. She immediately felt intoxicated. Now she understood why women rushed to procreate. Melody felt warm and full inside. Was this how unconditional love felt?

"Let me go change her." Harmony grabbed Aubrey and interrupted Melody's little moment.

Melody had to blink a few times to snap herself out of the little trance she'd fallen in. She chuckled nervously.

"Did I get carried away?" Melody released Aubrey back to Harmony.

"And you are?" Melody extended her hand toward Ron. She knew full well who he was. Melody had seen Ron appear in court alongside Harmony when Harmony had sued the record label and the group for back royalties and publishing rights. Melody had also paid top dollar for private investigators to find out all about where Harmony lived, whom she was married to, and all about the dance and acting school she had opened with the money Melody felt Harmony stole from her through the lawsuit. She also knew all about Ron's past as a child actor and his stint in drug rehab that Harmony had funded, also with money Melody felt Harmony wasn't really entitled to.

"Ron," he answered simply, taking her hand for a quick, firm, businesslike shake.

Melody felt something spark inside of her when he touched her hand. He wasn't just a normal good-looking man. He was movie star fine. Melody's cheeks burned. She flashed her gorgeous, shocking white smile and flicked her long hair.

"Nice to meet you, Ron. Should I call you brother-in-law? Baby daddy? What?" Melody asked sardonically.

"Definitely brother-in-law," Harmony interjected. "He's my husband," she said flatly.

Melody laughed. "Okay, okay. Don't bite my head off. Never can tell these days. Again, nice to meet you . . . *brother-in-law*." Melody sniggered, knowing that her antics were pissing Harmony off.

"Please do join us at my Hamptons estate this evening. It'll be the last of the homegoing events for our mother," Melody said to Ron directly, as if Harmony weren't standing there.

"Whatever my wife wants to do," Ron answered, putting his arm around Harmony's shoulders.

"Eww." Melody widened her eyes, feigning shock, and turned her attention to Harmony. "Whatever his wife wants to do. Sounds like he's a keeper, big sis." Melody chuckled, touching Ron on the chest playfully. "He defers to you for decisions, but you make decisions without him?" Melody asked, smiling at Harmony.

Harmony frowned. Ron looked at her and back to Melody.

"Oh, what? Your *wife* hasn't told you she'd be going out on tour with me in a few weeks? I'm having my sisters make an appearance on my 1 Night Stand tour. . . . You know, so they can make some money, get some of this spotlight, live a little," Melody said.

Harmony's nostrils flared open. Ron's eyes hooded and his jaw went square as he looked at Harmony expectantly.

"You did tell him. Right, Harm?" Melody winked.

"Melody, your car is waiting to take you to the burial. Everything has been delivered and set up for the party just like you requested," one of Melody's flunkies stepped over and said.

"Well, Ron, I have to run. I'm hoping I'll see you later," Melody said coquettishly, extending her hand toward his chest again.

Harmony stepped in front of Ron. "I'm not sure we will be able to come," Harmony said through her teeth.

"Aw, come on, sister. We've been through the rough stuff. Now come and let me show you all a good time. I mean, you do want to experience how the other half lives, don't you? You were the one who said we need to rebuild our relationships. Remember your promise to Lyric," Melody replied, smiling at Harmony.

Several emotions played across Harmony's face at once.

"That's what I thought. I'll see you *both* later."

With that, Melody's security team surrounded her and whisked her away, but not before she heard Ron say, "What the hell, Harmony?"

Chapter 12

Lyric

"Damn, this house is lit," Rebel said, craning his neck to look out of the limousine window as it snaked its way up the long winding road that led to Melody's East Hampton, Long Island estate. "This shit got more windows than the projects. Damn. She really live in this big-ass house with no kids, nothing?" He continued, completely amazed by the sprawling, red brick front mansion with its castle-like appearance.

Lyric wasn't impressed. Anything that Melody had, Lyric felt it was because of her sacrifices. "She probably don't live here. I'm sure she's got ten more like this all over the world," Lyric replied, a hint of resentment underlying her words. "Too bad none of the rest of us got on like she did. We never made the kind of money she made, even as a group. If we did, we—me and Harmony—didn't see a dime of it."

"Shit, the past it the past. You better make nice with her. If what you said is true about her taking you on tour with her, that could be a good look for you and for me. You could make some money, get our names back out there, maybe get me on a collabo with Sly or some shit," Rebel said, excitement building in his voice with each insane idea.

"Stop dreaming. A dude like Sly wouldn't even sneeze at your washed-up ass, and Melody inviting us on tour is probably all talk," Lyric said as the limo came to a stop a few luxury cars back on the circular driveway. Lyric tugged on the door handle before the valet could open her door and exited the limo. "Because Melody Love is all about herself," Lyric murmured.

Once inside, Lyric and Rebel looked around in awe. There were two rows of poster-sized pictures of Ava lined up on easels on either side of the grand foyer. Lyric recognized some of the pictures, but others were of Ava when she was much younger. Lyric shrugged her shoulders. If only Ava's outer beauty could've been turned inward, she might've made a wonderful mother.

Everything inside of the mansion was decked out in off-white and gold. It was just Melody's style—over the top. Lyric watched as servers walked around with trays. She noticed carving stations and the elaborate food spread. There were so many people milling around that Lyric got dizzy trying to figure out who they all were.

"This shit look more like an industry party than some after-funeral dinner," Rebel commented as he bopped his head to the old school disco music blaring through the built-in sound system.

It was Donna Summer's hit song "Last Dance" playing. Lyric knew every word to that song by the time she was just two years old because her mother played it so much. It was fitting for Ava's last dance.

"Trust me, this is how Ava would've wanted it," Lyric said, snatching a drink from the tray of a passing server. She would need a drink and then some to survive this.

"Shit, this is better than some of the top industry parties I been to," Rebel said as he shoveled a handful of bacon-wrapped shrimp into his mouth. "This is that shit," he mumbled with a mouthful, heading straight for one of the six bars situated around the estate.

Lyric shook her head. "This dude. Always looking for free food and a free high."

She didn't care if Rebel got lost. That would mean she could get high in peace. Lyric gave her bag a squeeze.

Just me and you later.

Lyric finally dissected the palatial living space and spotted Harmony sitting on a beautiful white chaise lounge, holding Aubrey on her lap. Lyric's shoulders eased with relief. She rushed over, smiling.

"Hey." Lyric sat down.

"Hey." Harmony seemed to light up at the sight of Lyric. "How are you feeling? You had rough morning," Harmony said all in one breath.

"I'm good. You officially blew my high," Lyric joked. "Hi, cutie pie. Oh, man, she is so adorable, Harm. She looks like a little angel," Lyric said.

Harmony didn't answer; instead, she looked at her baby sadly. Lyric took her eyes off of the baby and looked at her sister's face. She immediately noticed the sadness that had suddenly crept into Harmony's eyes.

"What's up? Are you okay?" Lyric asked.

"I'll be okay. Just a little disagreement with Ron," Harmony replied, shifting the baby so she was facing Lyric. Lyric put her pointer finger in Aubrey's little fist.

"Hey, pretty girl," Lyric sang. Aubrey kicked her legs and smiled at Lyric.

"Why? What happened?"

"Melody happened." Harmony sighed.

"What the hell did she do now?" Lyric asked, biting down on her bottom lip.

Harmony sighed loudly. "We can talk about it later."

"No. Tell me now," Lyric pressed.

Harmony shook her head. "Back at the chapel, Melody told Ron we were going on tour with her," Harmony said.

Lyric's eyebrows furrowed.

"Melody made it seem like you and I had agreed to go on tour with her. Like we had a discussion about it and that I had made a decision behind Ron's back. Ron is upset because he thinks that I didn't discuss something as big and important as that with him. We always talk about anything that affects the other person before making a decision.

"I tried to explain to him that Melody was jumping the gun, that neither you nor I had agreed to go with her on tour. I mean, look how we found out that it was even a thought—the damn paparazzi. We don't even know the terms of her offer yet. We don't even know if we can trust her after what we've been through. She doesn't have the greatest track record. But he just got so upset. It didn't matter that I told him I hadn't really made a decision, that I didn't know if it was something that I would even consider at this point in my life," Harmony relayed, shaking her head.

"But you're going to say yes to the tour, right?" Lyric inquired. "I mean, you said it yourself. We need to rebuild . . . everything. This would be the perfect opportunity for us."

Harmony closed her eyes and threw her head back. "Lyric, I don't know. Everything is happening so fast. I have to think about Ron and the baby. I have a business to run and— "

"You promised me." Lyric stood up abruptly. "I knew you were lying. I knew you would go back to your life and forget all about mine."

"Lyric, wait," Harmony called after her, but Lyric stormed off and got lost in the crowd.

Lyric went outside to one of the outdoor bars. She needed a drink. Now. She tapped on the bar's glass top to get the bartender's attention.

"Let me get Henny straight," Lyric demanded.

Lyric regretted even coming to the repast. She would've been fine going back to Harlem and getting wasted. She was kicking herself for letting Rebel pressure her just because it was going to be his first time in the Hamptons.

Lyric's mind raced with thoughts. When Harmony was gone, her life would go back to the same hamster wheel of partying, drinking, and drugging. The thought alone exhausted Lyric, but what else did she have?

She turned from the bar while she waited for her drink and looked out at the beautiful, sprawling green lawn and the different cliques of people huddled together talking, laughing, and drinking. Lyric scanned the crowd, thinking Ava didn't have nearly as many friends as were in attendance at the repast. Half of the people there probably had never met Ava.

Lyric had to wonder how so many people gathered for a woman they didn't know. She wondered if all of these people were there in support of Melody or just to say that they'd attended an event that Melody the megastar had thrown, even if the event was as morose as a funeral repast.

Lyric shook her head. Nothing was small and private when it came to Melody. Not even her mother's funeral.

As Lyric examined the strangers, something caught her eye. She squinted, stood up straight, and stretched her neck out for a better look.

"Ain't this about a bitch," Lyric mumbled under her breath. She watched as Melody giggled in Ron's face like a teenage girl with a crush. Ron had a drink in his hand, and he didn't look so uncomfortable entertaining his wife's sister either. In fact, he looked a bit too comfortable.

Lyric's insides immediately heated up. Hadn't Melody caused enough trouble between Ron and Harmony already?

"Here you go, Miss." The bartender interrupted Lyric's concentration.

She grabbed her drink. As Lyric stomped toward Ron and Melody, she grew angrier and angrier. She had watched Melody take things from Harmony all of her life. Most of the time, Melody wasn't even interested in the things Harmony had; she just wanted them because Harmony had them. Lyric knew Melody so well.

Melody and Ron stood so engrossed in conversation that it took them a few seconds to even realize Lyric had approached and was standing there.

"What's this all about?" Lyric interrupted rudely, taking a big swig from her snifter.

"Oh, hey, Lyric," Melody chimed, flashing her winning smile as if she didn't have a care in the world. "Have you met your brother-in-law, Ron?"

"Of course I have," Lyric replied. "But do you remember that he's your brother-in-law?"

Melody laughed. "Of course I do," she came back sarcastically. "I was just getting to know him better since I seem to be the only one that wasn't invited to the wedding."

"Looks to me like you've gotten to know enough," Lyric said, grabbing Ron's arm and pulling him aside.

"You're mad at your wife so you make pals with her sister who caused your argument in the first place?" Lyric asked, her tone serious.

"It was nothing like that. She approached me. I was just listening." Ron pled his case.

Lyric wasn't buying it. "Your wife is inside with your baby, feeling pretty terrible," Lyric whispered gruffly. "She would feel worse if she saw you right now. That is not a road you want to go down." Lyric nodded in Melody's direction. "That's a dangerous game that, trust me, you won't win."

"I'll go check on Harmony," Ron said, quickly taking Lyric's cue. He set his drink down on one of the satin-wrapped high-top tables. "Excuse me," he huffed as he walked away in a hurry. He pulled out his pocket-sized breath spray and squirted it a few times into his mouth.

Lyric turned her attention back to Melody, who had moved on to giggling and flirting with another handsome guest. Melody was just like Ava, always there for any attention from a man. Lyric grabbed Melody's shoulder and forced her to turn around.

"Excuse me for a minute," Melody said to her guest, followed by an awkward laugh. When she was finally face-to-face with Lyric, she pursed her lips.

"What do you think you're doing?" Melody gritted.

"The one thing I won't see you do is destroy Harmony again," Lyric whispered harshly.

"I don't know what you're talking about," Melody shot back, her voice just as harsh.

"You know exactly what I'm talking about. We are not kids anymore. You can't keep taking everything from her. Especially not *this*," Lyric said with feeling.

Melody chortled. She looked at Lyric through narrowed eyes. Lyric could see fire flashing in Melody's eyes. "If I were you,"—Melody grabbed Lyric's arm and turned it over so that her track marks were face up and visible— "I'd worry about my own problems."

Lyric wrestled her arm away and pouted. Her chest moved up and down, and her hands curled into fists at her side.

"You better remember something. Everybody has a price, little sister, and I just happen to be wealthy enough to pay the price when I really want something," Melody said, storming off.

Lyric's heart pounded. She could see herself running after Melody, wrestling her to the ground, and pounding her face with her fists. Lyric had wanted to do that for years. She hated that Melody held so much power over all of them.

Lyric took the rest of her drink to the head and winced as the strong liquid burned going down. She could already tell that this reunion with her sisters was going to end up being a disaster.

Lyric rushed toward the house. She needed to find a bathroom and quick. The relief package she had in her purse was calling out to her. Lyric needed to escape and fast.

Chapter 13

Harmony

"I'm sorry." Ron moaned the words into Harmony's mouth as his hands worked furiously to unzip her dress.

"Me too." She breathed heavily, her words hot on his lips, her hands snaking down to the bulge in his pants.

"I missed you," he said, panting.

Harmony closed her eyes as her dress fell down around her ankles. She was so glad to be alone with her husband at last. Away from her sisters. The stress. The hungry-for-a story crowds. Harmony hated when she and Ron argued.

"Oh God, baby. I missed you so much too," she groaned, throwing her head back as he trailed his tongue down the ladder of her throat.

Harmony inhaled his scent. She embraced the fine sheen of sweat on his face as it dampened her own skin. Harmony hissed when Ron stopped at her weak spot—her breasts. He carefully lowered his hot mouth over the dark, rigid skin of her erect nipples. Harmony gasped.

Ron suckled her breasts at first gently, then slightly rougher. He walked her backward a few steps. She fell back on the hotel's couch and grabbed onto the back of Ron's head.

"Don't stop. Don't stop," she said, her breath catching in her throat.

Ron dropped to his knees and wedged himself between her legs. He moved his tongue from her breasts, down the curve of her abdomen to her inner thighs. He kissed the insides of each thigh gently.

Harmony moved her thighs apart wider, giving him full access. The anticipation of what was to come made her mouth water.

"Oh," Harmony belted out, arching her back as he blew on her gently. "Oh my God, I love you, Ron," Harmony huffed, her voice gruff with lust. Electricity pulsed through her entire body. Harmony began panting through her slightly opened lips. Her heart was racing and her thighs trembled.

Harmony let out a small gasp as her body became engulfed in the heat of desire. She reached down and pinched her erect nipples, sending an even stronger electric sensation flooding all over her body. The combination of what was going on below her belly button and the pressure she was putting on her nipples was almost too much to handle.

"Yes," she whispered lustfully, lifting her hips slightly toward his mouth.

Ron thrust his long, wet tongue deeper into her warm, gushy center. He used his hands to gently part the petals of her flower, carefully lapping up every bit of her nectar.

"I want to feel you," Harmony whispered. "All of you."

Ron stood up and took off his pants. Harmony shivered just looking at his washboard abs and strong, muscular legs.

Ron lowered himself down in front of her. "You ready for me?" he teased, licking his lips lustfully.

Harmony shook her head and licked her lips too. Ron pulled her closer to him until her hips were hanging off the edge of the couch.

"Ah," Harmony winced as Ron used his steel-hard member to fill her up. Harmony's body was on fire. She lifted her pelvis in response to Ron's rhythmic thrusts. Their bodies moved in sync, each feeling the buildup in their loins. Harmony's hands splayed across Ron's back like a pair of wings.

"Oh God!" Harmony crooned. Her inner thighs vibrated from the explosion of pleasure filling her body. She could feel the pressure building in her loins, just on the verge of climax. Her screams urged Ron on. He grinded into her pelvis with longer, deeper strokes. Her slippery walls responded immediately, pulsating and squeezing him tight. Ron growled as his body picked up speed. He was at his tipping point.

"Is it all mine?" he huffed in Harmony's ear. The heat of his breath sent stabs of heated sparks down her spine.

"Yes. Yes." Harmony gasped, losing her breath as Ron slowed down and began grinding into her slowly again.

"You ready?" he huffed.

"Ah!" she screamed out, tightening her legs around his waist as her walls pulsed in and out.

Ron followed with a muscle-tensing climax of his own. He collapsed on Harmony's chest. She reached down and stroked his head gently.

"I'm sorry I yelled at you." Ron was the first to speak.

Harmony closed her eyes. She just wanted to cry. She loved Ron so much. "It's my fault. I should've told you about the little trick Melody pulled with telling the reporters we were going on tour before even discussing it with us. I should've also told you about the promise I made to Lyric," Harmony said regretfully.

Ron lifted his head so that he could look her in the eyes. He tilted his head slightly, waiting for her to explain.

"I promised her I wouldn't leave her again. That I'd be here for her until things got better," Harmony said. She could see Ron's eyes narrow.

"Here? Meaning in New York . . . in Brooklyn?" Ron asked, looking directly in her eyes for clarification.

"Yes," Harmony replied, her voice just above a whisper.

"I can't believe you." Ron blew out an exasperated breath. He moved from between her legs and sat on the floor with his back against the couch.

"Wait. Just let me explain." Harmony sat up. She touched his shoulder gently.

Ron shrugged his arm away from her touch. "It just gets deeper and deeper, the lies," Ron grumbled. "All it took was a trip back here to fuck everything up, huh? To change your priorities just like that. All the while you were worried about seeing your sisters, I should've been the one worried."

"No. Baby, please listen to me," Harmony pleaded.

"I've been listening to you." Ron raised his voice. "All I hear out of your mouth is things you've kept from me. All I hear is that you made a commitment to someone other than me and Aubrey."

"I was going to tell you. I just have to make sure Lyric is going to be okay. She's really not doing well," Harmony confessed, her words coming out in a rush of breath. "Ron, I have to save her. I feel responsible for the way things are with her right now. I feel responsible for her, especially now," Harmony said, her voice cracking.

Ron palmed his head. "She's grown!" His voice went up.

Harmony jumped. Her entire body trembled. "I can help her."

"So after everything that happened—the turning their backs on you, leaving you broke and in the cold, cursing you out—you're really considering going on your sister's tour and being away from the life we've built because you think you can save your other sister?" he repeated for clarity. "You know damn well you can't save someone who doesn't want to be saved." His eyes narrowed to a pinprick.

"It's not that cut and dry, but I made a promise." Harmony swallowed. She felt like she was being ripped apart, like each of her arms were being pulled in opposite directions.

Ron got to his feet. "Oh, yeah, you made a promise, Harmony, and what about us?" Ron asked, pointing behind him to the hotel bed where Aubrey slept soundly. "What about our life at home and our business? What about the promise you made to me? You just abandon us for the sisters that didn't give a fuck about you or your feelings these past three years?"

Tears ran down Harmony's cheeks. She was so conflicted. She shook her head, trying to find the words to explain her obligation to Lyric or her need to somehow feel connected to Melody now that Ava was dead. She had never told Ron about the things Lyric had endured at the hands of Ava and for the sake of the group. It was the one thing she had found hard to discuss with him.

Harmony closed her eyes and sobbed. She couldn't stop the images of Lyric, that night, screaming over and over again after Andrew Harvey suffered a heart attack and died while he was having his way with her. Lyric was inconsolable. Harmony remembered her little sister's deafening screams of, "I killed him! I killed him!" Harmony had tried desperately to calm Lyric to no avail. Eventually, the ambulance had to be called. They had put Lyric on a 72-hour hold in the psychiatric ward of Kings County Hospital.

Outside of the hospital, Harmony had gotten in Ava's face and accused her of ruining Lyric's entire life. Melody had come to Ava's defense. It had all turned for the worse.

Harmony owed this to her little sister. She had to save her in order to save herself. Harmony knew that if she didn't at least try, she would be no good to herself or Ron and Aubrey.

Ron started putting his pants on in a fury. Harmony stood up. She tried to grab him.

"Wait," she cried. "Just let me explain, Ron. I can make this work."

"Don't touch me," he gritted, moving so she couldn't lay her hands on him.

"Where are you going?" she called after him as he roughly yanked his T-shirt over his head. He glared at her as he snatched his jacket from the back of the chair.

"You don't care where I go. You only care about yourself, remember. Harmony's needs come first now," Ron accused, his chest heaving. "Well, I have a confession too, Harmony. I had a drink today. There. All of this bullshit made me want to run back to it, Harmony," he spat.

Harmony reacted as if she'd been slapped in the face. She opened her mouth to speak, reaching her hand out toward him.

"Don't," Ron growled. "Yeah, at your sister's wonderful party, I had my first drink in three years, and you know what, Harmony? It made me feel good. The house, the party, the music, all of the rich folks: I felt like my good old self again. Yeah, that drink eased my mind. It took my mind off of you and your deceit. That's what you want, right?" he continued.

Harmony shook her head no. She couldn't even speak. What had she done?

"Yes, I got you figured out. You want someone to take care of so you can fulfill your sick need to care for people? You want me to be the old Ron again. . . . That's what it takes to get your dedication, right? You were only happy when I was a project, a drug addict for you to save. A broken man for you to fix," Ron spat cruelly.

Harmony doubled over, unable to breathe, unable to control the onslaught of emotions threatening to take her down. She was losing everything right before her own eyes. How could she have let this happen?

"Go ahead on tour with your sisters. You deserve it. You deserve the money and the fame and to live that life again." Ron's voice cracked.

"I'll be around . . . maybe. Maybe I don't deserve you, Harmony." He put his hand on the doorknob.

"Wait," Harmony cried out. "Ron, wait."

"I've waited long enough," he said, his voice hoarse. With that, he flung the door open and stormed out.

Harmony jumped when the hotel door slammed. Aubrey started to cry. Harmony fell to her knees and sobbed. Why couldn't she just let them go? Why was she destroying her life to take care of her sisters? Why did she have to save everyone? Harmony's body quaked. The answer hit her all at once: because sacrificing and giving up everything for others was all she had ever been taught to do. That's why.

Chapter 14

Melody

Melody reached over and grabbed her home phone off of the receiver. Without even opening her eyes, she grumbled her "hello" into the phone.

"Who?" Melody opened her eyes this time and looked around her room, confused.

She twisted slightly and looked over at the empty spot on the other side of her bed. She closed her eyes and shook her head. Sly had snuck out after their wild sex session without so much as a good-bye.

"Um. Yes. I'm here. You can send him up," Melody said, her voice still thick with sleep.

She sat up, looked around, and placed the phone back on the receiver. She touched her cheeks to make sure she was not dreaming. Melody squinted at the beautiful, glass-encased wall clock hanging on the wall across from her bed.

"Its four in the morning. What the hell?" she whispered out loud.

All sorts of wild thoughts ran through Melody's mind as she rushed up from the bed and practically ran into her expansive en suite. Melody quickly splashed water on her face and swished around a cap full of mouthwash. She took a quick look at herself in the wall of mirrors over the sinks.

"Yuck. A face with no makeup is not a face at all." She mumbled the words Ava had said to her many times.

Melody didn't have even a minute to apply as much as a sheen of lip gloss to her lips before she heard the loud knocks on her door. Melody slid into her furry, high-heeled slippers, and as she hurried to the door, she tied the waist belt on her long, white silk kimono-style robe. She ran her hands over her hair and tucked the loose strands behind her ears. She cleared her throat.

Before Melody could open the door, another round of knocks reverberated from the other side.

"Okay, okay!" she yelled in response. Melody yanked the door open. Her doorman, Ralph, stood with his face contorted in disgust.

"This guy says he's your family?" Ralph droned, his white-gloved hand holding onto her visitor like he was contagious.

Melody's cheeks flamed over and her face immediately contorted into a frown.

"What? What the—" Melody was dumbfounded.

"Listen, I . . . I know I'm the last person you . . . suspect, I mean . . . expected to see," Ron slurred, his words drifting out of his mouth on an alcohol-scented cloud. "But I . . . I . . . need to say some . . . some things to you." Ron's left pointer finger moved unsteadily in front of his face.

"My God, Ron. You're a mess," Melody said, eyeing his twisted, untucked shirt and the big wet spot on the front of his pants. Ron could barely stand up on his own.

"You are . . . you . . . fuck . . . fucked uh . . . up. Fucking up . . . my marriage," Ron warbled.

"You're pissy drunk," Melody said, fisting the material of her robe at the chest, frowning.

"You can't break up . . . no . . . break up my marriage with your stupid . . . tour," Ron said, dribble running out the side of his mouth.

"Ms. Love, I can call your security and have them come if you need me to. I can have him removed as well," Ralph said, still holding onto to the collar of Ron's shirt with one hand. With the other he held Ron's jacket between his thumb and pointer finger, like it was contaminated.

"No, no. Trust me, he's not a threat. Look at him. He couldn't harm a fly right now even if he wanted to. He just needs to dry out," Melody replied, shaking her head.

"You just need to get out. Get out . . . out . . . of my marriage," Ron said indignantly.

"Ron, just come inside and dry out. You're not yourself right now," Melody said evenly. She was not going to take his mess much longer.

"No. I came to say . . . I love . . . love my wife. You can't do this to uh . . . us." Ron leaned forward toward Melody and almost fell.

"Whoa!" Melody and Ralph both reacted at the same time, keeping Ron on his unsteady feet. Melody's face reddened. She nodded at Ralph.

"Thank you, Ralph. I'll take it from here."

The doorman looked at her skeptically.

"Honestly, it's okay," Melody assured.

Ralph shrugged his shoulders and slowly released his grip on Ron. Melody stood aside as Ron staggered into her place.

"I came here . . . here to give you . . . a piece of my . . . my . . . mind." He almost hit the floor again.

"Listen. Concentrate on staying on your feet." Melody grabbed onto his arm and guided him to her white leather couch. She tossed his jacket down first then helped him onto the couch. Ron was mumbling something that Melody could barely understand.

"Sit down. You are a complete mess right now."

"I . . . didn't have any place left . . . I mean . . . else to go," Ron garbled almost incoherently. "I . . . I didn't . . . have anyone else to tell. She . . . hurt me. She . . . hurt me bad. You caused all . . . all of it."

Melody immediately wondered if he was talking about Harmony. Melody couldn't imagine how Harmony would've let Ron out of her sight long enough for him to get like this. And how would Ron have ended up at her place, of all places?

"Where are you coming from this time of the morning? A bar? A party?" Melody pressed as she retrieved a bottle of water from her wet bar fridge.

Ron closed his eyes and lay back on Melody's couch for a few minutes. His mouth hung open and his breathing was labored.

"Does Harmony know where you are?" Melody inquired.

Ron groaned.

"What is going on, Ron? I mean, I don't even know how you knew where to find me. I'm only here once in a while. With Ava's death and all, of course I'm here this past week and a half. You come here in a complete mess, accusing me of doing something to your marriage, looking like you've been on a bender for a week, and, ew, smelling awful," Melody said, waving her hand in front of her nose.

Ron let out another low groan. Melody placed the cold bottle of water on Ron's forehead. That got him to open his right eye a crack.

"You probably need ten of these." Melody held the water out in front of her.

Ron looked like he couldn't even find the strength to accept the bottle of water from her. Within seconds, his eyes were shut again.

"I'm going to call Harmony," Melody said, flustered.

"No! Please. Don't," Ron shouted, the words falling heavily from his mouth. That had gotten his attention. Melody was startled by how adamant he was. Ron closed his eyes again and spoke.

"She can't know that I came to you. She . . . she can't see me . . . like this." Ron hiccupped a sob. "I wanted to fix it."

Melody rolled her eyes. Ron couldn't make up his mind if he wanted to be a mad, confrontational drunk who had come there to give her a piece of his mind, or a sad, sobbing drunk who was so ashamed of his behavior that he was hiding from his wife.

"I'm sure Harmony would understand what you're going through right now. She's your wife," Melody said, her voice trailing off as she stared down at Ron's gorgeous face. Melody tilted her head to the side and stared at him for a few long seconds. Something inside of her stirred. He might've been lying on her couch, dead to the world and drunk out of his mind now, but Melody had watched how he loved on Harmony at the funeral and back at the gathering.

Melody had tried to get to know Ron at the repast, but he seemed a bit distant and resistant at first. He had finally started to open up slightly when they were interrupted by Lyric. Melody thought about what Lyric had said, and then she thought about what it would be like to have a man like Ron or a gorgeous little baby girl of her own.

Melody stumbled back a few steps, dizzy with conflicted feelings. This man was her sister's husband. He seemed to be the source of great happiness for her sister. He seemed to be the complete opposite of Sly. Melody wondered what made him come to her house.

Ron snored so loudly. The sound snapped Melody out of her fantasy.

"Oh my goodness." She gasped, her hand flat over her racing heart. "No way. Stop it." Melody quickly shook off the thoughts. She was different now. She didn't want to hurt anyone, especially her sisters. She really wanted to try to be a family this time. But did they feel the same way about her? Did Harmony and Lyric really want to see her happy after Ava mistreated them to favor her? Melody had to guard her heart; she knew that. She couldn't be weak, not even for the love of her sisters.

Melody sighed. She set the water down at the side of the couch and rushed to her bedroom to retrieve her cell phone. Melody looked at Harmony's number in her contacts list and went to press the button several times but stopped herself. Ron had asked her not to call Harmony. Melody didn't really want to either.

"That's between them, Melody. Let him tell her." Melody spoke to herself out loud.

Melody rushed back into her living room, where Ron lay snoring like a grizzly bear, obviously in an alcohol induced coma-like sleep. Melody smiled for a few seconds. He was so damn cute, even with the piss stain on the front of his pants. She picked up her phone and snapped a few pictures of Ron, asleep on her couch.

"Just in case," Melody mumbled. "Just in case."

It was six hours before Ron groaned awake and tried to open his eyes. Melody had already showered, had her makeup artist Shannon come by to do her face, and her stylist Jetti to help her get dressed. She was flawless, as usual.

"Finally." Melody laughed, watching Ron slowly come into consciousness. His eyes were wild and dazed as he touched his chest and then his legs. Melody could see him struggling to recognize his surroundings.

"You had a rough night," Melody said as he struggled into a sitting position.

Ron swiped his hands over his face and blinked rapidly. When his eyes finally came into focus, they went as wide as dinner plates. He opened his mouth to speak, but the words wouldn't come. Ron blinked a few more times, as if he had to make sure that who he was seeing was actually there.

"You look like you've seen a ghost." Melody chuckled in response to the where-am-I, what-the-hell-am-I-doing-here look scribbled all over Ron's face. "Well, I'm not a ghost. Just little old Melody Love here," she said.

Ron touched his chest and then his legs again. He looked at her.

"Oh, if you're looking for your clothes, they're over there, folded on the floor next to you. I had them cleaned, because Lord knows between the sweat, the liquor, and the piss, you reeked so bad I couldn't stand to have you in my living room," Melody told him, crinkling her nose to drive home her point.

"Oh God," Ron grumbled, bracing himself on the edge of the couch. "How did . . . how did I—" He tried to stand, but his legs were like two wet noodles, and he fell right back down. "Oh God." Ron whipped his head around like a little lost boy. "What? Where?"

Melody was getting a kick out of seeing him so frantic. She swore she could see the vein in his neck pulsing even from a distance. She figured that must've meant that his heart was pounding.

"I guess you went on a bender and some way, somehow, you found my address and ended up here. It surprised me too, but I wasn't going to turn you away. I tried to call Harmony, but you wouldn't hear anything of it, so I'll leave the explaining up to you," Melody said, smiling like she harbored a deep, dark secret. She purposely left out that Ron had come there to give her a piece of his mind.

"Don't you remember anything? Anything that happened?"

Ron shook his head slowly and winced from the hangover headache. Fear danced in his eyes. He swiped his hand over his face several times again, as if he could make this all a nightmare. He put his palms on either side of his head and squeezed.

"Oh God. What did I do?" Ron croaked. He got to his feet this time. His eyes were wild, like a child lost at an amusement park.

"It's not that bad, Ron. I mean, at least you didn't end up in some *strange* woman's bed." Melody chuckled.

Ron looked over at her, his eyebrows knitted together. "What? I mean, did anything . . . " Ron started.

Melody busted out laughing. "You really don't remember anything, huh?"

"I have to go," he rasped, his throat and lips desert dry. "I have to get out of here."

Ron whirled around like he was caught at a fork in the road and couldn't decide which way to go. He grabbed his clothes in a heap against his chest. He spun around, not knowing which piece to put on first. He almost fell trying to put on his pants.

"Calm down. There's no rush. You've already been gone past sunrise. I think you should have some food or at least black coffee before you try to navigate these New York streets," Melody replied, shrugging like it was no big deal. "I can have Milly whip you up a quick meal, something healthy that will be good for the hangover I see playing out on your face. I mean, you were really a mess."

"No, no, that's okay. I'm fine," Ron said, panicking. He slid his shirt on in a hurry. "Did I have my . . . um . . . " Ron asked, patting his back pocket.

"Your wallet? No, I haven't seen it. When you arrived you were in pretty bad shape. I mean, you still look green around the gills, but much better than earlier this morning."

"Fuck! What time is it?"

Melody laughed. "It's ten o'clock in the morning, silly. Lucky for you this is the time I usually get up and head out to rehearsals. I mean, I was so shocked you showed up here at four o'clock in the morning. I would never turn you away, but I was shocked nonetheless. I don't think you could ever imagine how shocked I was. You coming to see *me*," Melody rambled.

"Fuck!" Ron shouted, cutting her off. "I can't believe this. I have to go," Ron said, snatching his jacket and rushing for the door.

"Okay, but my breakfast offer still stands," Melody told him.

"Thank you, but I really have to go," he said, shrugging into his jacket. "Harmony is going to be worried sick. I can't believe I—Oh my God. Harmony," Ron huffed, clutching his chest like just saying his wife's name was going to make his heart explode.

Melody's stomach dropped at his mention of Harmony's name. Melody walked Ron to the door. Before she opened it, he turned to face her.

"I'm sorry for intruding on you. I don't even know what made me come here or how or—I mean . . . I . . . I was out of my mind. I . . . I'm really—Please don't tell," Ron stammered.

In one swift move, Melody boldly crushed her mouth over his, her tongue sending his words tumbling back down his throat.

"Mmm," Ron moaned.

His body stiffened, and he jumped back and pushed Melody away like she had bitten him.

Melody jumped too. She didn't know what had gotten into her. She put the back of her left hand against her mouth and lowered her head in shame.

"I didn't mean to. I . . . I know you're—" Melody stuttered, her heart pounding so hard she felt nauseous.

What are you doing? What are you thinking?

"I have to go," Ron said for the final time.

He snatched the door open and hurried out, still staggering. Melody stood in the doorway and watched him race toward the elevator. She felt like her insides were being run through a meat grinder. Melody hadn't wanted something or someone so badly since the days when she had longed for fame and fortune.

"Ron!" she called out to him.

He froze and looked over his shoulder. His eyes were wide and wild, like he was looking back at his worst nightmare.

"There's a reason you ended up here in your drunken state. Remember, the drunk mind is the true mind," Melody proclaimed.

Ron whipped his head around and raced to the elevators.

"Maybe you were thinking about me," Melody murmured as she watched until he disappeared. She stepped back inside of her loft and closed the door. She leaned back against the door and closed her eyes.

"He's not yours, Melody. He can't be yours. He belongs to her. He belongs to your sister."

Chapter 15

Lyric

Lyric held her left nostril closed as she used her right nostril to inhale the small mound of white powder laid out on a pocket mirror in front of her.

"Whew!" She flinched as the drugs hit her system. Her eyes snapped shut by themselves, and her body went limp for a few seconds. Lyric slumped over, nearly kissing the floor.

"Hey. Hey, be easy on this shit, girl," Lyric's friend Kim said, grabbing Lyric before she face-planted.

"Damn," Lyric huffed. "That is the shit!"

"I told you." Kim laughed. "This is premium. Not that stepped-on shit you and Rebel are used to. Now be easy because this is not to be messed with," Kim said as she stepped between the little mountain of white powder and Lyric.

"I'm a pro." Lyric waved her off. "Let me hit that again. That shit is better than sex and chocolate and chocolate and sex." Lyric laughed and pranced around.

She opened her eyes and looked in the mirror. She finally liked what she saw. Lyric flipped the long side of her hair and rubbed the lipstick off of her teeth. "I'm ready for the next one." Lyric loved how she felt: invincible, beautiful, happy. She'd finally found that high again.

"Lyric, I'm telling you, girl. You have to get used to the kick of this shit. You can't be blowing through it. You're a lightweight when it comes to this straight-off-the-boat product. Take one more quick sniff and that's it. I mean it," Kim warned. "I am not trying to pick your ass up off the floor or be in the damn morgue," Kim joked.

"You worry too much, girlie. We came to have a good time. Shit, if I end up in the morgue, at least you can stand up at my funeral and say, 'That bitch went out hiiigh as a motherfucker,'" Lyric replied, raising her hands above her head for emphasis.

Kim laughed. She had been Lyric's friend for six years, and she had watched Lyric's entire life change, not for the better. Lyric had told Kim all about how the singing group had broken up and how Lyric desperately wanted to still be famous, but Lyric had never told Kim everything that she was battling inside.

"One more. Dead ass," Kim said sternly, stepping aside to give Lyric access to their little party stash.

"One more," Lyric acquiesced. "I promise. Just one more." That was the famous drug addict line—it was always just one more, or one last hit.

This time Lyric held her right nostril closed and vacuumed up the powder with her left nostril. When the tiny line of white powder was all gone, Lyric threw her head back and shook her shoulders. The pure, uncut cocaine hit her central nervous system with a bang. Lyric saw colorful fireworks erupting behind her eyelids. This was better than any heroin high she'd had in years.

Lyric's drug addiction had taken on a life of its own over the years. It had started with the pills Andrew Harvey fed her every time she was forced to be with him. At first, Lyric tried to resist, but she quickly learned that the pills made it and him easier to deal with. Then, after he died with his dick inside of her, Lyric had graduated to using heroin. Her first time was with Rebel. When that high wasn't strong enough for her to escape reality anymore, Lyric began mixing things and using whatever she could get—alcohol, pills, meth, cocaine and/or heroin. Lyric didn't care so long as she didn't have to feel any pain. So long as she didn't have to live with reality.

Lyric let out a high-pitched squeak and cackled somewhat maniacally. Her head hung down until her chin was touching her neck, causing her hair to spill forward wildly. She could feel the vibration from the club's music pounding in her chest. Lyric felt good.

"That's some primo shit." Lyric giggled.

She kept complimenting Kim on her new drug because she couldn't get over how good it was. Lyric swayed her body to the sound of the loud music filtering through the club's bathroom.

"It's a celebration, bitches," Lyric joked. She danced over and planted a playful kiss on Kim's cheek. "Thank you for celebrating with me, best friend. That's my best friend. That's my best friend," Lyric sang.

Kim giggled. "Well, you getting back out there, making moves is cause for celebration," Kim said. "And a tour with Melody Love is fucking big. I mean, she's your sister and all, but to the world she's like a god. I've been waiting for you to patch things up with her so I could just meet her one time. I think if she shook my hand I wouldn't ever wash it again. I am definitely part of the Melody Army."

Lyric had told Kim all about the fact that she was going back out on tour, and how it wasn't going to be long before she had her own money, her own big house, and a Tribeca loft.

"Naw, forget Melody. That good shit you got right there is cause for celebration. That's what we should be worshipping. You can change the world with that," Lyric replied joyfully. She felt damn good. Lyric didn't think she had felt this great in years. She danced around some more.

"I told you," Kim said, bending down and sniffing up her own dose of her supply. "My guy told me this is what his richest clients use. He hooked me up. I mean, I had to give him a little something, but it was worth it."

"He hooked you up for real. That shit so good, I'd give him some ass too. I'm ready to take on the world now," Lyric cheered, raising her hands over her head and clapping.

"You just graduated, chick. This is better than that depressing-ass smack. That shit is a downer, and it makes you look terrible too. Uppers, girlfriend. You can't beat this high. This is the new wave shit, and I made sure you had it first. You can't be stopped now," Kim said, cheering Lyric on even more.

"Let me have one more hit," Lyric begged, spinning around like a ballerina, her dress riding up her thighs.

"No more hits yet. You need to take it slow. You can't hit this like it's that regular half-pure street junk," Kim warned for the third time.

"Let's go party. Shit, you know I can get us into V.P. I mean, you are celebrating, right?" Kim said, leaning over the bathroom sink so she could apply another coat of lip gloss to her full lips.

"Ah, VIP. We big time again?" Lyric giggled, holding her fist up as a show of power. "I can definitely dig it. I could really dig it if I could hit again." Lyric winked.

Kim looked at Lyric and smiled. Lyric hadn't been this excited and happy in a long while. Kim had seen Lyric at some of her lowest points, including Lyric's suicide attempt that had scared the shit out of Kim and made her fly right for a few months. Kim was definitely happy that her friend was finding a renewed sense of fulfillment. Kim wished she could keep Lyric happy like this for life.

"Okay, look. One more tiny line before we go get our party on," Kim said, dumping a tiny hill of drugs on the mirror.

"Hell yeah," Lyric cheered, rushing over to the sink.

She quickly snorted the line. Within seconds, she was ready.

Kim watched as Lyric's eyes rolled back in her head. Lyric's back went straight and stiff for a few seconds.

"Lyric? You all right?" Kim shook Lyric's shoulders.

Suddenly, Lyric seemed to come back. Her eyes returned to normal. She sniffled and brushed her nostrils off. "I'm good! I'm real good!"

Kim's face eased with relief. "C'mon. Let's go have some fun. Let's go celebrate your rebirth," Kim said, pulling Lyric's arm through her own as they exited the bathroom and headed into the bowels of the club.

Lyric and Kim sauntered through the club, attracting a lot of attention. Lyric hadn't felt attractive or beautiful in a long while, but now, with the drugs giving her a newfound dose of confidence and courage, Lyric stopped on the dance floor and began dancing up on several strange men. She let the music reverberate through her body and soul while she made herself forget about Rebel, Ava's death, Harmony, Melody, her past . . . everything.

As Lyric bucked her body vigorously to the beat, she remembered all of the times she and Melody had partied in their girl group days. Harmony had never been one to go out and party, but Lyric and Melody had done enough for all of them. When Ava finally let them out, they were like animals out of a cage. Industry parties had been everything back then—the expensive drinks, the high grade weed, the special treatment from club owners, and just the rush of the nightlife had been a form of escapism for Lyric. She used it to escape thoughts of Andrew Harvey touching her. She used it to escape the fact that her mother hated her.

When Melody went solo, she focused on her career and left Lyric behind like she had never mattered. Lyric had missed the fun days after that. She had missed the days when she didn't have to worry about having money, or when people still recognized her as Lyric Love and not as Melody Love's sister. Lyric had missed being able to say she was actually a celebrity. Those days were the only times she could put the abuse out of her mind. Lyric needed the attention like she needed air, food, and water.

Lyric was getting all of the attention now. She closed her eyes and let the music soak into her soul. "Ow!" she sang, rocking and letting all of her problems fall away, even if just for that moment. Lyric shook her hips and sandwiched herself between two dudes. One grinded her from the front, and one grinded her from the back. She was loving it. She didn't care about their hands on her thighs, on her ass. It was the attention she craved. Lyric pulled the dude behind her in closer and threw her arms around the neck of the dude in front of her—until Kim rushed over and grabbed her arm like a parent chaperone at a high school dance.

"What? What's the matter? I'm having fun." Lyric's eyes popped open.

Kim clutched onto her tightly and dragged her off of the dance floor.

"I'll be back, cuties." Lyric flirted with her two confused dance partners.

"Girl, no. You are about to be a big name again. You can't be dancing with the local yokels, looking like a thot out here. We fuck with VIP status dudes only. Did you even look at those lames you were dancing with? Had their damn hands all up your dress and on your ass. Yuck, Lyric," Kim scolded. "You and I have a reputation to uphold, and it is of style and class, not ratchetness. Do I have to teach you everything? Better start getting back in that A-list celeb mind set. You think Beyoncé would be out here on the dance floor, grinding up with some lames with her ass all out?"

"First of all, I'm not Beyoncé. More like Solange, or not even Solange. Shit, right now I'm more like that washed-up-ass Michelle."

Lyric busted out laughing at her own joke. "And why the hell else did we come to the club if it wasn't to get our dance on? I damned sure didn't come to sit around and be cute, acting like some stuck-up celebrity prude like my sister," Lyric replied sassily.

Lyric loved to party hard. Her idea of coming out was to dance and have fun, not sit like a princess on her throne, decked out in the latest fashions with a high-priced purse in her lap, just to make other women jealous.

Kim sucked her teeth and continued dragging Lyric toward the VIP. "I come to the club to listen to the music, have a few drinks, and do a few lines. In *VIP*," Kim stressed.

"Stuck up," Lyric mocked. "You could've been Melody in another life."

"Yes, call it what you want, but I keep it classy all the time. I don't let people make me sweat, and I certainly don't dance with club regulars who come to the club with five dollars in their pockets and try to get a free feel," Kim answered. "Shit, they ain't even have to buy you a drink and you gave them free feels!"

"Yeah, yeah, Mother-may-I. You sound like Harmony with the lectures. I need a hit," Lyric grumbled. "You blew my high all the way. Shit,

I might as well have come out with Rebel, the biggest hater of all."

"One more hit and that's it for the night," Kim warned, storming back into the VIP section. "And I mean it, Lyric. Don't ask me for anymore after this."

Lyric followed Kim to a darkened corner in the VIP section like a horse following a carrot. Kim looked around to make sure they were all clear, then she dug into her bag and handed Lyric a small glassine envelope.

"Hit it easy. A little bit at a time," Kim instructed. "I already told you this stuff is not to be fucked with."

Lyric waved her hand dismissively. "You worry too much. Damn. If I wanted to be out with my sisters, I would've invited those bitches," Lyric grumbled.

"Just hurry up before someone sees." Kim spoke directly into Lyric's ear.

"Okay. Okay."

Kim turned her back so that she could play lookout just in case any of the club's security guards wanted to get nosey. Kim listened as Lyric snorted a couple of lines.

"Lyric, I told you a tiny bit. You sound like you took too—" Kim spun around to warn Lyric again about the potency of the product, but

Kim's words got stuck in her throat. Her mouth hung open in an O before any words came out.

"Lyric! Lyric!" Kim screeched at the top of her lungs.

Lyric was at Kim's feet, her body twitching like she was being electrocuted. White foam bubbled from Lyric's lips, and her eyes were wide open, glassy, and even in the darkened club Kim could tell they were staring at nothing. Dead.

"Lyric!" Kim fell to her knees and began shaking Lyric's limp body vigorously.

"Oh my God! Help! Help!" Kim shrieked, pulling Lyric's head into her lap. "I need help! Help! Please! Call an ambulance! Lyric! Please don't die! Lyric!"

Chapter 16

Harmony

It seemed like Harmony had just fallen asleep when she heard the click of the hotel room door. She jumped up and off the bed in one swift motion.

"Ron. Oh my God. Where have you been?" Harmony rushed to him and threw her arms around his neck. "I was so worried." Her words came out in a breathy rush and her tears spilled in fast streams. "I'm so glad you're okay. I'm sorry." Harmony clutched him like she didn't believe he was staying. "I want to make things better."

"I'm . . . I . . . I'm sorry," Ron said as he tried to fight back his own regretful tears.

He didn't lift his arms to return Harmony's embrace; instead, he sobbed.

Harmony inhaled and released her hold on him like he'd suddenly turned into a venomous

snake. "You've been . . . you." She stumbled
backward a few steps, shaking her head no. She
smelled the alcohol reeking from his pores.

Ron put his hands up in front of him. "Harm,
let me explain."

"What have you done?" Harmony screamed.
"Ron, what have you done?" Aubrey began
crying, but it was as if neither Ron nor Harmony
could hear her.

"Ron, what have you done?" Harmony's legs
got weak. She bent at the waist like she'd been
gut-punched. "Oh God," she cried out, crawling
to a chair. "Ron!"

"A few drinks . . . nothing more. It . . . was
just—" Ron stumbled over his words. "I swear,
Harm. I will never do this again. I'm okay."

Harmony couldn't bring herself to look at
him. She hid her face in her hands. She knew his
story. When they first met, Ron had admitted
that his addiction started with alcohol. The free
drinks at the industry parties were the gateway
to his drug use.

"No drugs, Harm. I . . . promise. Just the
drinks." Ron pled his case. "I'll never do it again.
I swear. I'm okay, Harm. I promise. I can control
this. I swear."

"No. God, why is this happening? Why?"
Harmony wailed. She had heard all of his prom-

ises before. It had taken two tries before Ron had gotten clean and sober. Harmony had witnessed him relapse. She had dealt with the lies, the secrecy, and the total rock bottom behavior before. She'd stuck by him, but this time, after everything, this relapse was something she didn't think she could endure. It was a long rough road before he'd gotten clean and stuck with it. Harmony knew how hard Ron could fall. She'd cleaned up his mess enough times to know that it had gotten worse each time. Now this.

Ron rushed over to Harmony and grabbed her wrists. "Harm, listen."

"Get off of me," Harmony screeched, recoiling from his touch. "All that I've been through with you. You threw it all away. You threw it all away." She yelled so loud her throat itched.

Ron pulled his hands back in surrender. His jaw rocked and he had to fight to slow his rapid breathing. He swallowed hard and blew out a hard puff of breath.

"Harmony, just listen to me." Ron tried to level with her. "After our fight, I was upset. Emotional. I felt like you were betraying me. I felt hopeless. I didn't mean to have those drinks; it just happened. I felt lost. Alone. I was walking the streets, and I don't why, but I just wandered into the bar. It . . . it was the place that felt most like home to me at the time," he explained.

Harmony belched out a few sobs.

"I swear, Harmony, if we just leave now and go back home, it won't happen again," Ron implored. "We can fix it. I can fix it."

Harmony looked up at him, her eyes sagging at the edges. She shook her head in disbelief. "All it takes is this to get you all the way back to the beginning, Ron. I don't know if I have it in me to do it again. Going home is not going to change the fact that you . . . "

She couldn't say the word *relapse*. She couldn't conceptualize the idea that she might have to watch her husband crawl around on the floor of their home, searching for a crack rock, or that he might clean out their bank account and go missing for three days.

Harmony threw up her hands and stood up. She snatched her cell phone from the small hotel desk and her jacket from the back of the desk chair. She headed for the door without any regard for Ron or her baby. She just needed to get away from him, from everything and everyone.

"Wait, Harm. Where are you going?" Ron called after her.

"I need some air. I don't know what's happening to me . . . to us. I'm so . . . we are so . . . lost,"

Harmony said through her tears. With that, she let the door slam behind her.

An hour after she'd stormed out of the hotel wearing a pair of joggers that doubled as pajamas, a head scarf, and a workout jacket, Harmony found herself standing in front of Ava's house. She didn't know why she felt so compelled to go there after her fight with Ron. It was like she had been drawn there. Harmony lifted the rickety front gate up and entered the yard. She moved the old, weather-stained and cracked adobe flowerpot at the bottom of the stoop and retrieved the house key. Harmony shook her head at the fact that Ava had never moved her key from that old spot.

Harmony entered the house and closed the door behind her. She stood still for a few minutes, her heart drumming in her chest.

"You came here. Now deal with the feelings."

Harmony set her jaw and slowly climbed the stairs, each one creaking under her feet. She remembered how many times those creaking stairs had warned her that Ava was coming. The same thunderbolt of fear that used to hit her back then hit her now. She shuddered.

Harmony made it to the top of the staircase. She blew out a shaky breath and shook her arms. She fought to be brave as she entered Ava's bedroom. Harmony stepped over the mess—scattered clothes, broken perfume bottles, and shattered picture frames.

"What happened here, Ava?" Harmony whispered, bending down and picking up one of the shattered frames. She removed a piece of the cracked glass so she could see Ava's face clearly. Harmony's stomach knotted.

"Why, Ava? Why did you do this to us? We can't even stand to be sisters; we're so screwed up. I can't be a wife or the mother that I really want to be. I'm so scared of being hurt. All I ever wanted was for you to love me. Why was that so hard for you, Ava? What mother can't love their child? I can't remember you ever giving me a hug or a kiss or telling me that I was beautiful. Beautiful? I never heard that word as a kid unless you were saying it to Melody. No, all I ever heard from you was how black and ugly and terrible I was. Sometimes, even now, I can't stand to look at myself in the mirror because all I see is that tar baby, jiggaboo, nigger-naps, escaped slave you always talked about. Why? I can't ever remember you ever telling me I did a good job at something. No, I was always the worst at everything that I did. So, I was your ugliest child and the worst at everything? That's impossible. Everyone is good at *something*. Why, Ava? And let's not even get into what you did to Lyric." Harmony's voice caught in her throat. She had to swallow a few times to find her voice again.

"Lyric . . . she . . . was a baby. She didn't fucking deserve that. She didn't deserve to be sold off like some sex slave. You stood there while that nasty bastard sized her up and played out in his sick mind what she could do for his sordid pleasures. You gave him permission to rape her over and over again. Your child. Your baby. For God's sake, why? She was a baby. She was a goddamn baby, Ava. Why? What happened in your life that would make you capable of such evil things? What could've possibly made you so heartless? Tell me. Tell me."

Harmony screamed as if Ava could somehow telepathically hear her or answer the questions she had been holding in and wanting to ask most of her life.

"I hope God has mercy on your soul, Ava. I'll never get to tell you face-to-face just how much you ruined us, and that's my fault. I should've come back. I should've made sure you got the message. I should've wrote you a letter. Maybe that would've helped me. Maybe it would've helped Lyric. It's my fault that she's suffering. I should've stepped in and been a mother to her. I should've picked up your slack because I benefited from her pain too.

"I'm going to save her, Ava. I'm going to be better to her than you ever were. I just want you to know that I am trying to find it in my heart to forgive you. I can't have a good life if I don't forgive you, but I just can't. I want to, but . . . "

Harmony collapsed onto the edge of Ava's bed. She clutched the broken picture frame so tightly the veins in the tops of her hands rose to the surface. Harmony stared down at the picture. In it, Ava was dressed in a glittery show costume, smiling like her life was perfect. Harmony sniffled the snot threatening to drop from her nose. She lowered her head over the pictures and laughed, but not the kind of laugh that came out because something was funny; instead, it was an angry laugh, bubbling up from the deep pit of hurt in her soul.

"If only you could've loved your daughters as much as you loved the music, the fame, the attention. We would've been all right. If only you could've stopped hating us and seeing us as a burden and just love us. Every single one of us, even your favorite Melody, wanted your love. Real love. Not love based on musical talent, or light skin, or so-called good hair, or how you could use us to live out your fantasy of being rich and famous. No, not that kind of flimsy love. We wanted the kind of love mothers give freely and without condition. The kind mothers just have inside of them because their kids are alive and healthy. Just the plain kind of love that comes effortlessly to a woman once she pushes a life out of her body and into this cruel, mean, cold world.

"Where did yours go, Ava? Did you not feel it? Was something inside of you so walled off that you didn't get God's gift of unconditional love? Ava, we didn't need anything special like extravagant birthday parties and trips around the world to make us believe you loved us. A good night kiss or an occasional hug would've done the trick. One hug or one 'I love you' from my mother, in all my twenty-eight years of living, would've done the trick, Ava. One fucking hug from my mother in my lifetime would've set me free from all of these feelings swirling around in my brain right now. One hug." Harmony's voice cracked and her stomach quivered. She sucked in her snot and licked the salty tears from her lips.

"Goddammit, Ava. We were good kids. We didn't get into any trouble. We did whatever you said . . . like little loyal robots. We were just normal, regular good kids that wanted you to see us, to recognize our individuality. I loved math and writing wild stories that I thought up with my imagination. I hated broccoli and kale, but I loved Jolly Rancher candy. Lyric loved jumping rope, and she was fascinated with the ocean and the things in it—sharks, octopi, whales. She hated meat, meat of any kind, but chocolate cake was her favorite. I think she could've survived off of chocolate cake alone if you had let her."

Harmony chuckled at the thought, and in her mind's eye she could see Lyric's face all covered in chocolate. Harmony used the edge of her sleeve to swipe away some of her tears, but within seconds, her face was wet with them again.

"And what about Melody? She was your favorite, yes, but did you even know that Melody dreamt of being a makeup artist? She would steal blush and lipstick and eyeliner from the small beauty section at the supermarket. She used to sneak and make our faces up at night. I bet you didn't know your favorite was such an adept thief, did you? She hated tomatoes, but at least you let her get away with picking them out of her salads. You let her have her favorite strawberry ice cream occasionally too. I guess you thought Lyric and I didn't know about that. Oh, we knew. Melody made sure that we knew."

Harmony chuckled again. This time she let her tears fall onto Ava's picture.

"Did you even know any of that, Ava?" Harmony's eyes went dark and her jaw stiffened. She shook her head in disgust.

"What kind of mother doesn't even know her kids' likes and dislikes? What kind of mother? What kind of mother hates her own kids? You weren't a mother at all, Ava. You were not our mother!" Harmony screamed so hard and so loud the veins in her neck roped against her skin and the back of her throat burned.

Harmony threw Ava's picture against the wall, and the remaining pieces of glass that made up the picture frame shattered into tiny pieces.

"I just wanted you to love me," Harmony whimpered.

Exhausted, she fell back on Ava's bed, feeling like someone had taken a giant straw, stuck it in her heart, and sucked all of the energy, life, and love out of her. Harmony lay staring up at the ceiling.

"I just wanted you to love me. I just wanted you to love me." Harmony didn't even remember when the darkness of mental and physical exhaustion finally engulfed her.

***

Harmony roused to her cell phone vibrating against her chest. She popped up on Ava's bed, bewildered. "Shit," Harmony whispered, wiping the drool from her mouth and cheek.

Panic caused her hands to tremble and her temples to throb. Her phone rang again, startling her. Harmony fumbled with her jacket pocket and wrestled her phone free. Her eyebrows dipped on her face.

"Two-one-two?" Harmony's first instinct was to ignore the call.

She remembered her fight with Ron and figured it was probably Ron calling from somewhere in the hotel trying to find her. "Hotel is in Brooklyn. That's not him." She took a deep breath and pressed ACCEPT.

"Hello?" Harmony answered, her voice gravelly. "This is she." Harmony stood up. "What?" Harmony's voice rose two octaves. "Oh my God." Her hand flew up to her mouth. "I'll be right there." Harmony's heart thundered against her chest until it ached. Without another thought or a minute's hesitation, she raced out of Ava's room, down the steps, and out of the house.

Once outside, Harmony felt lost. She looked up and down her childhood block. What would be the fastest way? She couldn't walk to the city.

It was impossible. She didn't drive. The bus and train would take way too long. Harmony shook her hands in front of her—what she did when she was trying to focus.

"A cab. I need a cab." Harmony moved her hands to her head and tugged at the sides of her wild, tousled hair. "Yes. I need a cab." She looked up and down the block again. Had it been that long since she lived in Brooklyn? It had at least been long enough that Harmony definitely didn't know any cab company phone numbers.

"Okay, Harmony. Stop and think. Calm down." She flexed her neck and shook her arms at her sides like she was preparing for a track meet. Taking a few deep breaths, Harmony finally broke out running toward the corner, as she remembered that in Brooklyn you could hail a cab on most street corners. With fear gripping her around the neck, Harmony stuck her right arm out and frantically flailed it until an old burgundy Lincoln Town Car stopped in front of her. Harmony yanked on the door with fury.

"I need a ride."

"Miss, I am not supposed to pick up here," the cab driver was saying.

Harmony ignored him and threw herself into the backseat of the car. "Mount Sinai hospital.

Hurry up. I have to get there now," Harmony yelled, pounding her right fist on the Plexiglass partition. "Please, I have to get there. It's a matter of life and death."

Chapter 17

Melody

"Ron—"

His name didn't last a second on Melody's lips before Ron grabbed her by the neck and slammed her against her own wall.

"Did you think you were being smart? Did you think you were being funny?" Ron growled, slamming Melody against the wall again, this time so hard things around her went blurry.

His hand was a vise grip on her throat, cutting off her air supply until her lungs burned. Melody hissed and spit, trying to get air. Instinctively, her hands flew up to her neck and she clawed at his fingers.

"You thought this would be more important to me than my wife? Huh?" Ron used his free hand to lift the tiny baggie, dangling it in front of Melody's face.

"You fucking tried to set me up?" he said, biting off each word and spitting them in her face. "You know damn well I am in recovery, so you leave this in my jacket."

He held the evidence in front of Melody's bulging eyes. She tried to shake her head, but the movement only managed to send a searing pain from the base of her skull straight down her spine. Ron clamped down harder. Melody could see that his pupils were ringed with a fiery orange tinge.

"What if I was weak enough to fall for this? What if I had sniffed this whole fucking bag of coke? Huh? Would that make you happy? You think that would make me want you? I would be fucked up for the rest of my life. Do you realize that? My wife . . . my fucking daughter," Ron yelled, trembling hard with emotions. He slammed her head against the wall again. Hot, angry tears sprang to his eyes.

"You were trying to kill me," Ron accused.

Melody's eyes rolled up into her head until only the whites were visible.

"You thought I would relapse or maybe overdose and it would destroy my wife. Is that why you did it, Melody? You want to destroy Harmony because even with all of this fame and money, you're still a weak bitch that hates herself and everything she stands for."

Melody opened her mouth, but she couldn't get one word out. That just made Ron angrier. He slammed her harder against the wall, forcing the tiny bit of air she had left in her lungs to blow out of her mouth. This time, her eyes snapped shut and she felt herself floating.

Melody saw tiny squirms of light flash behind her eyelids. Suddenly her body crumpled in a heap onto her beautiful, shiny hardwood floors. An audible crunch resounded through her loft as her skull connected with the floor. Melody's chest ignited like she'd sucked in a ball of flames. She rolled onto her side and curled into a fetal position, coughing and gagging. She tried in vain to get her lungs to fill with air.

Melody could feel Ron looming over her, brooding. He wanted to kill her. He clutched the drugs in his hand so tightly his muscles bulged.

Melody's eyes slit open a crack just as her security team stampeded into her loft and pounced on Ron. Their timing was nothing short of divine. She'd called Virgil and the team to accompany her to an obligatory charity event in Midtown and had been waiting for them. It was the reason Melody had opened her door so easily and without checking the peephole when Ron banged on it.

Melody looked up as Virgil and two other broad-shouldered men carried Ron, his mouth bloodied, to the door like a pig going to slaughter.

"This is not over," Ron grumbled, blood dripping from his nose.

Virgil helped Melody up from the floor. "I'll call the police. Make a report and ask for a protection order. I'll put someone here twenty-four hours."

"No," Melody rasped, running the tips of her fingers over her throbbing neck. She could see the confusion in the creases in Virgil's forehead. "It's okay. I'll handle it," she croaked.

Virgil stared at the purple rings cropping up on Melody's throat, and his jaw went square. He reached out to touch her. "What do you mean, no?"

Melody recoiled. "I said no! I said it's okay and that I'll handle it!" she barked.

Virgil snatched his hand back, shocked by her outburst.

Melody staggered to the back of her loft and into her bedroom. She threw herself onto her bed, buried her face in her custom down pillows, and sobbed.

What did you do? Why can't you stop being so evil?

***

Melody got the call about two hours after her run-in with Ron. No amount of makeup could cover the necklace of handprints she wore around her neck. In a frantic rush, Melody draped a silky brown-and-tan monogrammed Louis Vuitton scarf around her head and neck, Jackie O style. It hid the remnants of her attack, and it made her look sophisticated at the same time.

"That works," she whispered to herself while staring in the mirror.

Melody had Virgil and two more members of her security team rush her to Mount Sinai Hospital. When she arrived, the doctors were working on Lyric. There was a lot of running and screaming and code language for "shit is going from bad to worse." Melody stood, surrounded by her security, with her knees knocking together. She tried to ask several of the nurses that were rushing in and out of the tiny emergency treatment room what was going on, but they all seemed to be laser focused on what was happening behind the curtain. Melody's teeth chattered together and she began pacing. She wondered if Harmony knew anything. Melody pulled out her cell phone and hit Harmony's number. No answer.

"Oh, come on, Harm. I'm not calling to brag or get on your nerves this time," Melody said under her breath, ending the call before Harmony's voice mail picked up.

Finally, after what seemed like a year, a young, sweaty-faced doctor emerged from behind the curtain. Melody shivered. There was something about the doctor's eyes that sent a chill down her spine. His eyes were dead, blank.

"Ms. Love, we are doing our best to save your sister's life. She's in pretty bad shape. We will keep you updated," the doctor said, his voice tremulous.

Melody felt like the air in the room had all been sucked out. Her legs grew weak. Everything in her world seemed to be falling apart. She wondered if staying away from her sisters all of those years had been better. For the first time in years, Melody said a silent prayer.

Virgil grabbed her arm to keep her up. As they made their way to a small waiting room down the hallway from the emergency treatment rooms, Melody heard a small commotion behind her. She turned just in time to see Harmony running down the long hospital corridor with terror etched on her face.

"Where is she?" Harmony huffed, her lips white with fear.

Melody raised her hands. "Harm, we have to be strong."

Harmony sucked in her breath as she came to an abrupt stop in front of Melody. "Where is she?" Harmony wheezed, her chest pumping up and down.

"Listen, Harm—"

"Where is she, goddammit?" Harmony didn't give Melody a chance to finish. She pushed Melody out of the way and rushed to the nurse's station.

"Lyric Love," Harmony said. "My sister. Where is she? Where is she?" Harmony demanded, banging on the counter in front of the station. The four nurses behind the counter all looked up at the same time.

"Don't all answer at once," Harmony snapped.

"I'm sorry, ma'am. Which patient?" a short, Asian nurse answered, looking straight at Harmony.

"Lyric Love. I got a call."

"Are you related to her?" the nurse asked.

"I just said three times she's my sister," Harmony boomed.

Melody walked over and touched Harmony's arm. Harmony yanked it away.

"I'm trying to find out what's happening since you don't seem to know." Harmony rounded on Melody.

Melody could tell this behavior was a true indication of her sister's emotional turmoil. "If you calm down I will tell you what's going on," Melody gritted, losing her patience. "The doctor came to speak to me. They're trying to save her life, Harm. From what I've been told, it's pretty bad." Melody softened again.

"What? How?" Harmony couldn't seem to find her words.

"Overdose," Melody whispered.

Uttering the word seemed to drive it home for Melody. Overdose. It was like a curse word. Ron had just accused her of trying to cause him to overdose, and now her baby sister was clinging to life from an overdose.

"Overdose," Harmony repeated. Harmony shook her head and pinched the bridge of her nose. "My mind was so scattered. When I got the call from the hospital, I didn't listen to everything. I didn't even bother to check my phone for missed calls. All I heard was Lyric . . . hospital . . . emergency . . . life or death." Tears ran down Harmony's cheeks.

"Shh. I know," Melody comforted.

She moved close to Harmony and wrapped her arms around her. At first, Harmony stood stiffly, but within a few seconds the gravity of the situation seemed to hit her. Harmony turned around and embraced Melody too. Melody squeezed Harmony tight, and Harmony did the same. They held onto one another like they thought they'd never see each other again, and sobbed. Melody couldn't remember the last time she had hugged either of her sisters, especially Harmony. Now, she clutched Harmony so tightly she could feel the beating of Harmony's heart against her chest. Their tears danced down one another's necks and shoulders.

"I'm so sorry," Melody cried. "I'm so sorry for everything. Everything."

Ron's scowling face flashed into Melody's mind. Some of the things he'd said to her played like a record on repeat in her ears: *I would be fucked up for the rest of my life. Do you realize that? My wife . . . my fucking daughter. You want to destroy Harmony because even with all of this fame and money, you're still a weak bitch that hates herself and everything she stands for.*

"I'm so sorry. I'm so sorry." Melody cried harder, running the palms of her hands over Harmony's back.

"Me too." Harmony spoke through her tears. "I'm sorry too."

It seemed like they had been holding onto each other for an eternity before the doctor returned.

"Ms. Love?"

"Yes," Melody and Harmony answered in unison.

"This is my other sister . . . our older sister," Melody explained, looking at Harmony proudly. It was something Melody had never done before. All of their lives she'd made herself the most important person, because that was what Ava had preached.

The doctor nodded, acknowledging Harmony. "We have stabilized your sister, but I want to warn you. This first twenty-four hours is going to be critical. The good thing is she didn't lose a lot of oxygen to her brain when she lost consciousness, so we don't expect there to be brain damage."

"Oh, thank God." Harmony sighed.

"But," the doctor continued, putting his left hand up in a halting motion, "we can't tell how much damage has been done to her other organs until we can get her stable enough for a CT scan and some other tests. From what I can tell, your sister ingested a fairly large amount of drugs. Another one of these and I can assure you both she will be dead."

Melody reached down and grabbed Harmony's hand. They huddled together as the doctor gave them good, then bad, then good news again.

"Can we see her?" Harmony asked.

"Yes, but we ask that you keep the traffic to a minimum and keep things quiet so she can rest and her body can repair itself."

Melody held Harmony by the elbow as they slowly entered Lyric's room together. Harmony gulped and froze. Her hands flew up to her mouth and she shook her head no.

"All of that? I can barely see her face," Harmony cried.

"I know. I know," Melody agreed, staring across the room.

Lyric had tubes coming from her nose, mouth, neck, and both arms. Her head was wrapped in white gauze ,and there were two more gauzy wraps—one on her right pointer finger, and one on the top of her right hand. The IV pole that loomed just behind the head of Lyric's bed had four different clear bags hanging from it—some small, some large. There was a heart monitor at the left of her bed. The sound—*blip, blip, blip . . . blip . . . blip, blip*—made Melody's skin crawl. From the looks of it, Lyric was in worse than critical condition.

"Is she dying?" Harmony asked. Melody shook her head no.

"Come here." Melody comforted her, putting her arm around Harmony's shoulders. "She is going to pull through, Harm. Trust me. I will make sure she gets the best care. She just needs us to be strong right now. You can't break down, because all of these years, you've taken the best care of her."

Harmony looked at Melody like she couldn't believe it was her saying those things. Melody parted a tiny smile and put her head on Harmony's shoulder like a small child would lay on her mother's.

"I always thought you were the strongest, Harm." Melody spoke directly into Harmony's ear. Saying the words felt like a ten-ton weight suddenly lifted from Melody's shoulders. "I always admired how you stayed so strong through it all. I know I wouldn't have been so strong if it were me."

The hard spot in the center of her chest seemed to soften. "I am sorry for what Ava did to you . . . and to Lyric. You were better than me to be able to take that." Melody's voice cracked.

More pressured eased in her head and her heart. She took a deep, cleansing breath. Melody felt lighter by the minute. It was the first time she had ever admitted to herself or anyone else that someone, namely her older sister, was better at something or more successful than her.

Melody swallowed hard and shook Harmony's shoulders in a show of support. "You're stronger than all of us, Harmony. You're stronger and better than me," Melody said.

For the first time in her life, Melody didn't have to pretend. For the first time, something she said out of her mouth felt sincere and in line with what she really felt. For the first time, Melody felt free.

Chapter 18

Lyric

"No. Please," Lyric screamed. Her screams fell on deaf ears. Her head jerked back and pain daggered through her scalp.

"Please, don't," Lyric screamed again, but again her pleas were to no avail. Lyric raised her hands to her head, trying to loosen the painful grip on her hair. Her defiance just made him clamp down harder, increasing the thunderbolts of pain that lit up her scalp.

"I . . . I will obey," Lyric whimpered. *"I . . . I . . . promise this time, I will obey,"* she cried.

He roared, laughing maniacally, as if her pleas and her pain were amusing him. He pulled her head close to his. She saw fire flashing in his eyes. Pure evil.

Lyric moaned and squeezed her eyes shut. She couldn't stand to look at the rough mask that was his face—Andrew Harvey's face. Tears *spilled down her trembling cheeks. She felt something cold and wet on her lips. Lyric slowly opened her eyes and came face-to-face with a two-headed snake. It was coming out of his mouth, where his tongue was supposed to be.*

"Kissss me," the snake hissed.

"Ah," Lyric screamed and screamed and screamed and screamed.

Lyric's eyes fluttered open. Each part of her body seemed to come alive inch by inch. Her vision was blurry, but she could see and feel someone next to her. Lyric felt something in her left hand. She curled her fingers around it, one-by-one.

Harmony's head popped up from the side of Lyric's bed. "Lyric? Baby sis?" Harmony squeezed Lyric's hand in return. Lyric had to fight to keep her eyes open. She felt herself slipping away again.

"Lyric, I'm here. Just like I promised, I'm right here," Harmony said in a rush of breath. "I'm here, sweetheart. Open your eyes. Let me know you can hear me." Lyric slowly opened her eyes again.

"Oh, thank God." Harmony lifted Lyric's hand and kissed the back of it. "I'm so happy you're awake. I've been here since it happened, and I'm not leaving your side. I swear it."

Lyric groaned and tried to lift her head. Something pulled her back down onto the pillow. Lyric lifted her bandaged right hand and touched the side of her head. She ran her hand down the side of her face to her mouth.

"That's helping you breathe," Harmony told her.

Lyric groaned again. She tugged on the breathing tube protruding from her lips, held in place at the corner of her mouth with white surgical tape. In response to the tugging, the monitors next to her bed rang off, squealing like a burglar alarm.

"Lyric, don't do that. You need that to breathe." Harmony panicked. She stood up and tried to move Lyric's hand from the breathing tube. Lyric kicked her feet and moved her head side to side.

"Lyric, keep still. You're going to pull out your IVs and make this much worse," Harmony warned, her face crinkled with fear.

Within seconds, a team of nurses burst into the room. "Ma'am, we're going to have to ask you to step out for a few minutes," a nurse said to Harmony.

It took all of the strength Lyric had to hold onto her sister's hand. She would not let go.

"Lyric, I'm here. I am not leaving you," Harmony called to her as the nurses tried to move her away from Lyric's bed.

"Miss, please," a different nurse yelled at Harmony. "We can't help her if you're in our way. It's for her own good."

"I am not leaving her. Do whatever you need to do, but I am not leaving her," Harmony said.

With that, Lyric stopped fighting to yank out the breathing tube. The nurses rushed around, checking her tubes, pushing buttons, and one injected Lyric's IV line with something from a syringe. Lyric's body went limp and her head lulled to the side. She was knocked out. Again.

Chapter 19

Harmony

Harmony's eyes burned, and her muscles ached in places she never knew existed. She had been holding vigil at Lyric's bedside for over fifteen hours without moving to even go to the bathroom. When Lyric finally came to, Harmony was glad that she'd made the decision not to move.

She eased her hand out of Lyric's. Confident that the sedation meds they'd pumped into Lyric's IV would buy her some time, Harmony slowly stood up. She bent over and planted a light kiss on Lyric's forehead, took one last long look at her baby sister, and turned to leave the room for a much-needed bathroom and stretch break.

Harmony tugged on the door handle, and just as she went to step through, she bumped into someone. "Oh." Harmony clutched her chest.

Her face immediately flattened and her eyes hooded over.

"You have some fucking nerve coming here," Harmony said through clenched teeth. She pulled Lyric's room door closed behind her and blocked the entrance with her body.

"I—I need to see her," Rebel stammered. Harmony could tell from his eyes that he was high. He moved side to side restlessly.

"How dare you?" Harmony gritted, pushing him hard in the chest.

Rebel stumbled backward a few steps, clearly caught off guard by Harmony's aggression.

"You feed my sister so much drugs she almost lost her life, and you have the fucking nerve to show your little dirty, disgusting face?" Harmony backed him down, fire flashing in her eyes.

Rebel shook his head no. "It—I . . . it wasn't me. I wasn't there. I didn't give it to her," Rebel said, his hands shaking.

Harmony stopped moving and squinted at him. "What are you talking about? She lives with you."

"Yes, but she went out with some friends. Said she needed to get away from me. We argued. She stormed out," Rebel explained.

Harmony's scowl softened into a confused grimace.

"Look, I know you all don't think that highly of me, and yeah, I'm a stoner." Rebel opened his arms wide as if to say "Look at me."

"But I love your sister," he confessed in a shaky voice.

Harmony swallowed the ball of emotion that suddenly lodged in the back of her throat.

"We fight. We argue. And we get high together sometimes, but I'm telling you, I love Lyric. I really fucking love her." Rebel broke down.

Harmony was at a loss for words. Suddenly, her own situation sprang to her mind. She realized she was yearning to see Ron. She needed to feel his touch and hear him tell her he loved her. She wanted to tell him what happened to Lyric, and she wanted him to hug her and tell her it would be all right.

"Would you stay with her until I come back? I don't want her to wake up alone."

Rebel's eyebrows shot up on his face. He nodded his head. "Yes! I promise I won't move from her side," Rebel agreed gratefully.

"I'll be back," Harmony assured, stepping aside so Rebel could access Lyric's room.

Right before he entered the room, Rebel touched Harmony's shoulder and nodded. "Thank you. I really meant what I said. I love Lyric."

Harmony cracked a weak smile. "I love her too."

Harmony crept into the darkened hotel room and gently shut the door behind her. She stood inside the small foyer area for a few seconds, trying to find her nerve. She took a deep breath and moved further inside, stopping and smiling when she saw Ron asleep with Aubrey on his chest. A burst of warmth filled Harmony's chest and stomach at the sight. She realized that Ron was right—being back in Brooklyn had made her lose sight of what was really important to her.

Harmony stared at her husband and baby for a few long seconds. She walked to the bed and placed her hand on Ron's forehead. Her eyebrows dipped, looking at Ron's bruised eye and split lip.

Ron's eyes opened.

"Hey." Harmony smiled at him.

Ron parted a lazy grin and pointed to the baby. Harmony picked Aubrey up, kissed her chubby cheek and put her down on the bed. Ron sat up. He stretched and yawned.

"Are you okay? What happened to your face?" Harmony inquired, her head tilted.

Ron waved his hand. "Just a little accident. No big deal," he assured.

Harmony didn't press the issue. She didn't have the mental fortitude to cause another argument.

"I heard about Lyric on the news," Ron said, changing the subject.

Harmony knew that was his way of breaking the ice and moving on from their two big fights. She wanted to forget too.

"Yeah, she's in pretty bad shape." Harmony sat down next to him. As a way of saying sorry, she placed her head on his shoulder.

"I'm really scared, Ron. Everything seems to be out of control. I want to run and run and never stop," Harmony confessed. Ron grabbed her hand. She recognized that it was his way of apologizing.

"You can't run, Harmony. That's not you. I understand that now. I support you. I want you to take whatever time you need to care for her, Harmony. Whatever time you need to do what makes your brokenness heal," Ron said.

That caused Harmony to lift her head from his shoulder and look up at the side of his face. She placed her hand under his chin and urged his face toward hers. Harmony looked deep into his eyes for a few long, meaningful seconds.

"No matter what, I will not abandon you and Aubrey," she assured. "Even if I have to run back and forth between Brooklyn and Jersey, I will not let you down. I will find a way to do both."

Ron closed his eyes and nodded. Harmony knew that meant that, just like her, he knew better. They both knew that their lives would never be the same again, but at that moment, neither of them had the courage to tell the other the truth. Harmony and Ron both needed to pretend things were going to go back to normal in their lives, because pretending was easier than facing the truth.

Chapter 20

Melody

"My hero. You are my hero. I can see my life through your eyes. My hero. You are my hero. Every breath that I take is because of you." Melody held onto the side of the headphones that covered her ears and sang every note with heartfelt feeling. She didn't need to read the words on the loose sheets of paper in front of her; the lyrics were etched in her mind now. The music filtering through the headset and into her ears touched her soul.

Melody kept her eyes closed and held her last note as long as her diaphragm allowed. The music was soothing the aching spots in her heart. It was just what she needed.

Although she was running on little to no sleep, Melody had rushed to the studio straight from the hospital. Seeing Lyric in such a horrible condition and having that heartfelt, touching moment with Harmony, Melody had become overwhelmed with all sorts of pent-up emotions. She had felt like the feelings were choking her. The guilt of it all weighed on her like someone had tied a chain with a cinderblock attached around her neck. Melody had told Harmony she would be back, and she ran away from the hospital like it was the deadliest place on earth.

Melody had screamed at her driver several times as he tried his best to navigate the New York City traffic. Melody needed a release before she burst. The studio was empty when she arrived, just like she liked it. That was one of the times Melody realized how valuable it was that she owned her own studio. It had been her best investment to date. There weren't many female artists who owned their own studio, music production company, and almost all of their songwriting publishing. Melody was a rare breed in an industry filled with pretty faces and empty heads. The entire building that housed her music studio, dance rehearsal studio, and business center belonged to her.

Melody inhaled once she walked into the studio's control room. Every single button on the control room mixing console and every piece of melamine foam in the sound booth belonged to her. Melody didn't need her producers, her writing team, or any other artists to be there with her like she usually did. Instead, she got behind the large, multi-track mixing console and created a beat that spoke to her heart.

The boom of the 808 fell in line with Melody's heartbeat. The tune was reminiscent of an old school love ballad, but the words that were swimming around in Melody's brain were different, more like a song of redemption. She wanted to let her feelings pour out of her until she collapsed. Melody had closed her eyes and let it carry her away. When she had finally stepped into the booth, she felt ready to conquer anything.

Melody threw her head back and swayed. "Oh, my hero. You are my hero."

The tiny soundproof booth in the studio rocked with the sound of her melodic voice. Every single bar of the song held a strong meaning for her.

"My hero."

Music and singing had always been Melody's release. Shortly after Sista Love broke up, Melody had started missing Harmony and Lyric horribly. Sometimes the longing would make her hide in her enormous closet and cry at night. Melody felt she couldn't confide in Ava, for fear that Ava would call her weak and stupid. Ava didn't think Melody needed anything but the fame and the money.

Even then, Melody would go to the studio and compose to make herself feel better. She would scribble her feelings—whether angry, lonely, sad, or happy—onto a yellow legal pad, and then she'd turn those feelings into beautiful, soul-stirring, chart-topping songs.

Melody may have appeared to be a bitch on the surface or an unappeasable diva to the public, but she was really a broken girl inside. The sincerity and authenticity of her music was all that saved her from completely losing her mind. The music became all that she had that mattered to her. It was the reason she was so successful. Melody wrote songs and sang them based on her emotions—emotions that hundreds of thousands of women around the world could relate to—and they loved her for it.

Melody realized that her music had saved her life on many occasions. On those days when she missed Harmony and Lyric so badly, she contemplated ending it all, but the music had brought her back from the brink. When she was in the studio and in that booth, Melody shed her tough-girl exterior like a snake shed its dead skin. It was a rebirth of sorts.

"My hero. I want you always and forever. Oh, you are my hero." Melody could've dedicated the song to so many people, but in that moment, she could only picture her sisters. Melody sang so loudly and the words were so powerful that she was shaking.

Her chest filled with air as she prepared to belt out another verse, but an abrupt disruption caused her to go off key and choke back her words. The music had suddenly died. Melody opened her eyes to tapping on the sound booth glass. Her heartbeat quickened. Melody snatched the headphones from her ears and glared through the glass.

"What the hell?" she snapped. *How dare he?* Her nostrils flared as she watched Sly waving at her, signaling with his hands for her to come out of the booth.

Melody stood there, staring at him for a few long seconds, and felt her insides heating up. Sly wore that stupid, guilty grin that Melody had seen so many times. Now it made her stomach sick. Melody sucked her teeth and hung the headphones on the hook next to her. She pushed the microphone aside and closed her songbook. Clearly she was stalling. Melody hadn't seen Sly in the three days since he'd snuck out of her bed like she was some sort of call girl.

"'Sup?" Sly grinned as Melody stepped into the control room from the booth. "That beat was fire, ma. You still got it," Sly complimented with his gorgeous smile.

Be strong, Melody. Don't let him sweet talk you, Melody. Be strong, Melody.

The scent of Sly's cologne made her stomach flutter. Melody knew she had to put her foot down, but looking at Sly in his sleek, fitted jeans, swagged-out dark green Buscemi sneakers, and black Givenchy shark tee was making it hard for her to keep up her attitude. That was the one thing Melody always loved about Sly—his swag.

"What do you want, Sly?" Melody's words came out in an exasperated breath.

Be strong, Melody. Don't let him sweet talk you, Melody. Be strong, Melody. Damn, he is fine. Be strong, Melody.

"Why you acting like that?" He smiled again, moving toward her for a hug. Melody side-stepped. Sly looked surprised by her bold dismissal.

"It's like that now, ma?" He chuckled. Melody could tell he was trying to fight the embarrassment of her rejection. That made her feel good for a second.

"Yes, it's like that. I'm busy," Melody said flatly.

Sly got serious. "I heard about Lyric."

Her gaze snapped to his, and her eyes burned into his. "Is that what you came here for? After three days of no call, no texts, not one fucking thing, you came to tell me you heard about my sister's unfortunate drug overdose?"

She was fighting the tears welling up in the backs of her eyes. Why couldn't Sly just love her the way she needed? Why couldn't he just love her like Ron loved Harmony?

"Nah. You're right. That's not what I came here for," Sly said, his voice taking on a somber tone.

"Okay?" Melody replied quizzically, turning over her palm as if to say, "What?"

"Honestly, Mel, I came to tell you something else." Sly let out a long breath. "Something that needed to be said in person and not through a punk-ass text or over the phone."

Melody felt an ominous feeling in the pit of her stomach, and a wave of nervous nausea made her weak. She flopped down in the rolling chair in front of the mixing console. Sly took a seat at the edge of the black leather couch behind it. Melody swung the chair around so she could face him.

"I'm listening," Melody said, twisting her lips to the side and wringing her hands in front of her.

Sly cleared his throat and lowered his head into his palms. He took off his Yankees fitted cap, scratched his head, and set the cap back on it. He repeated that three more times.

"You're playing right now, Sly. I really don' have time for it today." Melody tapped her foo expectantly and folded her arms across her chest.

"Okay, okay," Sly relented. He set his cap on his head and lifted his head a little bit so that he was stretching his eyes to look up at Melody.

Melody melted inside as soon as she looked down into Sly's gorgeous, puppy dog eyes.

Be strong, Melody. Don't let him sweet talk you, Melody. Be strong, Melody. Whatever he has to say, you stay strong. No matter what it is, stay strong, Melody.

"I wanted you to find out from me and not some blog or paparazzi magazine," Sly said, his voice unusually mousy.

Melody hugged herself tighter. All of a sudden, she was so cold her teeth chattered. "Find out what?"

"First let me just say this, Mel." Sly lowered his eyes to the floor like he had to choose his words carefully.

"No. Don't caveat your news with a bullshit line about how you love me and how you want o be with me. Tell me what you need to tell me now, Sly," Melody demanded, her patience wearing thin.

Melody had endured years of this type of bad news sit-downs. Her mind raced in a million directions now. Melody could only imagine what blog had caught Sly with what stripper this time, or what paparazzi had spotted him coming out of what club with what model hanging on his arm, canoodling like they were a couple. Melody had heard it all before—or so she thought.

Sly's shoulders slumped. "A'ight. I'm just gonna come out and say it then," he said, stalling some more.

"Fucking say it already, Sly!" Melody exploded. Her nerves were already shot to hell from everything else. "I mean, what haven't I heard before? What did you do now and with who and—"

"Terikka is pregnant," Sly blurted, cutting her off mid-sentence.

Melody's lips snapped shut. She met his gaze. "And?" Melody's head jerked back like he had just thrown cold water in her face. "Terikka is pregnant? And?" Melody repeated Sly's words so that they settled in her mind.

Terikka was Sly's little female protégé who he'd taken under his wing and signed to his record label two years ago. The girl was a beauty from St. Thomas with a sexy little accent and a beautiful face. Terikka had talent, and in the two short years she'd been signed to Diamond Records, she had eight number one hits. The girl was hot and had literally blown up overnight.

Melody always acted as if she didn't care Terikka still hadn't caught up to her when it came to hit songs, net worth, and music awards but Melody also knew that if anyone could; it would be Terikka.

When Sly had first introduced Terikka to Melody, she thought the young girl was cute kind of skinny, kind of homely, and definitely had nothing on her. Of course at that time Terikka was fresh off the island with four outfits to her name and a bad weave that looked like it was done in someone's basement. Melody hadn't felt threatened at all, but Terikka didn't stay the homely, innocent little young protégé for long.

Terikka quickly made a name for herself as the pop culture bad girl. She had sex appeal, and she was unapologetic about it. Terikka wasn't trying to have that pop diva reputation like Melody. No, Terikka was the new Grace Jones.

It wasn't long before Melody had started to hear rumors in the media about a salacious romance between the much older Sly and Terikka. Sly had always vehemently denied it.

Sly had even had Terikka and Melody at his industry events together to prove to Melody and to show the media that there was no beef in their camp.

Melody played along, but deep down in her gut, she had never fully trusted Sly and Terikka's relationship.

"And, Sly? What does that have to do with me?" Melody pressed, her heart racing so hard the movement was visible through her clothes. Every nerve ending in her body was tingling.

Sly lifted his cap from his head and scratched his head again. Melody recognized that nervous tic. She knew it all too well. Melody slid her chair closer to Sly. She bent down and got in his face. "What does that have to do with me, Sly?" Melody asked again through her teeth.

"A'ight, man, I'm just going to say it." Sly paused.

Melody narrowed her eyes to a pinprick and held her breath.

"Terikka's pregnant and she is keeping the baby. I'm the father. I had to tell you now because she is planning on announcing it at the awards next week at the end of her performance." Sly rushed the words out.

Melody fell back in the chair, sending it rolling backward a few inches. She felt like Sly had just kicked her in the chest. Melody tilted her head, and her teeth closed down around her bottom lip so hard she tasted her own blood.

"Mel, listen." Sly reached his hand out toward her.

Melody leapt from the chair and charged into Sly with wrecking ball force. She was on top of Sly before he could react. Melody growled and hissed as she clawed at his face.

"Shit!" Sly exclaimed as the searing pain hit him from Melody's nails connecting with his left cheek.

"I hate you. I hate you," Melody yelled, flailing her arms, throwing wild punches at Sly's face and head. Melody bared her teeth like a rabid dog and tried to bite Sly, but he was able to wedge his hand between her mouth and his face.

"Yo! Stop it," Sly yelled at her. "You're acting fucking crazy!"

"I hate you." Melody caught Sly with a fist to the left side of his head. She was a scorned woman possessed. "I hate you. I fucking hate you. How could you do this to me? How could you? You knew I wanted a baby. You fucking knew all this time I wanted a family more than anything, Sly," Melody screamed so loud her voice echoed off of the walls. Melody lifted her knee swiftly and caught Sly in the balls.

"Oh, shit," Sly groaned, covering his private parts with his hands.

"You knew I wanted a baby," she cried, the sheer pain of her hurt evident behind every word.

In that quick moment of his weakness, Melody caught him across the neck, her nails cutting into his skin like razors. Sly's hand flew up to his neck. He felt the blood on the tips of his fingers.

"I hate you," Melody screeched. She went to attack him again, but this time Sly caught both of her wrists.

"Stop," he gritted. "Stop."

Melody tried to break free from his grasp.

"Stop it," Sly demanded, roughly flipping her down onto the couch. He pinned her wrists at the sides of her head and her body to the couch.

Melody tried to kick, but Sly's weight held her legs down. He loomed over her as her chest heaved like a madwoman. Her eyes were wild, feral. Sly looked down into her face, the blood on his cheek and neck painting his skin deep red. Melody closed her eyes. She couldn't stand to look at him. Every muscle in her body was tense and cording against her skin.

"Listen to me, Melody. I didn't mean to hurt you."

His words made Melody try to free herself again. She turned her head to the left and tried to bite Sly's hand so that he would release her. That just made him clamp down harder.

"Listen to me. I have been trying to tell you for years now that you needed to put down that wall you have up with everybody. Don't say that I didn't try, Mel. I fucking tried over and over again. I tried to soften your hard heart. I tried to love you, but you were unlovable most of the time," Sly said, his words painfully true. "The only time you let yourself be a woman was when I was having sex with you. You know how that made me feel? I wanted you to be my lady . . . not my competition." His words stung like open-handed slaps to her face.

Melody came alive again, kicking and trying to free her arms. She moved her head side to side, and like a crazy psych patient, she tried to bite Sly again.

"I tried, Mel. This news could've been about us. The world wanted to see us have a kid and make that billion together. I wanted that more than anything, but I couldn't do it no more. Your mother turned you into a real fucked up, hardened person. Don't be like her, Mel. Find that soft spot and open up to the next dude. Maybe you'll get that family one day."

Melody belched out sobs. Sly's words were cutting into her like a surgical scalpel.

"I wish you all the best, but I wanted someone who would let me in. Someone who didn't base her entire life on things. Material things. Money and fame don't mean shit if you can't love. I wanted a woman that could be vulnerable, not one that always wanted to be in charge or competing with me," Sly continued, clutching her tighter.

Melody finally stopped moving. She closed her eyes and tried to slow her breathing. Tears drained out of the sides of her eyes and pooled in her ears. She wanted to die. She literally wanted God to take all the breath from her body. She had never felt anything like this, not even after she'd found out her mother was dead. She felt like someone had her heart in their fist, squeezing it.

"All I want is someone to love me," Melody whispered. "All I ever wanted was someone, anyone, to love me."

Melody knew at that moment that the old, evil, selfish Melody was back. She didn't care anymore who got hurt. From that moment on, she was going to protect her own heart. She was going to make them all pay for her pain. If she couldn't be happy, then no one would be happy.

Chapter 21

Lyric

"Come on. Open up for the airplane," Rebel joked, making airplane noises and waving a spoonful of applesauce in front of Lyric's mouth. She was finally breathing on her own and had the tube removed.

"Get out of here." Lyric giggled and turned her head to the side. They both laughed. Lyric was so happy to wake up and find Rebel at her bedside. He usually put up a hard, tough-guy act, but Lyric always knew he had a soft spot.

"Yo, you scared the shit out of me," Rebel confessed, putting the spoon on the hospital tray at the side of Lyric's bed.

Lyric lowered her eyes. "I know. I scared the hell out of me too." She shook her head, ashamed. "But I remember that high, yo. It was like nothing I ever had before, Reb. I was wishing I could share that shit with you the whole time. I mean, I was flying so fucking high."

Rebel reached out and squeezed her hand, halting her words.

Lyric looked down at the skull and crossbones tattoo on the top of his hand and then at his face. "What?" she asked softly.

"I want you to kick, Lyric," Rebel said. "This is the end of the line for you and the life. You gotta get clean."

Lyric pulled her hand away, put her head back on the pillow, and stared up at the ceiling. "Not you too with the lectures," she groaned. "My sisters are going to be on that rehab shit. I already know. Not you too."

"This shit ain't for you, Lyric. You almost died and for what? Going on tour with your sisters. Singing and dancing. Being a beautiful young girl and living, enjoying life. That's for you. That's what you been trying to get back to all this time. I mean, you got the support right here, all around you." Rebel opened his hands to drive home his point. Lyric sucked her teeth and closed her eyes.

"I'm serious, Lyric. Your sisters are in your corner for once. You should've seen how Harmony was ready to kick my ass when she thought I was the reason you OD'd. Man, she was ready to rip me apart with her bare hands. That means something, Lyric. That means you're loved, even more than you know. Don't blow it."

Lyric swiped at the tears rimming her eyes. Thinking about rehab and having nothing to help her escape her pain made her stomach knot. Lyric couldn't imagine life without getting high.

"I don't want to lose you," she said, "so if kicking means I can't be around you, then I'm not going to fucking do it."

Rebel sighed. "Look at me," he demanded. He met her gaze. "I ever tell you how I got hooked on this shit, Lyric?"

Lyric thought for a second. "No," she murmured, embarrassed that she had been with Rebel almost two years and didn't really know that much about him. Their relationship, very early on, had become about partying and getting high. Rebel's eyes burned into hers.

"I was a kid when I took my first hit. When I say kid, I mean a twelve-year-old kid. My pops gave me my first one," Rebel said, swallowing hard afterward like saying those words hurt his tongue.

Lyric's shoulders quaked as she listened. The pain was evident in Rebel's words.

"That fucking coward told me it was for my own good, but really, he forced it on me because he was afraid. He was afraid to be alone in his fucked up, miserable world. When my moms

OD'd and died, he didn't have nobody else to get high with, so I was the next best thing. I had already started dabbling in the music with a couple of my friends at school. My pops told me the smack would make me better." Rebel's voice cracked. He blew out a long, hard breath, like he was trying hard not to cry. Lyric noticed the dagger tattoo on Rebel's neck moving in and out with the pulsing of his heart.

"It did for a while, you know? I was flying high all of the time. I could perform for a couple days straight, non-stop. The record label and my pops benefited off that shit. Everybody was collecting checks. I would get high and go like the Energizer bunny, show after show. My pops kept the drugs coming, and I kept going. When my single blew up, I was riding fucking high, literally.

"Then I started crashing. My body needed the smack to stay regular, not just for me to perform. I needed to hit it more often. I didn't care about shit else but a hit. I started seeing the little bit of money they gave me disappear faster than I could blink. My brain got all fuzzy. I couldn't write rhymes. I couldn't go on stage. I couldn't get in the studio. All I wanted to do was chase the high and keep myself from being sick. Then that stupid fuckhead pops of mine

ups and dies. Endocarditis, the doctors said."
Rebel poured out his soul. He lowered his bald,
tattooed head into his hands.

Lyric cried hard for him. She felt every ounce
of his pain.

He lifted his head abruptly and parted an
awkward smile. "Then I met you. From the gate,
you were the best thing that happened to me. I
know I did some foul shit to you, Lyric. It was
because I am sick. It was because I didn't know
how to fucking love someone as innocent and
pure as you. I grew up around shitheads all my
life. But you, Lyric, I have loved you from the
day we met. It's so fucked up that the only way I
ever learned to express love was to get a person
high. I thought by giving you that first hit I was
showing you what my father showed me —love.
That's bullshit." Rebel's resolve finally broke.
His bottom lip quivered, and hot, angry tears
ran down his face.

"I know you love me, Rebel," Lyric cried.

"That's bullshit, and don't you ever believe
that me fucking up your life with this poison
meant that I loved you," he said through his
teeth.

Lyric could see that he was angry at himself
for everything. She reached out for his hand.
Lyric looked down at the big, silver skull ring on
Rebel's left ring finger.

"I love you, Rebel."

"I want you to kick, Lyric. I want you to know real love, and your sisters are going to show you that," Rebel said, pulling his hand away.

Lyric's eyes went wide with surprise. Her heart throttled up until it felt like it was beating in her throat. "We can do it together. I'll only do it if you do it with me," Lyric said, anxiety lacing her words.

Rebel stood up. He was shaking his head. "I'm never going to get better. But you have to, Lyric."

Rebel backed away from Lyric's bed. The jingling from the chains hanging from his pants pocket sent an ominous feeling over her, like she'd been tossed into a dark, haunted house alone.

"Rebel, don't leave me," Lyric begged, trying to muster her strength to go after him. "I won't stay here. I won't kick. I'll find you. I'll fucking hunt you down," she screamed until her face reddened.

"You have to stay and get the help you need. I can't be helped," he said with finality.

Lyric threw back her hospital blanket and tried to yank her IV out. The monitors next to her bed began wailing and ringing. Lyric's heart was pounding so hard she felt lightheaded and weak. She had to throw up.

"Rebel," Lyric screamed, her arms tangled in the tubes and wires as she fought to free herself.

"I'm no good for you," Rebel said through his tears. With that, he headed out the door.

"Rebel! Rebel! Don't do this to me! Rebel!" Lyric screeched. "Rebel! Rebel!" Lyric's entire body shook.

Two nurses rushed into Lyric's room just in time to find her frantically trying to unhook herself from all of the monitors and IV.

"Ms. Love, please. You will hurt yourself," one nurse pleaded.

"Rebel," Lyric sobbed. The nurse grabbed her right before she hit the floor. Lyric's body went limp, and she sobbed.

"Rebel," she muttered. "Please don't leave me."

Chapter 22

Harmony

"I promise it won't be longer than a week," Harmony said as she tossed the last of her clothes into her suitcase. Ron didn't answer. He had his back to her, busy packing his own bag. Aubrey kicked her legs and cooed happily.

"I'm going to see to it that she gets out of the hospital and into some kind of program. You know?" Harmony called out to him. Ron grumbled and continued folding and packing.

"If I can just get her in somewhere good that specializes in young people, and if Melody will pay for it so that our options are not so limited, that would be ideal. You know in the world of rehabs, the more money or the better the medical coverage, the better the program. Lyric can't do this without a strict rehab. Maybe someplace far away. I'm hoping that she can leave New York altogether. You know?" Harmony rambled,

trying to ignore the thick tension stifling the air
in the room.

Ron didn't mumble, groan, or say anything
this time. Harmony sighed. She threw the shirt
she was holding into the bag without folding
it, and turned around to face her husband. Ron
kept busy, like he didn't see her staring at him
with her arms folded.

"Ron, please stop ignoring me," Harmony
said, flustered. "I need your support now more
than ever. I'm under enough stress as it is."

Ron stopped what he was doing, turned, and
shot her a look. Harmony could see annoyance
in every line of his creased forehead.

"What do you want me to say, Harmony?
Huh?" Ron tilted his head. "You want me to
say I'm looking forward to going home without
you?" Ron asked. "You want me to tell you that
I am not feeling anxious about taking care of
Aubrey alone . . . babysitter or no babysitter?
Is that what you want, Harmony? To lie and
pretend that I'm okay when really I'm scared as
shit?"

"I thought you said—"

"I did," Ron said, cutting her off with his
hands up. "I did say that it was okay for you to
stay and handle your business here. And I meant
it. I do want you to take care of your family and

make sure they're okay so that you can get back home. If that is what will make you happy, make us happy, then yes, I support it. But that doesn't mean I don't feel anything over leaving without you. I feel anxious and kind of abandoned and just plain alone right now. But that doesn't mean I don't support your decision. I am in my feelings. That's all," he explained, softening his tone at the end. "I think with everything that has been sprung on me, I'm entitled to be in my feelings about missing my wife."

Harmony's shoulders slumped with one part relief and one part sadness. She didn't want to argue with Ron anymore, but she understood where he was coming from at the same time.

"I don't know what other way to get this done so that I'll be able to live with myself, Ron," Harmony said. "I feel so torn. It certainly doesn't mean that I don't love you and Aubrey more than anything in this world. I just have to do this one thing. I have to do it for myself, but more so, for Lyric."

Ron walked over to Harmony. She turned to meet him halfway. Harmony's heart broke looking at how the edges of Ron's mouth were sagging with sadness.

"It's all good. I'm a big boy. I'll handle things, just like I always have my entire life. I'll get over it."

"I promise, Ron. I'm going to take care of Lyric, the sale of Ava's house, and those loose ends and then be back home in no time," Harmony said, trying to convince herself more so than Ron.

"Shh. You don't need to keep explaining and promising things." Ron looked into her eyes. He moved her hair behind her ear and palmed the back of her head. He pulled her head into his, lowered his mouth over hers, and kissed her deeply.

Harmony fell into him, his love filling her up inside. It was the fuel she needed to keep on going, to keep on taking care of everyone else.

"Thank you," Harmony whispered as their faces moved apart. She meant it. It had been a rough couple of weeks for both of them, but Ron's support at that moment made her happy and relieved.

"Anything for you." He stood up straight and looked across the hotel room. "Now let's go before me and the little lady get stuck in all sorts of rush hour traffic on the turnpike."

"Yes. Yes," Harmony acquiesced, although her heart was breaking to have to let them go.

Harmony put her small bag down next to her while she stood at the hotel's front desk to check out. Ron had gone to load the baby and the bags into the car. Harmony was speaking to the front desk clerk when out of her peripheral vision, she saw Ron rushing toward her. Harmony turned and noticed the panicked looked on his face.

"Ron?" Harmony didn't get a chance to say anything else.

"Hey. Hold Aubrey. I forgot something upstairs," Ron huffed.

Taken aback, Harmony's face crinkled.

Oh . . . um . . . okay," she stammered, caught off guard as he dumped the baby in her arms and took off toward the elevators.

"Ron," Harmony called after him. He turned and looked over his shoulder at her, his eyes bugged out. "What the hell did you forget that has you going so crazy?"

Ron's back went stiff, and he struggled to ease the tension in his face. "It's just my phone charger. No big deal."

Harmony's gut clenched. Something about Ron's behavior nagged her. He had gone from complete panic to trying to convince her that it was no big deal. Harmony wasn't buying it.

"Ma'am, I'll be right back. Can you watch my bags, please? We forgot something upstairs in the room," Harmony said to the front desk clerk. The woman nodded and smiled.

Harmony bounced Aubrey on her hip as she waited for the elevator. When the elevator doors opened, Harmony rushed forward so fast that she ran straight into someone.

"Oh, sorry," Harmony apologized, catching glares from the elevator occupants trying to get out.

"Supposed to let people off first," one man grumbled.

Once inside, Harmony stabbed the fourth floor button repeatedly. Sweat burned the pits of her arms, and her stomach did flips as she watched the little red numbers over the doors change. She tapped her foot. It seemed like it was taking a lifetime.

When the elevator dinged open, Harmony ran out. Aubrey giggled like she did when Harmony played the bouncy game with her.

Harmony made it to the room door. Her hands shook so badly and she was so winded that she fumbled with the key card until it dropped.

"Dammit."

Harmony struggled to bend down with the weight of the baby making her feel like she would tip over. Skillfully using the tips of her fingers, Harmony picked up the key card. She stood up, blew out a long breath, and swiped the card against the electronic door lock. The little light on the door turned green, and Harmony heard the lock click. Harmony took a deep breath and stepped into the room. A hot feeling came over her body when she didn't see Ron inside. It was fear, sheer terror, she was feeling.

Harmony's instinct told her not to call out to Ron. As she moved, her breath came out rough and fast. Her nerves were on edge so bad that she had to take each step carefully to keep her legs from giving out.

Harmony approached the bathroom door. It was the only place Ron could be. She found the door closed but for a tiny crack. Harmony stood back, trying to see through the small sliver. The sound she heard next told her that Ron was in there. Harmony jumped when she heard the snorting again. Harmony held her breath. She craned her neck, and there he was, bent over the sink, snorting something.

Harmony became so weak she almost dropped the baby. Aubrey giggled. Harmony's heart seized, and her hand flew up to the baby's mouth.

"Harm?" Ron shouted from the bathroom.

Harmony jumped, her knees knocking together. She could hear him fumbling around. It sounded like glass shattered, and then there was bumping, frantic moving. Ron was trying to clean up his mess—literally.

"Harm, is that you?"

Harmony could hear him sniffling. She could only imagine how frenzied and crazy he looked trying to get his nose clean. Harmony whirled around, not sure what to do next. Her heart ached so badly that she felt like it would explode. Her temples throbbed. In that moment, everything became different. Harmony felt like she'd been pushed out of an airplane and she was freefalling to her death.

"Harm?" Ron emerged from the bathroom, a tiny dot of white powder still rimming his right nostril.

Harmony's eyes were stretched as wide as they would go. She moved backward like a killer from a horror movie was coming toward her.

"Harm, wait," Ron said, his left hand out in front of him. "Let me just tell you what happened." His eyes were watery. His brow was wet with sweat.

Harmony had seen him in this condition before. She knew what it meant. Harmony stumbled backward into the desk. Her baby laughed joyfully again, oblivious to the doom and gloom Harmony felt.

"Just hear me out, Harm."

Harmony opened her mouth to speak, but no sound came out. She couldn't find the words.

She couldn't cry. She couldn't yell. She couldn't do anything. The devastation she felt was like nothing she had ever experienced in her life. Harmony felt like she was standing in quicksand. No matter what she was going to die—either trying to escape it or by drowning in it. There were no wins in this situation.

"I got it under control, Harm," Ron said. "I'm telling you. I was a little stressed out with everything that was going on with us, but I know once things are back to normal with us, I can stop."

Now Ron was blaming her for his relapse. *How dare he?* Harmony turned swiftly and bolted for the door.

Ron raced around her and blocked her from leaving. Harmony tried to go around him, but he shifted sideways to stop her.

"Da-da," Aubrey cooed, stretching her chubby arms toward Ron. It was the first time she'd said the word. Harmony felt a sharp pain in her stomach. Her daughter would grow up just like she did—fatherless.

"Harmony, just listen to me. I promise. I can handle it. I swear it won't be like before," Ron begged. "It's not like you didn't drive me to this."

In a knee-jerk reaction, Harmony reached up and slapped him across the face with every ounce of strength she had in her body. Aubrey started crying. Ron stumbled sideways from the impact. Without a word, Harmony yanked opened the door and stormed out, her screaming baby in tow.

"Harmony, wait!" Ron called after her. "Just give me a minute to talk to you."

Harmony didn't bother to turn around. Her legs felt lead-pipe heavy, but she forged forward as fast as she could.

"Harmony," he called after her again.

Harmony didn't hear his footsteps behind her or sense his presence. She knew that Ron wouldn't chase her. Harmony was well aware that so long as there was even a tiny bit of drugs left in that hotel room, they would be more important to him than anything else—even her.

Chapter 23

Melody

"Mel," Gary called out, just above a whisper, as she shook Melody's shoulder. Melody moaned, lifted her hand, and swatted at him.

"Mel, you can't stay in this godforsaken, dark-ass room for another day," Gary said in his best parental tone. "You have to get up now. I know you're hurting, boo, but this is definitely not helping."

Melody buried her face further into the pillow. She had been hiding from the world since Sly broke the news to her. He was going to be a father, but she was not going to be the mother of his child. Just thinking about it again made Melody's stomach swirl.

"Okay, what about just sitting up? Washing your face? Getting some sun?" Gary made his way over to the large bay of windows in her bedroom and yanked her room-darkening curtains apart. Melody groaned louder.

"Mm-hmm. I hear all of that, but as your self-appointed get-yo'-life coach, I will not let you lay here rotting away. Besides, I spoke to Lyric and she's being released today. They're expecting you at the hospital for the big release." He walked over to the bed and yanked the thick, pure white down comforter off of Melody's body.

"Gary, please don't get cursed out," Melody croaked, her voice hoarse and gruff from all of the crying and screaming she'd done over the past three days.

Gary sat down on the edge of her bed and sighed. "Mel, I have all the respect in the world for you, but the only way to show the world that this thing with Sly is not going to destroy you is to bounce back. Get outside. Let those nuisance-ass paparazzi snap some pictures of you looking fantabulous. C'mon, you don't have to be a PR expert to know what you have to do to keep yourself from being embarrassed. We have to act like this shit doesn't faze miss Melody-fucking-Love, hunty," Gary said with feeling. He snapped his fingers and drew an S in the air with his hands to drive his point home.

Melody parted a weak smile. It was the first time she felt anything other than grief in days. "You're right." Melody sat up.

"Oh God." Gary frowned. "I ain't never seen that hair in such a mess. Girl, you look like the bride of Frankenstein mixed with Marge Simpson and Lady Gaga on steroids," he joked.

Melody smiled again. "Why the hell can I picture all of those mixed together?" Melody chuckled, kicking Gary in the leg playfully.

"There's my abusive BFF. Kick me, hit me, spit at me—whatever you want to do to let me know you're back." Gary laughed.

"Okay. Call the style team. I'm going to get up and get out. I'll make a show out of picking Lyric up. She'll love the attention anyway," Melody said.

She was ready to go back to her façade of a perfect life. She was ready to go back to evil Melody, because being soft and having those sentimental moments had gotten her just where Ava always told her it would—hurt and alone.

"Melody, is it true your sister almost died from a drug overdose?"

"Melody, are the rumors about Sly and Terikka true?"

"Melody, is Sly having a baby with your nemesis? Did you think it would be you?"

Melody almost paused her steps when the question about Sly and Terikka hit her ears.

"Don't you dare feed into it," Gary warned, trying to shield Melody from the cameras. Although he had called the paparazzi himself, he had to play it off.

"Melody! Melody! It's me."

Melody paused. Her entire body stiffened and a cold chill shot down her back. Gary pushed her down into the waiting car.

"Unh-uh. What the hell you want, Floyd Mayweather? I heard about you," Gary shouted, pointing an accusing finger in Ron's direction. Melody's security was ready to pounce.

"Let him in," Melody yelled to Gary from the car.

"What? After what he did?" Gary's eyebrows shot up into arches.

"Gary, I said let him in," Melody demanded.

Ron fought his way through the crowd of cameramen. Gary folded his arms across his chest and snaked his neck at Ron. "You're lucky I'm feeling like a lady today," Gary gritted.

Ron slid into the backseat of Melody's car. "Thank you," he huffed.

"Driver. Move the car," Melody said, tapping the back of the driver's headrest. As the car pulled out, Gary banged the side, and Melody's security team could be seen scrambling to their vehicles.

"Just drive," Melody commanded. She needed to get away from the prying eyes of the cameras. Melody turned her attention back to Ron.

"What do you want? To come and tell me how terrible I am again, or to try to choke the life out of me again?"

For some reason, this time Melody wasn't scared or worried about Ron getting violent with her. There was something in his eyes that was kind of sad.

"Look. I'm sorry about that. I was out of my mind," Ron said.

"I didn't put the drugs in your jacket," Melody lied. "It must've happened in the bar when you were too drunk to notice."

Ron seemed to contemplate what she was saying. "It doesn't matter now. I've lost Harmony forever." His voice waivered.

Melody whipped her head around so she could look at him. "What are you talking about? What do you mean you've lost—"

Before Melody could finish, Ron lurched over and put his mouth on top of hers. Melody tried to moan, but Ron's tongue was in her mouth before she could get the sound out. Her mind went blank, and her body tingled in places she hadn't felt in a long time, even with Sly. Ron had her pushed against the car door. His hands moved over her body.

"Wait," Melody whispered over his lips.

She tried to push him away, but he was determined. Ron ran his tongue down her neck. Melody tried to push him away again, this time her force weaker than the last.

"I need you," Ron said, panting. "I need you now. This is what you wanted, right?" His hands worked feverishly at the buttons of her jeans.

Melody's mind swirled. *Harmony. Sly. Lyric. Aubrey.* She thought about all of them.

Ron had her pants off. The motion of the car, his muscular arms, and the possibilities all made her dizzy. Melody was battling the devil and the angel on her shoulders.

He is your sister's husband, Melody. He doesn't belong to you.

Your sisters have their bond and they never included you. Who cares how they feel?

He just beat you up. He is just trying to use you now.

Maybe he realizes that you are way more beautiful than Harmony and you have way more money than she does.

He doesn't want you. He wants money. He is Harmony's husband.

From the moment you met him he wanted you. Maybe he realizes that he loves you and not her.

Melody screamed out as Ron grabbed her up and forced her to straddle him. She couldn't listen to the competing voices in her head anymore. It was happening. It was happening faster than she could control.

"Oh, shit!" She gasped as he lowered her dripping wet hot box down onto his swollen member. Melody felt a shockwave of pleasure mixed with pain. Ron used his powerful hands to clutch her hips and force her up and down. Melody was singing with the high-pitched sounds of ecstasy coming from deep inside of her.

Within ten minutes Melody had reached her peak.

"Oh God!" she screamed, digging her nails into Ron's shoulders. Ron followed. Melody fell into the seat next to him.

"Exactly what the fuck was that?" Melody huffed. She banged the seat next to her. Guilt quickly trampled on her mood. She turned her face away from his, embarrassed that she had been so weak.

"The coke. I need more," Ron said, his voice devoid of emotion.

Melody shot up in the seat. "You fucking bastard. Get out!"

Ron ducked her slaps and punches. "You wanted me. I knew it since the funeral. You wanted to see me like this." He sniffled and rubbed his nose.

"Fuck you. Get out. Driver, stop the car," Melody shouted. The reality of what she'd done made her head pound. If Harmony ever found out, the hurt would kill her.

"I don't have anything now. You wanted me, and now you have me." Ron put his hands up. "I need the name of your dealer."

"Get out!"

Melody fell back against the seat as he got out of the car. Her mind raced. She had purposely hurt Harmony so many times. Melody closed her eyes and thought back to the night she'd entered Ava's room and tiptoed over to her mother's bed.

"Ava. Ava." Melody shook her mother.

"Huh, what?" Ava had stirred, lifting her eye mask. "What's the matter, Melody? What's going on?"

Melody knew Ava hated to be roused from her sleep.

"I can't sleep. Harmony keeps crunching on something in her bed and waking me up," Melody whined, rubbing her eyes. *"I'm going to look all puffy tomorrow for the talent show."*

"What you mean, crunching? Like she eating something in the bed?" Ava asked.

Her legs were already over the side of her bed. Melody stepped back out of her way. Ava slid her feet into her furry pink high-heeled slippers.

"I think it's candy," Melody said in a babyish voice.

"Oh, yeah," Ava snorted, shrugging into her robe.

"Don't tell her I told you," Melody begged, using the same baby voice.

She followed Ava out of her room but slipped into the bathroom. Melody looked at herself in the mirror and squinted her eyes devilishly. The next sound she heard was Harmony screaming.

Melody opened her eyes now, recalling how getting Harmony in trouble had brought her great satisfaction at the time. This time Melody felt different. She had crossed the line in a way she knew she could never fix. But she couldn't stop thinking about Ron either.

Chapter 24

Lyric

"I can't believe how many paparazzi were outside of the hospital." Lyric was amused. She was famous again.

"You like that?" Harmony asked, her brows furrowed.

"Hell yeah. I'm all over every social media site, the blogs, all of that. Famous again, and all it took was an overdose and a very famous sister."

"All attention is not good attention," Melody interjected, walking into the parlor of her huge Saddle Hill, New Jersey mansion.

Harmony and Lyric turned around.

"Thanks for inviting us," Harmony said.

Melody waved her off. "You're not guests. You're family."

"Yeah, we are family," Lyric followed up, smiling. "Famous family. I like how that sounds."

Within an hour, Lyric and her sisters had changed into the new matching pajamas Gary had picked up for them. Melody had her staff lay out oversized beanbag chairs and huge, fluffy pillows. Lyric couldn't stop digging into the buffalo wings, loaded fries, cocktail shrimp, and hand-made dumplings that were laid out on silver platters.

"This food is one part bougie, one part ghetto," Lyric joked.

"Just like me," Melody replied. "I may have all of this now, but I remember our days of having nothing."

"You realize we never had this kind of slumber party as kids," Lyric mumbled with her mouth full of food. "Ava never let us be kids. No friends. No slumber parties. No birthday parties."

"Well, we are having one now, and we can have them whenever we want from now on," Melody said. She stood up. "I want you both to hear something." She rushed to the music system that was built into the wall. She hit a few buttons and a beautiful tune filtered through the room.

It seemed to hit Harmony first. She scrambled up from the floor, closed her eyes, and swayed her hips. "This is beautiful. Makes me think of my baby and—" Harmony paused without finishing her sentence.

"I love you more than you know," Melody crooned, right on time with the beat break. "I love you more, more than you'll ever know."

Lyric got to her feet, holding a tiny chicken drumette to her lips like a microphone. "I need you to love me too." She moved close to Harmony and they harmonized the words.

"I . . . love you." Melody led, as usual.

"Love me too," Lyric and Harmony followed.

They got into their old triangle formation, moving their bodies in sync like they'd rehearsed it. Lyric looked over at Harmony as they crossed and changed positions. Lyric shook her head at the tears streaming down her sister's face. They sang and danced like they had never been apart. Lyric hadn't felt this good around her sisters in years.

"Yes," Melody cheered as the beat faded out. "We still got it."

"As soon as you get out of rehab, the 1 Night Stand tour is going to be the best thing that has happened to you in a long while," Melody said, smiling at Lyric.

Lyric flopped down on one of the beanbag chairs. "About that."

Harmony put her hand up. "Lyric, rehab is not an option. It's a must."

"I'm fine. Look at me. I don't even feel like getting high right now."

"That is because we are here and we are having a moment, but when you have to be alone again, then what?" Harmony said, looking at Melody.

"I can't have you on the tour messed up, Lyric. Rehab or no tour," Melody said, widening her eyes at Harmony.

"So now it's gang up on Lyric day." Lyric folded her arms across her chest.

Harmony bent down next to her and put her arm around her shoulder. "Nope. It's get Lyric healthy day."

"And that place I have set up for you is like paradise," Melody added. "So let's enjoy our last night together."

"Yeah." Harmony got back to her feet and started dancing around, making silly singing faces. She picked Aubrey up and danced with her. Melody laughed, but Lyric tried to stay serious.

"Girl, you better get your ass up and dance and sing," Harmony said in her best Ava imitation.

"Yeah. Get your black ass up and put them heels on," Melody followed, sounding more like Ava than Harmony did.

"Girl, you been eating candy?" Lyric mocked too. They all busted out laughing. It was the first time they'd made light of their abusive childhoods. Maybe it was a sign of a real breakthrough.

Chapter 25

Harmony

Harmony held onto Lyric so tight they both struggled to breathe. Lyric was crying, and Harmony was fighting back her tears. It was another one of those times she had to pretend she wasn't hurting in order to make things better.

"It's not the end of the world. I promise. Life will be so much better when you're clean," Harmony comforted.

Lyric didn't say a word. Melody stood aside, looking as if she didn't know whether to join in their embrace or run away.

"Ms. Love, it's time," said Ms. Shay, the counselor from Paramount House, her voice calm and soothing.

"It's okay. I swear I'll be right here whenever they say I can come," Harmony assured. She finally released her hold on Lyric. She reached out and wiped tears from Lyric's cheeks.

"We don't allow the family inside. We take them from here," Ms. Shay said, touching Lyric's shoulder.

Harmony exhaled. She had the same stomach-sinking feeling she'd had when she took Ron to rehab the first time. "I love you, Lyric."

Lyric didn't respond. She lowered her head, turned swiftly, and walked away with Ms. Shay. Harmony wrapped her arms around herself.

"She's going to be fine," Melody said, walking over. "She better be."

Harmony smiled weakly. "It's not easy getting clean. And she will always have to fight to stay clean."

"Maybe the tour will help keep her out of trouble. Have you talked to your husband about it?" Melody inquired.

Harmony shuddered at the mention of Ron. She hadn't told her sisters about Ron's relapse. "He said he supported whatever decision I made about it," Harmony lied. "I'll do it just for Lyric."

Melody's face folded into a frown. "Just for Lyric?"

"Wait, no. I didn't mean it like that. I just meant that if it will make things better. Better between all of us." Harmony stumbled over her words, realizing her mistake.

"It's fine. I'm used to you being there for Lyric only. I understand. I'm a big girl, with lots of money. I don't need many people," Melody said, shrugging.

"I didn't mean it like—"

"Harmony, save it. I said I understood. Ava did a number on us. I get it. I don't have any expectations anymore. People have been hating me my entire life. I've learned to accept it. I can afford to buy my own happiness. One thing Ava taught me that was right is all I need in the world is me," Melody said with feeling.

"Wait, Mel."

Melody put her hand up. "The driver will take you wherever you need to go. I'll ride back with my security team. Let me know when Lyric is out. We can talk about the tour then."

Harmony opened her mouth to speak, but Melody had already stormed off. Harmony's shoulders slumped. She looked down into the stroller at her sleeping baby. "It's just you and me against the world, Aubrey. Just you and me."

Chapter 26

Melody

Melody held the tiny baggie out in front of her. Ron reached for it, but she pulled it back.

"For the record, I probably could've had you even if you weren't hooked again."

Ron shook his head. "Maybe," he agreed, licking his ashy lips.

"Do you miss Harmony?"

Melody could see Ron struggling with his emotions. It made her feel good inside. *Fuck Harmony. She never cared about me anyway. Lyric was the only one she cared about. Some sister.*

"Answer me." Melody dangled the baggie in front of her face.

Ron lowered his head, causing the tiny beads of sweat lined up at his hairline to run in streaks down his face. "No. I don't miss her. She just abandoned me," he answered.

Melody laughed. "You're such a damn good actor," she said with disgust. She tossed the baggie at him.

Ron rushed over to her glass-top bar and went to work snorting the cocaine.

"You should go back to her, you know," Melody yelled to him from across the room.

Ron turned toward her, wiping the powder off his nose. "I'm where I want to be," he said.

"No. You're here because you need to be here. There's a difference. I know you said she froze all of your accounts and she probably changed all of the locks on the house, but I know my sister. She still loves you. You still love her too. As for me, I guess I just wanted to see if I could get you. I had a nice night with her and Lyric the other night, and I didn't tell her about you . . . how you seduced me for drugs. I didn't have the heart to tell her. You should go back to her. Get yourself clean again. I get bored too easily."

Ron rushed over to Melody. "I'm where I want to be."

Melody felt a warm sensation in her chest. She wanted so badly to believe that Ron loved her.

He reached out and touched her face, then he kissed her. Melody's insides ignited. As Ron ran his hands over her body and began removing her clothes, the angel and devil in her mind began speaking to her again.

He's only here because he needs you to supply his drugs.

He might just love you more than he loves Harmony.

Impossible. You saw how much he really loved Harmony.

That means nothing now. You have this to hold over her head.

It's wrong. He belongs to her.

It doesn't matter. He said he wants to be with you.

Melody screamed out in ecstasy when Ron entered her. She dug her nails into his shoulders. Soon their bodies moved in sync with the music, as if this was meant to be.

When it was over, Melody buried her face in her hands. The shame was too much. She felt Ron get up and walk over to the bar. She listened as he snorted more lines of cocaine. Melody shook her head, disgusted with herself. She'd let her loneliness drive her to the lowest point—plying her sister's husband with drugs just so he'd be with her.

You're pathetic, Melody Love. Pathetic.

Chapter 27

Lyric

"Wait here," Lyric told the Uber driver. "My sister has a lot of money. Just let me go get some."

The driver grumbled something as Lyric scrambled out of his car. She rushed up to Melody's door and rang the bell.

"Hi, um . . . is my sister home?"

The housekeeper shrugged and stepped aside like she didn't understand English.

"Melody. Your boss. Is she here?" Lyric asked, annoyed.

The short, round Hispanic woman shrugged again.

Lyric shook her head and pushed past the woman. She took the stairs on the spiral staircase two at a time. Lyric rushed down the long hallway toward Melody's wing of the house. As she got closer to the tall, ornate French doors, Lyric heard voices.

"Good. She's here," Lyric mumbled. She was almost to the doors when suddenly one door swung open.

"I don't have to listen to this," a man's voice boomed.

Lyric froze in place. Her mouth dropped open. "Ron?"

"Shit." Ron exhaled, rushing in Lyric's direction. "Lyric, listen to me."

Melody rushed out of her room just in time to see Lyric and Ron standing in shock.

"What are you doing here? Didn't we leave you in a rehab all the way in Pennsylvania?" Melody clutched the material of her gown, trying to cover herself.

"I can't believe you. I can't believe both of you," Lyric said, shaking her head.

"Just listen to me, Lyric." Ron reached his hand out toward her. Lyric slapped it away.

"Don't you fucking touch me. I can't believe that you're such a lowlife." She shook her head and her eyes hooded over.

"It was a one-night stand. It happened so fast. I didn't mean for it—" Ron rambled. "Please. Please don't tell Harmony."

"How much? What's your price to keep this quiet?" Melody interjected before he could finish.

Lyric jerked her head toward her sister, shocked. "What? What did you just ask me?"

"Let's face it, Lyric. You didn't leave rehab because you felt like it. You left because the urge to get high was too much to handle. Everybody has a price," Melody said.

Ron frowned.

"You selfish bitch. You're disgusting," Lyric said, barely able to get the words out. "Fuck you and your money." She turned to leave.

"Lyric!" Ron called after her.

Lyric paused for a few seconds, but she didn't turn around.

"Don't tell her. This would destroy her. Let me do it. Let me be the one."

Lyric picked up the pace of her steps. She didn't know how she'd pay the Uber driver or where she'd go next, but she knew that she needed to get far away from Melody before she did something she would regret forever—just like her last encounter with Ava.

Chapter 28

Harmony

"Come on, little ladies. One, two, three, four. One, two, three, four," Harmony yelled over the classical music. Her tiny dance students stood on their tiptoes and mimicked her movements. "That's it. Very good."

When the song ended, all of the tiny tot ballerinas curtsied like Harmony had taught them and ran to their waiting parents. Harmony couldn't wait until the class was over. She had been forcing herself to work, but each day without Ron was a struggle.

"Ms. Bridges," Serena, Harmony's newest teacher at Dance and More called to her. Harmony turned around, eyebrows up. "There's a girl in the lobby asking for you. She says she's your sister."

Harmony frowned. Lyric was in rehab, and Melody wouldn't be visiting unannounced. Harmony slipped her sweatpants on over her leotard and rushed toward the lobby.

"Lyric?" Harmony's heart sank. "What are you doing here?"

"Harm, I'm sorry. I couldn't do it." Lyric rushed toward her with outstretched arms.

"Shh. It's okay," Harmony comforted. Inside Harmony was screaming. She knew that Lyric needed to be in rehab.

"What happened? Why did you leave the program?" Harmony pulled away from Lyric so she could look into her eyes.

"I couldn't do it. I couldn't escape the pain. It wasn't for me," Lyric answered.

Harmony's shoulders slumped with disappointment. "Lyric, you have to get help."

"I . . . need to talk to you, Harm. It's real important."

Harmony's body went cold. The news couldn't be good. She could only imagine what Lyric had to say—what drug she had used now.

"Let's go to my office," she said.

"Wait. I need to pay the Uber driver."

"I have to get my wallet." Harmony shook her head.

Just as Harmony and Lyric turned to leave the lobby, they heard the chimes over the front doors sound off. Harmony and Lyric paused. Harmony turned first to find two men entering her place of business.

"Good afternoon, ladies. I'm Detective Brice Simpson, NYPD Homicide." A tall, handsome man stepped forward, accompanied by his trench coat–clad partner.

"Homicide?" Harmony repeated.

"What's this about?" Lyric dropped her bag at her feet.

"Are you the family of Ava Love?" Detective Simpson asked.

"Yes," Harmony and Lyric answered almost in unison.

"She's our mother," Harmony said. "Why? What is this about?" Harmony asked again, concern creasing her brow.

Detective Simpson cleared his throat. The other detective looked down at his shiny black wingtip shoes as if eye contact would've given away some top secret information.

"Your mother's death has been ruled a homicide by the medical examiner. I just received the final report," Detective Simpson said.

Harmony opened her mouth, but no words came out. Lyric flopped down into the receptionist's chair.

"What?" Lyric gasped. "Homicide?"

"But who would want to kill Ava?" Harmony asked almost breathlessly.

"That's what we are trying to figure out, ma'am. We'd like to speak to you about that," Detective Simpson said, his tone steely.

"Now?" Harmony asked. "We've already buried her weeks ago. You come now with this."

"With these things, sometimes it takes time for the medical examiner to make a determination that the cause of death was something other than natural," he replied.

"What do you need to know?" Harmony asked, her foot tapping.

"Which of you was the last to see your mother alive? And who would have a reason to want your mother dead?" he asked.

Harmony and Lyric looked at one another, neither wanting to answer first and both thinking about Melody. They had all wished their mother dead at some point, but who would have actually had the nerve to kill her?

"I'll need to know everything about all of you," Detective Simpson said.

Lyric lowered her face into her hands, and Harmony closed her eyes. Just when she thought things couldn't get any worse, now this.

"Where can we go to talk?" Detective Simpson asked.

Harmony pointed to her office. Before she followed the detectives down the hallway, Harmony turned to Lyric.

"Go call Melody, Lyric. We need her here for this."